NEXT STOP, BOSTON

Iris Dorbian

Next Stop, Boston
Copyright 2023 – Iris Dorbian
All rights reserved.
Printed in the United States of America

No part of this book may be used or reproduced, stored in a retrieval system, or transmitted in any form or by any means, electronic, mechanical, photocopying, recording, or otherwise, without the prior written permission of the author except in the case of brief quotations embodied in critical articles or reviews.

ISBN – 978-1-949802-35-1
Published by Black Pawn Press

First Edition

"There's nowhere you can be that isn't where you're meant to be..." – John Lennon

Preface

Every creative work is a collaborative effort and *Next Stop, Boston* is no exception to this notion.

In this vein, I extend a special thanks to Jessica McKelden, a talented young editor whose astute suggestions played a critical role in shaping and refining the manuscript in its earliest incarnation. Also, I must acknowledge Wendy Lee, a gifted author/editor, who came on board when the story was at a later stage of development. Her keen literary eye provided me with the perspective and guidance I needed to propel the narrative forward.

Last but certainly not least, I am especially indebted to Black Pawn Press for their unwavering belief in *Next Stop, Boston*. Bringing this novel to fruition was a labor of love, and I am grateful for their enthusiasm to publish it.

Next Stop, Boston is very loosely inspired by Fellini's cinema classic *La Strada*, with a sprinkle of Janet Fitch's *White Oleander*, and Thomas Hardy's *Tess of the d'Urbervilles* - a personal favorite from my teenage years –tossed in for good measure. The story merges my lifelong passion for rock and roll, particularly the tales of excesses and dissolute behavior as immortalized in countless rock star biographies and memoirs, with my interest in Hollywood gossip, fanfiction and soap operas.

Writing the story at the height of the COVID pandemic was a fun escape from the unrelenting grimness of that period but also hugely therapeutic. By drawing upon elements that had given me so much enjoyment throughout my life, I was emboldened to engage with the reality of that tragic time rather than shy away from it like some other authors. I am glad I did as I experienced a cathartic exhilaration that I hope you, too, dear reader, will feel as well.

Iris Dorbian
September 2023

Chapter One

Geri

April 2019

Her skinny fingers rippled across the strings. She played a G chord, one of the few chords he'd taught her in between gigs. She plucked it again, the twangy sound vibrating in her ears.

It was part of her nightly backstage ritual. Most important was polishing and cleaning his guitar. He was persnickety in the way he liked it. Lately, she had gotten the hang of it, but it had been rough going there for a while, as he was never satisfied with anything he asked her to do. Whether it was this task or another, she could never please him. Not until recently.

She'd thought being on the road would be a lot more fun. She didn't hate it, but she didn't relish it either. Time was a blur; it was as if school and her other life never existed, with every day seeming to stretch into an eternity.

She scanned the musty room, and when she was sure no one was lurking, Geri picked up the Gibson again and pretended to play the guitar like a rock god. Tossing her head back, she rolled her right arm like a windmill and closed her eyes, faking the strumming and picking motions.

It was dumb, childish as all hell. But, screw it. She needed to let loose.

Of course, if he saw her doing this, she'd never hear the end of it.

"*Gerrrrriiiiii!*"

Fear gripped her.

Oh shit.

Immediately, she put the guitar down.

"*Dez!*" she yelled back, her lower lip trembling slightly. "I'm in here. I'm in the dressing room."

The door barged wide open as he blustered in. He sighed loudly. "What the fuck is wrong with you?" He snatched the guitar away from her and started strumming.

"I'm sorry," she said sheepishly, her hazel eyes bugging out. "I was just doing what you wanted me to do, what you told me—"

"Shut up!"

Dez's gaze meandered toward the ceiling as he played the instrument, testing it before the sound check. His expression fluctuated between pensive and poker-faced.

"Not bad," he said, as he continued to strum. "Not bad at all. Maybe you can actually do something."

"Really?" She beamed, her smile radiating the heat of a million suns.

She had been wary of him early on; now his approval was all that mattered to her.

"Yeah." He cocked his head, fixing his sapphire eyes on her. "Really." His lips curled into a reluctant grin.

Her luminous smile engulfed her oval face, giving her peaches and cream complexion an almost Madonna-like glow.

He rolled his eyes, then placed the guitar back into the case before slamming it shut. "Come here," he commanded, in a tone not as harsh as before. Unfolding his arms, he enveloped her so tightly neither of them could breathe. "You stupid kid," Dez mumbled as he stroked her hair, inhaling the balsamic fragrance of the shampoo she'd used that morning. "I never know what's up with you."

Then he did something he never did: he kissed the top of her strawberry blond hair, which she always clipped up in a messy bun, making her look like a cross between a jailbait librarian and an unkempt ballerina.

His lips on her head touched her like volts of electricity. It felt like ages since anyone had kissed her. The sweetness of that sensation encircled her in a ring of warmth that dissipated as soon as he let go.

"You see how easy it is when you listen to me, Geri," he said, the sternness returning.

"I do, but sometimes," she shook her head, "I get confused."

"Because you don't listen," he shot back, a haughty smirk shading his finely sculpted features.

She scratched her mouth. "Can I go back to the hotel?"

"No," he snapped back, indignant. "You need to stay here."

"But Dez—"

"What did I say? I'm not going to repeat myself."

Maintaining his resolve, Dez crossed his arms. The sleeveless jean vest he wore nicely accentuated his muscles. Those sinewy biceps always distracted Geri, especially the tattoo that sported her sister's name on his upper left arm.

MICHELLE, 7/15/92–12/1/2018

Underneath her name and lifeline was a simple red rose. Michelle had been Dez's fiancée. If she hadn't been killed in a car crash in Milan, where she was modeling the latest Dior fashions, she and Dez would have married last New Year's Eve. Michelle had been in a car with another model, Selene, on their way to the airport, when their driver had been sideswiped by a drunken, middle-aged, off-duty police officer. They'd all died instantly on impact.

Geri was going to be her maid of honor. Last summer, while she was on her school break, Michelle had flown her to Paris for a special fitting with Henri, the finest wedding couturier in the business. Or so Michelle told her. She had modeled his designs in an issue of French Vogue a year before and was so smitten with his work, his name was the first that had popped into her head after Dez proposed.

The wedding was going to be held in a private Swiss chalet, a very small affair with a guest list that consisted of Dez's manager, Larry, acting as best man; Lanie, a model-turned-makeup-artist who was a close friend of Michelle's since their early go-see days; and Geri.

She couldn't believe it when Michelle had announced she wanted her, not Lanie, as maid of honor.

"Me? You want me?" she'd cried.

"Of course! You're my baby sister. Who else would I pick? All we have is each other."

Their bond, forged in DNA and loneliness, had been an underlying theme in both of their lives.

Their father, Jack, had died of cancer when Michelle was fifteen and Geri was five. Their mom, Lisa, had died four years later of a stroke, although Michelle always insisted she'd died of a broken heart, being that she and Jack had been as much in love when he died as they had been when they'd first met at the University of Colorado thirty years earlier.

Geri had been in the fourth grade at Grant Elementary School in Boulder when she found out that Mom was never coming back from the hospital. Michelle had flown to Boulder from New York City a week before when Lisa's health took a turn for the worse. She had been waiting for her sister in the principal's office.

"It's just you and me now, kiddo," Michelle told her.

She hadn't been wrong about that. Their mom was an only child. Both sets of grandparents had been dead for a long time. Jack did have a younger brother, who, last anyone had heard, lived in Florida. They hadn't been in touch with him in so long, he might as well have been dead.

Because Lisa had died in February and school wasn't over yet, Michelle had temporarily relocated from her Manhattan digs where she'd been a rising, in-demand model to tend to her sister. Her agency had almost dropped her until she'd reassured them she would return to New York City once her sister was done with the school year. Then Geri would move in with her and Michelle would enroll her in a school conducive to her needs.

As Geri was dyslexic, she had attended a special school for children with a myriad of learning and social disorders. It was considered one of the best in Colorado, and in the country. That it was close to the Boulder homestead made it even better.

Yet, as Michelle would tell Geri repeatedly, her sister had made a promise to her dying mom that she would take care of Geri and never abandon her.

"We're in this together, you and me," Michelle reassured Geri on the flight that would whisk her away from Boulder permanently to a new life in New York City.

Life had plodded along at a pleasant albeit unsurprising pace until Michelle met Dez. Then Geri's life had imploded as the whirlwind courtship to end all courtships began, only to end in tragedy months later.

Chapter Two

Dez

June 2018

He met her in a club in London, and knew instantly she was the one.

It was a cliché. Love at first sight and all that bullshit. But from the moment he saw Michelle glide into Heaven like a goddess on gossamer wings, he was mesmerized. No one else existed in that strobe-lit room other than her.

He nudged his friend, Pete, a local musician. "Who is that?"

"Who?"

"Her," said Dez, pointing to the angel. "The smoking hot brunette with the long, straight hair."

Pete squinted. "Who?"

Dez sighed. "The one with the silver dress. Do you know who she is?"

"Oh, her," Pete replied, barely stifling a yawn. "That's Michelle Randall. She comes here every time she's in town. She's a model. And a Yank, just like you. I'm surprised you've never met her. I thought for sure you two would travel in the same social circle."

"Yeah, well, you thought wrong," Dez answered, irked at Pete's insolence. *Jeez. What's with these Limeys? Everything and everybody is putdown material to them, isn't it?*

Before Pete could open his mouth in response—probably to say something bitchy—Dez made his way like a heat-seeking missile to his target: this tall and willowy vision.

"Ouch!" she cried out.

Without intending to do so, he had accidentally stepped on her dainty left foot, his sharp cowboy boot colliding with her silver Jimmy Choo pump.

He grimaced at his stupidity. *Deacon, what the hell is wrong with you?*

"Oh God, I'm so sorry," he said.

Pulling off her shoe, she glanced at the heel, which was slightly scuffed up by the momentary collision, and then laughed in a voice so sweet and melodic it flowed like a rhapsody in his head.

"If it's any consolation, I give really good foot rubs—the best this side of the Atlantic," he said. "In fact, I've been told my foot rubs are legendary."

A huge smile erupted from those luscious, rose-petal lips. "Hmm," she teased, her crystal blue eyes sparkling at him. "Maybe I'll take you up on that. You probably planned on stepping on my foot all along, didn't you?"

The corners of his mouth crinkled into a boyish grin. His stomach felt all fluttery, like he was a schoolboy in the throes of his first crush. For a second, he was tongue-tied. He couldn't remember his name.

Then it came to him. "I'm Dez Deacon. And you—"

Batting her thick eyelashes, she cut him off. "I know who you are."

"You do?"

"Uh-huh."

He threw his head back, shook it in frustration. "Ah. I guess you've heard the stories about me." The rapturous smile ebbed from his face, his finger stroking his slightly whiskered chin.

She shrugged, her eyes still shining, a constellation of stars. "I don't scare easily," she said in a tone so sultry that if he hadn't been hooked already, he was in that instant.

She was in the city doing a photo shoot for *Tatler*, while Dez was in the UK trying to revive a career that had stalled after he'd parted ways with the Prophets, the hard rock band he'd founded when he was still a teenager in Philadelphia. The split was due to "creative differences," according to his publicist. In truth, his bandmates had kicked him out after too many violent altercations with them over everything ranging from the direction of their music to Dez's ever-ballooning ego.

Booting Dez from the Prophets had been a controversial move for the remaining bandmates. He was lionized in the press and public mindset as a charismatic front man, whose swagger, style, and unbridled sex appeal made him a likely successor to such icons as Robert Plant, Roger Daltrey, and even Jim Morrison. But Dez, who had been raised in a tough neighborhood by a single mother, could also be prone to brooding moods and a powder keg of ungovernable rages, the likes of which made him anathema to both his bandmates and record company.

But not his Michelle. He had been with tons of models before, yet, as he would find out, none had ever captivated him the way Michelle did. And it wasn't because of her stunning beauty. She was introspective and sensitive, infused with a gentleness that was disarming. All this made it easy for her to probe into the hidden recesses of his soul and unmask all the lies he told himself about his life, lies he perpetuated to sustain this carefully vetted image of himself — the hellraising rebel — versus the reality — the lost boy from Philly. She peeled through all those layers of artifice and saw him in a way that no one had ever known.

By their third date, in a private room at Le Bernardin, a four-star seafood eatery in midtown Manhattan, he knew she was his soul mate. The only hesitation on Michelle's part was her sister.

"I'm responsible for her," she said mechanically, as if it were a rote answer to whenever the subject of her sister was broached. "I have to take care of her. I made a promise to our mother."

That prompted him to say something uncharacteristically selfless, but before he could check himself, the words poured out of his mouth.

"Bring her along with us," he said. "We'll figure it out as we go along."

It was an impulsive remark that he would later regret.

Chapter Three

Geri

August – December 2018

Fear overtook Geri when Michelle broke the news—she and Dez were engaged.

"What's going to happen to me?"

"We're going to have you live with us," said Michelle, placating her sister.

"I dunno," countered Geri, biting her lips. "Do you think this is a good idea?"

"Dez is all for it," Michelle replied. "In fact, he suggested it. Yeah, I know he doesn't know you well, but once he does, he'll love you. Trust me."

She wanted to believe her sister, but twinges of apprehension reinforced those doubts.

"Geri, look at me," insisted Michelle, grabbing her sister by her concave shoulders. They were standing in Michelle's condo in Greenwich Village. "What did I tell you when Mom died? It's you and me forever. We're a package deal."

During Michelle's fateful trip to Milan, Geri stayed over at the home of one of her teachers, Ms. Fenster, who taught English and history. She lived in Westchester, which was a short car ride outside the city. Geri had been staying there more frequently while Michelle was away.

Ms. Fenster was divorced, and had a daughter who was sixteen, the same age as Geri, and a younger son. As Geri's guardian, Michelle had met and befriended Ms. Fenster during an obligatory parent-teacher conference. The fact that Ms. Fenster had once been a model herself thirty years earlier, having posed for catalogs as a child, solidified the growing bond between the two women.

"I feel close to her," Michelle confided to Geri one day when she told her sister she would now be staying with Ms. Fenster during the times she was working and out of the country. "I know you like her too. So this is a good arrangement."

Then it happened: December first. The date would forever be sealed in Geri's memory. It was the day that Geri received a text from Lynne, one of Michelle's agents, to call her immediately.

"What is it?" she asked Lynne in a thin quaver of a voice that made Geri sound years younger than her actual age. There was something about that message, the ominous quickness of that alert, which gave Geri a funny feeling in her stomach.

She had just stepped out of Ms. Fenster's Honda at the Miller Educational Institute, a private school that catered to students with learning and social disorders, which wasn't far from Michelle's Village apartment.

"Honey, I'm so sorry, but Michelle—"

Geri heard a sob in the agent's throat. She tightened her grip on the phone while her heartbeat began to race like a locomotive.

Then it all tumbled out in a tidal wave of sorrow. "There was an accident in Milan. Michelle was in a car, right before she got to the airport. She's gone."

As Geri would later recall, one minute she was alert, and the next, she was lying on a cot in the school infirmary, her left hand clutching a wad of crumpled tissues.

Even after ingesting a tranquilizer given to her by Ms. Fenster, she couldn't sleep that night or the night after. By the third night, Geri fell into a comatose-like slumber that was so deep, it took Ms. Fenster and her children a good hour and several tries to wake her up the following morning.

Chapter Four

Dez

December 2018

Larry called him with the news. His wife, Tandy, an ex-model who used to be with the same agency as Michelle, had heard about it from one of her old bookers. She had told Larry, who'd immediately phoned Dez. He had to be told before the news would be released to the media, Dez and the sister.

He was waiting for Michelle at her apartment, expectant and thrilled like a kid on the eve of a birthday. He was going to be married, have a wife, maybe kids. The whole shebang. Hunker down and be friggin' normal. The American Dream.

Now, it had been snatched away from him. Just like that. *What the fuck? Well, God, I hope you're happy.*

The sister was in Westchester with that teacher. The plan was for her to stay away an extra few days while he and Michelle had some alone time after she got back from Milan. Then they were going to be like a family, with the family he and Michelle would create.

How could this happen? She had texted him hours earlier when she was still at the hotel, waiting for the car to take her to the airport. He had never been so in love in his life. Oh sure, he'd had infatuations, but never like this. He was running on air, mad with life, dizzy, reeling. Now it was all gone. He would never see her again.

His phone rang. It was Larry again. No, he'd heard enough for now. He clicked the phone off, then sank to the floor in Michelle's luxurious bedroom, with the French doors and the private terrace and the oversized walk-in closet.

For what seemed like an hour, Dez stared catatonically at a framed photo of Michelle. She was on a camel somewhere in the Negev desert wearing an embroidered white and gold tunic. Considering how young she looked, it must have been from one of her earliest shoots. He guessed it was an outtake, as Michelle was laughing hard, and models rarely laughed like that in photos. They always had this stuck-up, aloof pose, as if any other expression would take attention away from the clothes.

In the photo, Michelle was hunched over on the animal's humps, her arms firmly clasped onto its body. Dez marveled at her fearlessness. No doubt she had been trying to stay on top of the camel and not fall off and break her neck. Anyone else would be scared shitless, but not his Michelle.

Unlike other models who made self-worship an art in their homes, this was the only fashion photo of Michelle in the apartment. Instead, paintings and photos of her family, which included an old wedding shot of the parents, graced her creamy beige walls. Another big difference between Michelle and the other models he knew.

Once the fog of grief wore off, he picked himself up and trudged into the kitchen to open the fridge. Stacked on the top shelf was a bottle of champagne, a bottle of gin, and a bottle of Jack Daniels he had brought when he and Michelle first started dating.

He grabbed the Jack Daniels, twisted the cap open, and began guzzling it down. When he was done with that bottle, he tore through the other liquors and did the same.

After he polished off all the booze, he let out a loud belch and then wiped his mouth with the back of his hand. He pondered his options. He didn't want to go to the liquor store around the corner because if he did, he would have to brave the daunting spectacle of photographers and reporters and fans and other curiosity-seekers ready to ambush him and ask about Michelle. No way. He wasn't ready for that yet.

His phone was on top of Michelle's dresser. He staggered back to her bedroom and searched for the number of this guy Jojo, a musician he knew who lived on the Upper West Side. He did a lot of dealing on the side. He also did a lot of deliveries too. Dez knew this because he had made some orders with him the previous times he was in New York. It was safe scoring from Jojo, since he had a lot of clients who were celebrities and VIPs, and they certainly didn't want to get caught up in some sting operation by an undercover cop in Washington Square Park.

Jojo answered on the first ring.

"Hey, Dez! Oh man. I just heard the news. I am so sorry about Michelle. That's terrible."

"Thanks, I appreciate that," Dez slurred. "Lissen, are you holding right now? I need something, anything, I don't care. Whatever you have."

Chapter Five

Geri

January 2019

Two memorials were held in Michelle's honor. The first was a private funeral in Boulder that was attended only by a handful of people. In addition to Geri and Dez, they included Michelle's old pal Lanie, and Julian Rivers, the modeling scout and photographer who had discovered Michelle at a local mall when she was fifteen.

"She was a good person," said Julian as he gently touched Geri's arm, offering his condolences before the funeral. "A real class act. This is so unfair."

Maybe because she was still in shock, Geri didn't weep. Even after Michelle's casket was lowered into the grave, where she would be buried next to Mom and Dad, there were no tears.

The second memorial was an industry one in Manhattan honoring Michelle.

Unlike the funeral, which had been small and exclusive, the industry memorial was attended by everyone at Michelle's agency, Magnificent Models, as well as photographers, other models, journalists, designers, vendors, hangers-on—anyone who laid claim to being part of the fashion elite. The irony was that very few of these people had genuinely known Michelle, let alone uttered a single word to her.

"Fucking posers. Leeches," Dez snorted to Geri as he cased the crowd gathered outside the Cathedral of St. John the Divine.

They were inside a black stretch limousine that had picked them up from Michelle's Village apartment where both had spent the night—Dez in Michelle's bedroom and Geri in hers. Save for Dez knocking on her door that morning to find out if she was ready, neither had spoken to the other since leaving the apartment.

That changed the moment they stepped into the vehicle—even if it was one-sided. Eyes bloodshot and bleary, Dez reeked of liquor. Unlike the Colorado funeral where Dez had been, surprisingly on his best behavior thanks to consuming several tablets of Xanax—

one of which he'd offered to Geri, who declined, when they were outside their respective hotel rooms in the local Marriott—here, he was imbibing all forms of libation.

Dez grabbed a bottle of vodka from the minibar in the back of the limo, and guzzled its contents completely before seizing and draining another. "If I'm going to have to go through this farce for my baby, I may as well be shit-faced," he slurred to Geri, his breath especially pungent.

Cowering in the leather-upholstered seat, Geri inched closer to the right window, trying to put as much distance as possible between her and her dead sister's inebriated fiancé.

Seeing what she was doing, Dez snickered in between gulps of booze. "Don't worry. I'm not going to molest you," he snarled. "I may be loaded, but I'm not stupid."

Saying nothing, Geri continued to gaze out into Manhattan's busy, teeming streets, which were dissolving into one another in quick procession, a kaleidoscope of late-morning cityscapes. Traces of the snowstorm the week before feathered the ground while the exteriors of high-rises remained festooned with fading Christmas and New Year's decorations.

She felt a tap on her left shoulder. Jerking her head around, she saw Dez holding a fresh bottle of bourbon. The two other bottles he'd already quaffed and discarded.

"Want a swig, kid?" he asked, an impish glint illuminating his reddened eyes.

She shook her head before averting her eyes to stare out the window again.

"Suit yourself," he grumbled, then hiccupped. "I was just being hospitable."

He chugged down the bottle and tossed it into the pile.

When the limo finally braked to a halt, parking outside the landmark Morningside Heights church, the driver said, "I have to stop here. The cops won't let me go past the barriers. Are you two going to be okay?"

"Yeah, man. It's cool. We'll be fine. Thanks, buddy," Dez answered, raising his fingers in a peace sign.

Popping out from the limo, the driver walked to Geri's side and opened the door. As she emerged from the vehicle, she heard Dez shoot her a warning: "Get ready for the vultures, sis. They're going to be pouncing."

The first thing she did was adjust the silky black dress she had on. It was a custom-designed frock, replete with a frilly collar, which Michelle had insisted on buying her when they were in Barcelona two summers ago, right after school recessed for the year. Geri had told her sister she didn't want such a nice dress as she couldn't foresee when or what would prompt her to wear it.

"You never know," Michelle had said, overriding her sister's objection. "There could be an occasion in the future. Something unexpected. That's what makes life so interesting, Geri—when things out of the ordinary happen to us all of sudden."

Geri winced at the memory, her stomach constricting with pain that Michelle's memorial would be that event.

"Hey Dez, what do you think about Demon Records dropping you from their label, saying they would never work with you again because of your unprofessional behavior? Any comment?"

Dez glared at the reporter, who had a *Rolling Stone* press badge dangling from his neck by a lanyard.

"Let's go, kid," he whispered to Geri, gritting his teeth as he held her arm while they braved the horde of photographers and press hounds. "Ignore the trolls."

"Dez!" screeched another reporter, this one from *Page Six*. "Who's the jailbait? Isn't it a bit soon to be moving on from your dead fiancée? What would Michelle think?"

"Fuck you, you little prick," Dez flared. "This is Michelle's sister. Show some respect."

"Sister, huh? So you're keeping it within the family? Interesting," he leered, while jotting furiously in his pad.

That was too much. Without a second of hesitation, Dez knocked out the miserable scribe with a right hook that left the bottom-feeder bleeding from his nose and temporarily unconscious.

The media cacophony degenerated into bedlam.

"You're an animal!" shrieked one jackal while another hissed, "Michelle is so much better off."

Pressed into the crunch of madness, Geri tried to push and claw her way out of the lynch mob until she noticed her left hand was fastened in Dez's right.

She tugged her hand away. It was no use. He had her firmly in his grip.

Wanting to navigate her own path out of the insanity, she pleaded, "Let me go." But the din of the crowd drowned her out.

Minutes later, her wish would be granted when Dez was swiftly put in handcuffs by one of the police officers acting as security for the memorial.

"Go in," a shackled Dez hollered to Geri as she lingered at the church's entrance, watching her sister's never-to-be husband shoved into the back seat of the police car.

"Fuck me. He never learns."

Swiveling her head, Geri saw that the voice had come from Larry, Dez's longtime manager and fixer. Sporting a long, dark trench coat, elegantly coiffed white hair that grazed his shoulders, and a translucent pallor to a face marked by delicate features—chief among them deep-set grey eyes—he exuded sophistication touched with a smidgen of decadence.

As Dez would later tell her, Larry had discovered the Prophets at one of their earliest gigs in Philadelphia. They were opening for the Concussions, a far more popular group that merged rockabilly with rhythm and blues. At the time, Larry was scouting talent for Demon Records. When he got a flyer from the Concussions, Larry was so intrigued, he decided to hop on an Amtrak from Penn Station to check them out. He quickly forgot all about them when the Prophets strutted onstage. And the rest was history.

Larry edged next to Geri, their eyes following Dez being taken away to the local precinct. "So sorry, Geri."

Her pink rosebud lips contorted into a deep frown. "What's going to happen to him?"

"He'll post bail and be out in a few hours." He shrugged. "It's a damned shame. Poor Michelle."

Geri's eyes misted at the mention of her sister, but again, as in the case of the funeral, no tears were forthcoming.

"None of this seems real."

Her voice was barely audible. Larry shifted closer to hear her.

"I know," he murmured.

"I keep thinking she's going to come back any day now and it was all a mistake," Geri added in a choked whisper. At that point, the mere act of pushing out sound from her larynx was a challenge.

"I wish it were, sweetie."

Putting his arm around Geri's shoulder, Larry guided her inside the church. Geri stole one last sweeping look at Amsterdam Avenue. It was as if she expected Michelle to suddenly materialize, like a benevolent apparition, presenting proof that she was still alive and it had all been a dream. Instead, she spied one of the reporters who had taunted Dez argue with a cop about a parking ticket.

Geri shuddered, then walked inside.

Chapter Six

Dez

January 2019

Much to the consternation of Ms. Fenster, Michelle had stipulated in her will that Dez would be Geri's legal guardian.

Exasperated, the teacher filed a lawsuit against Dez, claiming that Michelle had been under his "harmful" influence and not in her right mind when she'd made that provision. But just as Dez had done years before when he claimed in an interview on *The Today Show* that he was an orphan until his mother got in touch with the network to share her side of the story, Ms. Fenster was paid off—handsomely—and the litigation was dropped.

As for his mother, Gloria, and her youngest son, Kevin, Dez's brother, they were living in public housing in Philly. Dez had abandoned them because, after a childhood marked by abuse and neglect, he wanted nothing to do with Gloria. Demon Records's savvy PR flack, Heidi, offered a *Today* producer a scoop on another hot young artist in exchange for not airing the interview with Gloria. The morning show accepted the bargain.

On his lawyer Lloyd's advice, Dez bought a luxury condo for his mother and brother and plied them with a significant nest egg, but it was executed with the implicit understanding that if Gloria stepped out of line again, Dez would cut them off. Mom agreed, even signing a contract prepared by Lloyd, and he never heard from her again.

Because he'd dropped out of school when he was Geri's age, Dez's first instinct was to pull her out so she could be with him on the road.

"School is bullshit," he declaimed to Geri after he found out he would be her guardian. "Algebra? Crap. Geography? Well…" He drew a long sigh. "Yeah, okay. I guess it can help when you're reading a map. English is cool. My teacher was a hottie. Had the nicest pair of legs—" Dez stopped short when he realized he was speaking to a kid, who was a virtual innocent, an obvious virgin, and whom he knew Michelle had sheltered. "She's different from other kids her age. She needs tender loving care, Dez. She's special," she always told him.

He knew special was a polite euphemism for retarded or someone with mental health or learning issues, but he didn't pry because it had nothing to do with him. It was Michelle's problem. Until it became his problem.

"Do you like school, Geri?" he quizzed her one night while they were having dinner in Michelle's apartment, another bequest to Dez courtesy of Michelle's will. "Do you want to stay?"

Both were scarfing down takeout—a vegan burger and sweet potato fries for him, and a cheeseburger and vanilla shake for her.

"I dunno," answered Geri, in between sips of the creamy drink.

"What do you mean, you don't know? Do you want to stay or not?"

"Can I have one of your fries?" she asked shyly.

He pushed the fries in front of her. "Yeah, sure. Take as many as you like."

Geri's eyes lit up with glee. "Thank you," she responded, her face transfigured by joy as she gorged on the fries.

Frustrated, he stared listlessly at her, then he furrowed his brows and put his right hand on the right side of his high cheekbone, as if he needed his arm as a pillar of support; otherwise he'd succumb out of boredom from dealing with this annoying kid who couldn't give him a straight answer.

"Geri, what about friends? Do you have any at school?"

"Not really," she piped back, as she continued to inhale the fries.

He rubbed the bridge of his aquiline nose, shutting his eyes.

"You're not going to make it easy for me, are ya?"

Geri shrugged as she polished off the remains of her cheeseburger.

He folded his hands as a germ of an idea entered his brain. "How about—and I know your sister did this sometimes—how about you go on the road with me when we head out in two weeks? I'll get you a tutor, arrange for you to study remotely, then you can do your lessons, tests, papers, whatever, and finish out the school year. How's that?"

The irises in Geri's eyes flickered. "I think Ms. Fenster might get upset if I don't come back," she said.

Dez stifled the urge to laugh. "Don't you worry about Ms. Fenster," he replied, thinking about the $500,000 Lloyd had forked over to get that hag to back off and drop that stupid lawsuit. What made it particularly laughable was how Fenster had originally held out for a million! *Greedy bitch. Everyone has a price, don't they? So much for her high-minded concern for Geri's wellbeing.* He scratched his chin. "I have a feeling she won't be a problem anymore."

"Really?" asked Geri, lifting her eyebrows.

Damn, she really is naïve, isn't she? he thought. It was as if she were a space alien visiting from another galaxy. He broke into a roguish grin. "Yes, really."

Geri sucked down on the straw, ingesting the remainder of her shake.

His fingers drummed on the table. "Okay, so we have a deal, then? Do you like the plan?"

Nodding, Geri put down the now-empty plastic container and gawked at him, impassive.

"It's okay, Geri," he chuckled. "You don't need to contain your excitement."

Her mouth twisted into a lopsided smile. He suspected she was feigning delight to please him. "I'm sorry. It sounds cool. It'll be fun to see all those places. Really."

"Okay, okay. I believe you."

What a strange kid she was.

He stared at her, scrutinizing her face and figure. She didn't look at all like Michelle. First, her hair color was different. Second, she was petite, about five foot six, which was practically elfin next to Michelle's towering five-foot-ten height, only two inches shorter than him.

But she did exhibit the same regal, reserved demeanor that Michelle had had, a similarity he found unnerving. While they also shared diminutive features, Geri's small, upturned nose and wispy lips gave her an earthy waif appeal that was the polar opposite to Michelle's ethereal, otherworldly airs. And yet, there were times when the kid would gaze at him in a certain angle, under a certain light, which would remind him of Michelle, breaking his already shattered heart.

It was too much to bear. He grabbed his leather jacket from the coat closet in the hallway, then padded back into the kitchen where Geri still sat, her large, ingenuous eyes gaping at him with a blank expression.

"I have to…" He groped for the right words, his hands flailing. "Do a couple things. I should be back in a while. "

He waited a moment for a response. It did not come. The girl was mute.

"Cool. I'll be back soon."

Chapter Seven

Geri

January 2019

He returned a week later. No explanation as to where he went. No apology. Nothing.

In the interval, when Geri hadn't been combing the streets of New York City searching for Dez, she was phoning and texting him on his cell. Silence.

Desperate, she had called and texted Ms. Fenster. Nothing.
She had even tried to get in contact with Lanie. Fortunately, her sister's bestie promptly replied. *What do you mean? Dez left you last week and he hasn't been back since?*

He's gone. I tried calling him, texting. He won't answer. I thought maybe he forgot to take his cell, but I searched his room and the apartment and can't find it. I don't know why he's ignoring me, Geri typed back, tears trickling down her face. She wiped them away, then continued.

Where are you?

I'm in the Bahamas on a shoot. I wish I could come get you, but I'll be here for another week. It's the swimsuit issue, for Sports Illustrated. Do you have Larry's number?

Geri texted back, *No,* and watched as the ellipsis forming under Lanie's name crystallized into a message.

Hold on. Let me find it. I'll text you in a few.

Ten minutes elapsed before Lanie followed up with another text.

Sorry, hon. I thought I had Larry's number, but I don't. I only have Dez's number, which doesn't do you any good. Sweetie, I'm so sorry. I loved Michelle, but she had no biz making that jerk your guardian. Damn. They're calling me. I have to go. I don't know what to tell you. I'd tell you to call the cops but you're still a kid. They'll put you in foster care and you don't want that. Pls hold tight. That asshole will probably be returning soon. I hope. Let me know if you need me to send you food or anything. Have to run. Stay strong, Ger.

"Miss me?" Dez rambled into the apartment, oblivious that he had been MIA.

Glum and dejected, Geri had been sitting with her laptop on the beige living room chaise for the last twenty-four hours. The dark circles that rimmed her insomniac eyes were so pronounced, they made her look like a raccoon.

He stared at her, folding his arms. "Say something." He lightly kicked her feet, which she immediately pulled away at his mere touch.

"Okay, I was gone longer than I thought. I needed to get my head together."

Ignoring him, Geri continued to eyeball the computer.

"You're not going to answer me?" he asked, growing increasingly flustered with Geri's uncommunicativeness. "Okay, I went to L.A. I needed some time away to chill. I have a place there, so I went."

"You should have told me!" Geri fumed. "Why didn't you call me back when I called you and texted you? I waited and waited."

"Come on. You're making more of this than what it is. I didn't think it was a big deal. There's food left here, right?"

He sauntered around the apartment. For realtors, this two-bedroom penthouse condo, with its panoramic windows, modern kitchen, wood-burning fireplace, and two private terraces overlooking Washington Square Park, might be nirvana for upscale bohemians or moneyed bon vivants, but right now, it was a mess.

Takeout bags and dirty napkins from Shake Shack littered the floor of the kitchen while some of Geri's clothes were scattered in a jumble throughout the living room.

Dez frowned. "What is all this shit," he picked up one of Geri's pants, before tossing it back to the floor, "doing here?"

Geri stayed mum, her eyes trolling through Selena Gomez's latest Instagram posts.

"When is Anna coming?"

Anna was a Polish woman in her 50s who would clean the apartment once a week and cook enough food that would last for a while. Michelle had hired her at the recommendation of the building's property manager.

Geri popped a strawberry Mentos in her mouth, sucking loudly on it.

"I asked you a question."

"She was here Tuesday," Geri mumbled, her attention mired in photos of Selena attending some film premiere in Hollywood.

She could feel the weight of Dez's unflinching stare on her. *Good. I'm glad he's getting pissed off. Let him know what it feels like. Asshole.*

"That was only a few days ago."

"What were you doing in L.A.?" Geri shot back, glowering.

"Getting my head together." He scowled. "Besides, it's none of your goddamn business. If I want to take a break from being your babysitter, I'm going to do it and there's nothing you can do about it. Let me tell you something—living here in luxury—well, what used to be luxury—it's still goddamned better than being in foster care. I was in foster care for six months when my mom was too wasted to take care of me. You don't know how good you have it, you stupid kid."

"Fuck you!" Geri spat out. She flipped him the bird.

"Oh yeah?" he retorted, glaring daggers at her.

"Yeah!" She sulked, arms crossed and defiant.

That triggered him. Without missing a beat, he snatched the laptop away from her and threw it onto the ground, causing a dent when it hit the edge of the coffee table. The screen went black as some of the keys popped out of their casings.

Geri's jaw dropped. *WTF????????!!!!!*

Before she could protest, Dez yanked her from the couch with as much strength as he could muster, then forced her into the kitchen. He then pushed her to the floor where her head nearly fell face-first in the food wrappers and dirty napkins.

The girl's bloodcurdling screams rang out, resounding throughout the apartment and in his ears.

"You're a monster! You totaled my computer!"

Rather than defuse his fury, her waterworks and yelping only made him more livid.

"I'll get you another one. I want you to clean up this mess! What the hell is wrong with you? I can't believe you're sixteen. You act more like three!"

And I can't believe my sister was actually going to marry you.

Still on the floor Geri looked up to see Dez looming menacingly over her, his finger pointing at her face.

"Pick up those wrappers now and when you're done, pick up your clothes in the living room!"

"I hate you!" she cried, her face flushed.

"I hate you too," he rejoined, mocking her. "Clean this shit up now or else. I fucking mean it, Geri. You are really testing me. Do it now or else."

"It's only a couple of food wrappers."

"That's not the point!"

"Did you ever treat Michelle like this?"

Suddenly, the wind from his bravado deflated. After composing himself, he said in a far calmer and measured tone. "Clean this up."

Grudgingly, she gathered up the food wrappers and dirty napkins, then tossed them into the kitchen bin. She glowered at him.

"And now the living room, por favor."

Bastard. I did nothing wrong.

Sulking, she picked up the clothes, one by one, while Dez stood vigil at the other side of the sprawling living room. She muttered profanities under her breath, scheming revenge scenarios. It vexed her to no end that Dez was acting like the wounded innocent and she the guilty party. Other than Michelle's old debit card, which hadn't been canceled yet, Geri had no money, even though Michelle had left a significant sum to her in her will.

Unfortunately, she had no access to it, as Michelle had stipulated that Geri would get it once she turned twenty-one. As Geri's guardian, Dez had complete control over it.

The more she dwelled on the unfairness of it all, the angrier she got. She wanted to fly to Boulder so she could visit Michelle's grave and yell, "Why did you leave me? And why did you leave me to *him*?"

But then Michelle obviously hadn't expected to die so young, and Geri had never expected to be alone. It was so unfair.

Chapter Eight

Dez

March 2019

He was at his wits' end. Everything he had to repeat. Everything he had to explain, more than once--even if it was how to order a simple goddam vegan salad. She still didn't get it! And now this!

"Crest?" he snarled at her, tossing the toothpaste onto the floor. "This has toxins! I told you I wanted vegan toothpaste." He overemphasized his enunciation of "vegan toothpaste," then growled, shaking his head in frustration.

Initially, she was all smiles when she padded into his room at the Peninsula Hotel, toting the plastic bag from CVS. Now, she was biting her lips, the color in her ruddy cheeks gone, the shiny glint in her hazel eyes dulled.

"I told you to go to Whole Foods," he ranted.

"I'm sorry," she said, still clutching the CVS bag, "but Whole Foods is closed. I had to go to CVS because they're open all night. Can't you use Crest until the morning?"

"No, I can't," he gritted his teeth.

"I'll go out to Whole Foods after I get up," she fretted. "I'll do that first thing. Before breakfast."

Arms akimbo, he glared at her. Then he strutted over to the bureau to glance at his Android phone. Blaring back at him was the time: two o'clock in the morning. Ordinarily, at this time, he'd be out partying and enjoying the company of a lady but after arriving in Columbus that morning, with rehearsals and all, he was so wiped, he decided to crash early.

Yeah, two o'clock wasn't an early time to crash but he wasn't a normie.

"I'll go back to CVS tomorrow," she said again. To him, it was as if she was repeating it more for herself and less for him.

"Maybe they have some vegan toothpaste in some secret compartment. In a stock room no one knows about. I'll go there and tell them I'm your assistant and you need it right away and then they'll—"

"Geri!," he shut his eyes, lifting up the palm of his right hand to her. "Stop!"

"But Dez—"

"It's okay," he said in a voice so low it sounded like a whisper. "Just go back to your room and you can get it tomorrow," he added, rubbing his eyes.

"I'm sorry, Dez," she answered downcast. A beat passed before she spoke up again. "But I'm trying," she gazed up at him with her large doe eyes. For a split second, he thought they were dewy with tears but he wasn't sure. "I really am."

"I know," he muttered softly.

"How are you going to brush your teeth?" she asked earnestly, her face as sweet and guileless as the purest cherub.

He nearly let out a belly laugh right there but stopped himself.

"Don't worry. I'll manage."

She nodded timidly, before scurrying out of his room like a petrified mouse.

He scratched his slightly whiskered chin before plopping down on the bed. He let out a long sigh. Still clad in the black T-shirt and jeans he had been wearing for the past 24 hours, he didn't bother dropping trou.

Guilt gutted him. Prior to this encounter with Geri, he had entertained serious thoughts of ditching the girl somewhere, anywhere, he wasn't particular. He knew it was wrong, a betrayal to Michelle but...good god. How much more was he supposed to take? He was already under a lot of pressure with his new record label. Now he had to be responsible for this weird kid, who always looked at him completely baffled even when he would ask her to do the simplest things.

He shouldn't have paid off that teacher. That was not one of his brilliant moves. But who was she to try and sue him like that? Who did she think she was dealing with? That teach needed to be taught a lesson. Yeah, he was an idiot.

No, he couldn't do it. Besides if he dumped the kid like in the middle of Ohio where they were right now--talk about nowheresville--she'd become a ward of the state, lost in the foster system. No, he couldn't dishonor Michelle's memory and wishes like that. After what he went through with Gloria, he couldn't do that to another kid.

In many ways, he saw a lot of himself in Geri, the same lack of family connections, the same loneliness, the same searching for belonging. For him, it was music that filled the void; for her, he didn't know. She was still young. She had a whole lot of time to figure that out. And she was now his family, whether he liked it or not. He'll have to be more patient. He couldn't give up on her. Not yet.

Chapter Nine

Geri

May 2019

She always found it next to impossible to peel her eyes off Dez when he was onstage. But then, considering he was the star of the show, her guardian and the reason she was even on the tour, did she have any other choice?

As she loitered in the wings, where she was on call in case Dez needed her, Geri wondered how this guy, the one who she saw hypnotize audiences on a regular basis, could be the same one who would complain to her nonstop about everything. Even shit she never knew existed, Dez would bitch about it. For someone who had accused her of being a baby that time in Michelle's apartment, he was proving her wrong cause he was the world's biggest baby himself.

Last night, for instance, the big problem was the cheap one-ply toilet paper in his hotel room.

"It irritates my ass, Geri," he told her. This was right before he sent her off to find two-ply toilet paper. Forget about the fact that it was two o'clock in the morning and the likelihood that she would be able to secure his heart's desire at that time of the night was practically nil. Nope. King Dez wanted that toilet paper now or she would never hear the end of it. Fortunately, an all-night convenience store ten blocks away turned out to be the godsend—thank you very much.

Offstage, he was a veritable borderline case, the way his moods swung the pendulum from rational to unhinged; but onstage, he was the epitome of a star.

Like tonight. With his bejeweled fingers stroking the microphone, Dez sang the final lyric of "Sweet Girl of Boulder." It was a love ballad he had written for Michelle when they were in their courting phase. It was so full of passion and emotion that not only did it make the fans swoon but her as well. She hated admitting that to herself because Dez could have been her brother-in-law. Also, it would probably swell his head and ego even more if he knew that. Like that was possible.

Geri had seen him perform that song countless times since the tour started. But what made this song—hell, the entire show—new and fresh, was the reception he'd get at each gig. Sometimes the audiences were loud and boisterous while other times, they were reserved and polite. Yet, each crowd in each city brought an excitement and electricity that could be so contagious very often Geri would feel their exhilaration in her bones—and this was after months of seeing the same show with the same playlist at every concert.

Of course, the common denominator here was Dez. As Geri saw him cast his spell over the audience, holding the crowd gathered in this 5,000-seat Chicago theater in his thrall—in a tour that began three months earlier and was winding its way through the Midwest before decamping to Boston and later New York—she wondered how this person, a "rock-and-roll shaman" as he liked to call himself, could be the same head case that unraveled in her presence on a regular basis?

It was an illusion, she knew that, but Dez Deacon, in all his glory, still riveted her.

Okay, the theater didn't have the 21,000-seat capacity of the United Center, which the Prophets, while fronted by Dez, had played six years earlier. But as he'd told Geri before he went on, it was the mere knowledge that after his thirty-four years of life, he could still pack them in and move a roomful of strangers with his music and charisma, that gave him a bigger higher than any drug.

A thunderous standing ovation followed when Dez finished.

"You've been a wonderful audience," he yelled out, bowing and jubilant. "Thank you, Chicago!" Lifting his eyes to the ceiling, he held his hands together, as if he was making a silent prayer. Then, with a flourish of his right hand, he motioned to his backup band. "Let's give a hand to these wonderful musicians," he added, naming them one by one.

Because of Dez's crappy reputation, Larry had to pay these musicians extra to induce them to go on the road with his proverbial loose cannon of a client. Of course, Dez hadn't told Geri that, but early in the tour when they were in San Francisco, one of their first stops, she had overheard Larry talking to his wife on his cell about the "hoops he jumped through, paying them double what they normally get" to land these musicians.

Perhaps because he feared a repeat of what happened between him and the other Prophets, Geri deduced that Dez tried to be on his best behavior with these top musicians, such as Gary, a bass player who had worked with such folks as Billie Eilish and Harry Styles; rhythm guitarist Big Man Louie, who got his nickname from his mammoth size and girth, having once been a linebacker in college before his childhood love of music steered him away from the field; and Mike, a veteran studio drummer who worked for real icons ranging from Machine Gun Kelly to Sting.

When the light streaming from the ceiling bathed Dez in a halo, he looked even more like a rock god. She wondered if that was the intention. Decked out in his signature leather pants and leather boots, his muscles rippling across his naked chest, the overall effect gave Dez this seductive, mesmerizing aura, as if he could get anyone to do his bidding at any time.

With an upraised arm, he tried to signal to the audience to quiet down as he wanted to say something more to them, but the more he tried to get them to pipe down, the more the clapping became ear-deafening.

"Okay, okay." Dez beamed. His handsome, chiseled face was aglow with bliss, like he was having a religious epiphany. "I guess you convinced us." He turned to his band, affecting a falsely modest gesture. "They've convinced us, haven't they?" The lights slowly came on. All nodded on cue, with Mike hitting the cymbals and Big Man Louie strumming a few chords in unison.

Dez broke into gales of laughter, his mirth ricocheting throughout the venue, thanks to the fierce clarity and decibel of the acoustics. She had no idea what the latter meant other than she heard the tour's sound engineer gush about it to Dez during the sound check.

A fan cried out, "Do 'Sweet Salvation'!"

It was the song that had catapulted the Prophets to the top of the charts, the one that had made Dez a celebrity or so he always told her.

"Oh," he teased the audience, his lips twisted into a sexy smirk. "So you want me to sing 'Sweet Salvation'? Is that right?"

The crowd roared in response.

Continuing to tease them, he cupped his right hand to his right ear. "I can't hear you," he joked. That unleashed a collective rumble so loud, Geri put her hands over her ears.

"That's better," responded Dez, as he continued to toy with the audience. "What do you say, guys?" he said, twirling and spinning back and forth from the fans to his band. "Do you think we can do it?"

Heads bobbing up and down, the trio grinned. It was especially funny seeing the perpetually Zen-like Big Man Louie try to force a toothy smile. That drew dry guffaws from Dez.

"You see that? Even Louie, the coolest rhythm guitarist in this hemisphere, in any hemisphere, thinks we should do 'Sweet Salvation.'"

Then, without warning, Dez boomed, "Let's go, boys! One, two, three, four!"

The band launched into the swelling overture of "Sweet Salvation," which the rapt audience lapped up with gusto.

No wonder Michelle fell in love with him, Geri contemplated as her hips swayed and undulated to the percussive beat and throbbing guitar driving Dez's husky vocals.

Clad in her ubiquitous black-and-red Dez Deacon T-shirt and black jeans, the uniform of all backstage employees, Geri tried to banish all thoughts of school from her mind. But it was hard. The trigger was the black-and-red T-shirt. It would always remind her of the dopey school uniform she had to wear when she was a kid going to that school in Colorado.

The memory of that uniform always made her chortle: a red-and-black plaid skirt and tie, a starched white shirt, and crisp black blazer with white trim. Thank god she didn't have to wear a uniform for the school in New York. Still, she always liked to remember that old uniform, probably because it was a remnant of her old life, when Mom was still alive, when Michelle would visit and regale her with stories of traveling to exotic locations on photo shoots, when her life seemed so secure and safe. She sighed. What's the point? *That life is over and all the people I loved are now gone.*

She hadn't gone back to school after Michelle died, or rather, Dez had never come through with hiring a tutor to help her finish out the year remotely. She thought about Ms. Fenster, wondering why, much to her dismay, her teacher had blocked her on her cell. She had thought Ms. Fenster liked and cared about her. How could she have been so wrong? Maybe she really was an idiot, totally hopeless, just like Dez kept saying she was.

To forget about school, she focused her attention on Dez, who had enlisted her to be his personal assistant. Duties consisted of performing errands such as picking up his dry cleaning, ordering gourmet dishes, polishing his leather boots, cleaning his guitars, and doing what needed to be done to make Dez happy. Anytime and anywhere.

Unfortunately, as Geri would come to find out, not a lot seemed to make Dez happy. Nothing but constant adulation, boozing, cavorting with groupies, and smashing hotel rooms when shows didn't go well—or when he simply felt the urge. It was a cyclone of mayhem and debauchery, and Geri was along for the ride.

She did find herself eavesdropping a lot on Larry and Dez while they talked business; it was hard not to, considering that constituted the bulk of their conversations. Apparently, Dez's solo album *Afterlife* had risen to the top of the Billboard chart during the first week of its release, but since then had slipped so drastically that it was cratering at the bottom. To make up for that shortfall in record sales, Larry had thought it would be good if Dez went on the road for the next two years, mostly in the U.S., with a few stints in Europe, as Dez was always popular there.

For this tour, the venues weren't as large as the stadiums that the Prophets had performed in when Dez was with them, but they were respectable theaters. And Dez had the reputation of always putting on a good show, or at least a show that would make fans flock to see what this unpredictable male diva would do onstage. That was, when he wasn't loaded or when something didn't set him off.

Tonight wouldn't be like that, she hoped as she watched Dez bask in the glow of adulation and applause. He'd be happy and not blame her for anything that went wrong. Tonight, he might actually thank her, or at least not act like she was the worst thing to ever happen to him. Tonight was going to be good.

As the claps died down and Dez and the band took their final bows, Geri sped to his dressing room to get his after-concert clothes ready: a short-sleeved black T-shirt with a red pentacle in the center and a pair of jeans. The first time he'd disrobed in front of her, it had been an unintentional goof. Peeling off his leather pants—he invariably went commando onstage to give the fans a better view of his equipment (after all, this was show business, he told her)—Dez had completely forgotten his dead fiancée's teenage sister was standing right there.

"Oh shit," he'd recoiled, his hands covering his penis with a fashion magazine that featured an article on his solo career. "Geri, get the fuck out of here!" he screamed at the top of his lungs. "Don't just stand there. Out! Vamoose! Now!"

Yeah, part of her was shocked. Another part was like, yeah, whatever. It did tickle her that Dez was far more horrified than she was.

To prevent similar embarrassing incidents, Dez had instructed Geri to lay out his post-show apparel in his dressing room and then exit. It was an edict she duly obeyed, even after it became apparent to her that Dez had stopped caring whether she saw him without clothes or not.

Humming "Sweet Salvation," she opened the musty dressing room and like clockwork, was about to make a scramble for the overnight bag she'd placed strategically on a chair by the mirror before the show, when the sound of a woman shrieking assaulted her eardrums. Nearly leaping out of her skin, Geri spun around to see a naked redhead behind her.

"Who the fuck are you?" the redhead screeched. "Where's Dez?"

"Uh, I'm, I'm—Geri," she stammered.

Relief seemed to overcome the redhead.

"Oh, yeah." Her mouth contracted into a half grin. "I know who you are. You're Michelle's little sister. Dez told me all about you. So how do you like being on the road? Quite a learning experience, isn't it? Different from school, huh?" She extended her hand to shake Geri's, while not even attempting to cover herself or put her clothes back on. "I'm Lily. Nice to meet you."

"Are you a model?" Geri asked timidly.

Throwing her head back, Lily howled, her open mouth revealing a wide gap between her teeth.

Geri was confused as to why her straightforward question would elicit a storm of laughter from Lily. Although she wasn't as tall as

Michelle, Lily was slender, had high cheekbones like her sister, a well-shaped jaw, and chestnut eyes. Other than her teeth, she didn't appear to have that many physical flaws, if any.

"Are you kidding me?" Lily's eyes danced with delight. "No, not a model." She chuckled some more. "You're sweet."

At that moment, Dez opened the door.

Geri squirmed. "I'm sorry, Dez," she stumbled, conciliatory. "I was going to lay out your clothes and…I….we….umm." Geri gestured to her and Lily, who still hadn't put on a stitch of clothing.

His face bathed in perspiration, Dez's jaw jutted out as his agate blue eyes widened so much, they looked like they were bulging out of their sockets. Coughing, he fixed a stare at Lily, his fingers pointing toward his body. Quickly, Lily reached out behind the couch to grab a gauzy teal mini dress, then squeezed herself into it.

Her pulse quickening, Geri was about to take Dez's clothes out of the bag when he stopped her.

"It's fine, Geri," said Dez as he grabbed a towel from a rack in the poky bathroom and wiped the sweat off himself, starting with his face, then his gleaming biceps and underarms. He took extra pains to clean his chest, which he dutifully shaved every day and varnished with body oil before every performance. "You can go. Thanks."

"So that's it for the night? You don't need me anymore?"

He tossed the towel back into the bathroom, where it landed on the fractured, white-tiled floor. "Yeah. It's cool," he answered, putting on the T-shirt. "You have the night to yourself."

Lily sidled up to him, whispering in his ear.

Geri was about to bolt when Dez stopped her. "Geri, wait." He raised his outstretched right hand, his left ear still cupped to Lily's sweet nothings. "You do?" he waggled his eyebrows at her.

Lily smiled, nodding.

He shifted his gaze back to Geri.

"Uh, Geri, why don't you wait for us in the green room and we'll go out and have dinner? Okay? Lily's an old friend of mine. Just give us a few minutes. It's been a while since we've seen each other."

"Okay," Geri said tentatively as she scampered out.

As soon as she closed the door, she heard peals of laughter inside. It was mostly coming from Lily, with Dez saying in between the intervals of cackling, "Now you see what've I've had to deal with the past few months."

The comment was yet another knife in her heart. If she was such a joke, then why bother to have dinner with her? Probably to make more jokes at her expense. The digs came so often, she knew she had to develop a thicker skin if she were to survive the tour and Dez. Still, every insult stung and every wound festered inside her like an open, infected sore.

Hearing the door lock from inside, Geri stepped away hurriedly, but not without hearing Lily purr, "Baby, you look so delicious, I could eat you up now."

Frowning, Geri stuck her tongue out in disgust and proceeded to the green room. As soon as she got there, she pulled out her cell from the pocket of her denim jacket, plopped down on a mauve velvet chaise, and began scrolling through her Instagram. Nothing but a collage of photos of Dez in concert, in a variety of poses. She scrolled through each and every one of them. Even though Dez had an official account—one that the social media manager at his new record label, Feral Records, was in charge of overseeing, and one to which she had no access, meaning she couldn't post on it—Dez insisted that Geri, as his personal assistant, should post photos of him and only him on her account to help drum up interest in the concerts.

She remembered Dez discussing this with her when they were still in San Francisco. She had been in his room at the Hyatt Regency when the subject came up.

"Why do I have to post only photos of you?" Geri grilled him. "Isn't that your record company's job?"

His mouth agape, he glared at her. "I really made a mistake pulling you out of school, didn't I? How can you be so goddamned stupid? The point of posting photos on social media, just like plastering posters all over the place, doing interviews on TV, radio, podcasts, magazines, newspapers, is to get publicity. Publicity is what helps sell tickets, Geri."

"I don't have a lot of followers, Dez," she said, shaking her head. "Just Lanie, a few old classmates from school, Ms. Fenster. No, sorry. She's not following me anymore for some reason."

He stared at her, his eyes devoid of expression.

"I don't know how my account, with its handful of followers, can help the great Dez Deacon achieve immortality."

"Are you mocking me?"

"No, I'm not," she replied. "I just don't see how I can make a difference here."

"Maybe if you use my name as a hashtag, you would get some traction. Did you ever think about that?"

"But they have to like you first, don't they?" argued Geri. "Otherwise, it won't make any difference, right?"

"You're a regular Einstein, aren't you?" he snarked. "Just do it. Okay?"

Jerk.

As she slunk out of his room, she heard him distinctly mutter, "Imbecile" within her earshot.

The memory of his insult yet again flashed in Geri's head as she posted photos of Dez that she had taken tonight to her Instagram account. She tagged them #BestConcertEver, #DezDeaconRules, #TheREALProphet, #GreatestFrontMan, #ChicagoThriller. For good measure, she added a row of red heart emojis. Embellishing the pics with the latter detail made her feel like a hypocrite, as heart emojis were not exactly what she felt about Dez these days. But she went along with it, and with whatever Dez wanted, because where else was she going to go? It seemed like she lived for him these days, and that's how he wanted it.

"That should do it," she muttered. Her mouth stretched into a yawn. She glanced at the time on her iPhone. It was almost 12:45 in the morning. The show had been over for a half hour. Did it really take Lily and Dez all that time to get "reacquainted" with each other? Come on.

If there was one thing she'd learned with this tour, it was that time operated on a whole other scale. It wasn't weird to go out and have a burger at two in the morning, or stay up until five, eat an early breakfast, and then crash until noon.

At first, she'd felt like a vampire, but after a month of this nocturnal schedule, she'd gotten so acclimated to the lifestyle, she wondered how she would ever be able to go back to a daily schedule that consisted of her going to sleep at ten o'clock at night, waking up at seven o'clock so she could arrive at school by eight-thirty, and be in classes until two-thirty in the afternoon. Then do it all over again the next day. Lather, rinse, and repeat.

"It's a soulless existence," Dez said to her a week into her attempt to adjust to life on the road. He was opining about the nine to five normies. "Absolutely brain-atrophying. These poor people are like ants. Hamsters on a wheel, doing the same thing over and over again. That's why what we do is so important to these people. For two hours, Ger, we bring them the excitement and adventure that's missing in their dull, defeated lives. We're like saviors to them."

Geri clicked on her personal photo gallery. She pored through an unending succession of shots of Dez, as well as shots she never would post on her account: various hotel rooms, desk clerks on phones or dealing with customers, piles of suitcases gathered in a mound in lobbies, regular people sharing drinks at a bar, working on their laptops. She loved the simplicity of these images, which captured life in hotels with an organic detail and vibrancy. She stopped at the bar shots, then zoomed in to snag a clearer view at the people in them. The barflies seemed to be swigging whiskey or scotch, she wasn't sure—an alcohol connoisseur, she was not; however, she'd seen so many adults in her young lifetime down gallons of liquor, she might as well be.

She studied their features to see if Dez was right about these normies. No, he wasn't. They didn't look defeated at all, only tired.

She moved on to a website she'd bookmarked when she'd done a Google search a month ago, while they'd been in Seattle. She'd finished her errands for Dez, who was hooking up with some groupie. Alone and bored and not wishing to barricade herself in her hotel room, she found soothing refuge in the lobby with her phone.

The website was entitled "Classic American Photography," and it featured the best work from the greatest masters in the genre. Geri's favorites were the Depression-era shots of Okies taken by

Dorothea Lange. She loved their weathered, non-Botoxed faces, and was shocked to read that the subject in Lange's most famous shot, "Migrant Mother," one of the most famous shots ever according to this website, had only been in her thirties when Lange took the shot. She had thought the woman, with her prematurely wrinkled, angular face, the planes of which were lined in desperation and hunger, was so much older than that. To her, the image was as haunting as it was tragic. During her down time on the tour, when she wasn't waiting on Dez or sleeping on the bus that would transport them from one destination to another, she would invariably go back to that website and seek out those Lange photos.

Maybe because she was dyslexic, she found it much easier to engage with visual imagery versus text. Despite years of going to the best schools to help her overcome this disability, she still found reading to be a chore, a formidable challenge she didn't enjoy. Sometimes she would see words moving in space, even though her teachers insisted it was her dyslexia acting up, that the words were static and inert.

Or worse yet, she would see letters rotating with each other, making it difficult for her to read the words as they appeared in their actual form on the printed page. Consequently, a piece of text that would take people with normal reading ability five minutes to read, would take Geri three times that span to comprehend.

To compensate, she found herself gravitating increasingly toward anything visual, particularly photography. To her, it contained a language she found far more meaningful than text.

Her stomach growled. A faint odor of meat pervaded the green room, no doubt the lingering residue of a meal someone had eaten hours earlier. The smell piqued her hunger. She hadn't eaten anything since one o'clock, right before sound check. She craved a tuna melt sandwich, her favorite comfort meal. She had developed an appetite for tuna melts while living with Ms. Fenster when Michelle was away. She loved them because they were so easy to make. Her mouth watered just thinking about them.

Dez said her taste in food was "hopelessly middle-class," but she didn't care. It was delicious. Certainly not like that vegan crap he liked to eat. That shit was tasteless the first and only time she tried it. After Dez forked over a sample of a vegan burger when they were having dinner in Vancouver, she had spat it out in her napkin.

She popped a couple of stale potato chips into her mouth from the white plastic bowl on the table in front of her. Next to it were white plates overflowing with candy. It was a regular smorgasbord of sweets: chocolate bars from Milky Ways to Kit Kats; licorice, both red and black; CBD gummies; caramels; and chewing gum. "Pure junk," Dez would call it.

After swallowing the chips, she grabbed a few of the red licorice sticks and gobbled them down, before snacking on a few caramels.

She yawned again, rubbing her eyes, which were feeling especially leaden. She hadn't gotten much sleep the night before. Dez had barged into her room in the interconnected suite they shared and woken her up. He hadn't been able to find his acoustic guitar and thought maybe she knew where it was. (It was in his dressing room, as they would later discover).

Her being in the adjoining room in Dez's suite was an anomaly. The hotel had made a mistake, and because there were no vacancies, she had been forced to take it. Not an optimal situation. Geri wasn't thrilled about it, given Dez's nighttime activities.

Someone nudged her, and her body jolted up with a start. The janitor stood in front of her, greeting her with a concerned, if baffled, expression.

"I'm so sorry, miss, but you're going to have to leave," said the man, who appeared to be in his upper fifties. It was hard for Geri to approximate his age. He definitely appeared much older than Larry, whom she knew was in his forties, as Dez would frequently reference his age when he made cracks about how old and out of touch his manager was.

"We have to clean the green room. We do it every day at this hour," he continued.

Geri wiped the gunk from the sides of her eyes. Alarm set in. *Oh fuck, Dez is going to kill me.*

She grabbed her cell phone. She tried turning it on. Nothing but a black screen. And the charger was back in the hotel room. "Shit!" she exclaimed. "What time is it?"

"Four-thirty in the morning."

She jumped up, frantic. "I have to go, but my phone is dead. I can't get an Uber because the app is on my phone. I'm with the Dez Deacon tour. We're staying at—um, shit! What's the name?" She kneaded her forehead, grimacing and hyperventilating. "It's the Chicago Hilton. Something like that. It's a Hilton, that I remember."

"I know the hotel you're talking about," he said, calming her. "Don't worry about it. I'll get you an Uber. Sit tight, young lady."

Bleary, she wiped her eyes again and thanked the janitor profusely.

When she finally got back to the hotel, she immediately raced up to her room. Then she pulled out from the left pocket of her black jeans a small folder containing her key. No key.

"Oh fuck!"

She racked her mind about its whereabouts. She hadn't lent it to Dez, so it must have fallen out when she was running errands for him.

A husky groan issued from her throat when she saw a red bandana tied around the doorknob. To underscore the point in case Geri was totally oblivious, there was also a "Do Not Disturb" sign hanging from the knob as well.

The red bandana was Dez's cue to Geri to make herself scarce, as he was currently preoccupied with some woman. In this instance, it was probably Lily. But who knew? It wouldn't surprise Geri if there was someone else in there. It wasn't as if Dez had been a model of abstinence since her sister's death.

He had tried being discreet around Geri for the first few gigs because she was Michelle's sister and Michelle had only been dead for two months, but after Geri accidentally walked in on him being orally serviced by some groupie in his dressing room right before a show, Dez banished all future attempts at discretion.

That didn't mean he was immune to embarrassment. She had almost been his sister-in-law, and a minor at that.

"I'm so sorry you saw that, Geri," he'd said, his face reddening. "Life is hard on the road, and sometimes you have to let off steam."

"That's how you let off steam? Letting some slut blow you? Wait, has this happened before? Did Michelle know about this?"

"Michelle was in the business. She knew the score and she accepted me. Maybe you should learn from her. Next time, knock before you enter, okay?"

No, Dez, she thought, *that's not going to work this time.* She was tired. She needed to charge her phone. She wanted to sleep in a bed, like right now.

She pounded on the door.

Nothing.

She pounded again.

More crashing silence.

She pounded some more.

"Dez! It's me. Open the door." She kept pounding. "Dez! Fuck you! You and Lily! This is bullshit. Please let me in. I need to sleep!"

Geri thought of the others in the tour who could help, then changed her mind. She didn't want to wake up anyone.

Who was she kidding? They were probably out partying at some local bar or club. Or getting laid. Ordinarily, she'd be up at this time, too, but she was bone tired and needed to crash ASAP.

She leaped into the elevator and headed toward the lobby, which was mostly empty except for three tourists from some foreign country, standing in a knot, all staring with bewilderment at a bunch of maps they were holding.

Geri approached the desk clerk, a prim young woman with a light brown bob. She looked about Michelle's age, mid-twenties at the most.

"Excuse me, I'm with the Dez Deacon tour, and I have a problem."

Peering up from her computer, the woman narrowed her dark eyes and shot Geri a suspicious glance. "Yes?"

Great. She must think I'm a groupie, Geri thought.

Geri pulled out the empty hotel folder with the missing key to provide evidence that she truly was part of the tour.

"The key must have fallen out when we were doing prep work for tonight's gig," she explained.

She felt awkward using that new term "prep work" in her vocabulary. It didn't seem very natural for her but Dez had taught her to say that when people asked her what she did, because her responsibilities were a hodgepodge and they varied with each gig and town.

The desk clerk, whose name tag read "Nancy," searched for the room number on her computer. Her eyes narrowed some more.

"This is Mr. Deacon's room," she monotoned.

"Yes, I know," answered Geri, quelling an impulse to roll her eyes. *No shit, Sherlock.*

The suspicious gleam in Nancy's eyes became more pronounced.

She was going to have to do some convincing.

"I'm his ward, Geri Randall."

No response. *Good God. Like speaking to a chair.*

"Dez is my legal guardian," she said, placing special emphasis on the last two words.

Again, Nancy was poker-faced.

Desperate, she blurted out, "My sister passed away in December. She was his fiancée."

Why was she babbling like this? Telling this stranger her entire life story. But what else could she do? She was tired and wanted to sleep.

"Can you charge my phone at least?" Geri begged, taking out her cell. Maybe then she could show Nancy a news story about Michelle's death and this annoying woman would believe her.

Ignoring the girl's request, Nancy's wariness escalated. "One minute," she said as she excused herself to go to another room. Two minutes later, she came out with another employee, a gentleman who appeared slightly older than Nancy. He was tall, and sported bland features and thin coppery hair. His name tag read "Ronald."

"Hello, Miss Randall. Nancy explained your predicament to me. Do you have any ID?"

Downcast, Geri shook her head. This was turning into a nightmare! "It's up in the room," she said, waving her hands.

"Your name is not on the reservation. Only Mr. Deacon."

Geri leaned over the desk to steal a glimpse at the reservation system on the front desk computer. Instantly, Ronald swerved it away from her.

"The hotel made a mistake! I was supposed to be on the list, but there was a glitch. There weren't any vacant rooms, so I'm staying in my guardian's room."

Ronald and Nancy gawked at her.

Finally, Ronald broke the stony silence. "I'm sorry, Miss Randall. But we cannot help you. I'm afraid we're going to have to ask you to leave."

"No! This is ridiculous!" Geri protested. "Um, buzz Larry, Dez's manager. He knows me. He can vouch for me." She raked her mind to remember his last name. "Shaffer! Larry Shaffer. He knows me."

Ronald and Nancy shared a conspiratorial look before eyeing Geri again.

"Miss Randall," said Ronald, in a clipped tone. He resumed his hospitality drone demeanor. "We need you to leave. Courteously and without disturbance."

Geri took a fleeting scan of the lobby. The foreign tourists were gone. Other than her and these two annoying hotel employees-slash-obstructionists, no one else was there.

"This is bullshit! Please buzz Larry Shaffer," she pleaded. "Or, um, the other guys in the band." Damn. She couldn't remember any of their last names. She only knew them by their first names or their nicknames. In desperation, she rattled them off. "Big Man Louie. Mike, he plays the drums. Gary, the bass player. Come on. You must have them listed in your little reservation system." She leaned over again to steal another glimpse.

Unfortunately for Geri, Ronald was steadfast in his obstinacy not to listen to her. "Miss Randall, how old are you?"

"I'm eighteen," she lied.

He whispered to a chagrined Nancy.

"Now?" she whispered back.

He nodded. Nancy crept back into the inner office where Ronald had initially emerged.

"You can take a seat." He motioned to the lobby, his face a mask of inscrutability.

Geri's pupils dilated. "What's going on?" She shivered with panic.

Ignoring her, Ronald turned his attention back to the computer. Nancy reemerged a moment later, again whispering into Ronald's ear. Geri distinctly heard her say to Ronald, "It's done. I just called them."

A realization dawned on Geri.

"You called the cops on me? You don't believe me!" Her voice became strident. "I'm not a groupie!" she yelled. "I'm really with the band."

Ronald and Nancy reversed positions. Nancy was now behind the computer while Ronald skulked back to the sanctum of the hidden office. Like Ronald, Nancy was acting as if Geri was part of the linoleum, her concentration now centered on whatever task she was doing on the computer, or pretending to do.

The more she tried to shut out Geri, the more the girl wanted to throttle her. But Geri checked herself. If she did that, she would be no better than Dez, and assault charges leveled against her, even as a minor, would be far worse than being picked up for loitering or whatever charge they were going to lob against her.

A scary thought seared itself into her brain. What if they tossed her into foster care? No one was looking after her. Her parents were dead. Michelle was dead. Ms. Fenster...well, she had ghosted her. Lanie was a flake. The few times she'd tried texting her since the tour started, Lanie had given her the bum rush by saying she was on a shoot in yet another remote location. After three foiled attempts at communication, Lanie was out.

Then there was Dez. Her so-called legal guardian. *Ha!* What a joke that was.

Last week, while they were in Portland and Geri had been in a local convenience store buying vinegar because Dez had read on the internet that it could clean leather, she had seen a sight that pained her: a father and daughter at the checkout line. The father was buying cleaning supplies. He was holding the hand of his daughter, who couldn't have been more than nine or ten. The girl had implored her dad to get her a doll that was on sale and on display by the counter. "Please, Daddy! I want it!"

Initially, the father was reluctant. "You already have enough dolls, sweetie."

Not relenting on her heart's desire, the daughter, clearly an ace at wrapping her father around her tiny, dainty fingers, overcame his objection. "Daddy, I want it. Puleeze."

The corners of his mouth widened into a crescent grin. "Okay, honey. You win."

Elated, the little girl glowed as her father added the doll to the conveyor belt on the checkout line.

A sweet, heartwarming scene between father and daughter. And one that Geri would never experience in her life. She knew it was wrong of her to envy that little girl. But the heart was not a rational muscle. She could barely remember her own father, since he'd died when Geri was so young.

She thought about rushing out of the hotel and running away, that way she would avoid tussling with the police, whom she was sure were on their way to relegate her to the netherworld of the foster system. She flinched, until a new thought infiltrated her head: maybe foster care was better than the alternative, which was Dez.

She had lived for him and only him since Michelle's death, and where had that gotten her?

She wished she had the wherewithal to live on her own, be a street urchin like those characters in old movies she used to watch on cable with Michelle, no longer beholden to adults. But she had grown up in comfort, and the idea of sleeping on a park bench or in a cardboard box like she had seen homeless people in New York City do, was not an appealing option.

She had to stick it out. In a year and four months, she would be turning eighteen, a legal adult. And there was nothing anyone could do to change that fact. She wouldn't be under Dez or any other adult's supervision. Money would be a problem, but she would figure out what to do when it was time.

Mired in reflection, Geri looked up at the door and sure enough, as if on cue, two police officers showed up. Geri scowled at Nancy, who was pointing her out to the men in blue. Stupid, considering she was the only person seated in the lobby.

"We understand there's been some trouble here," said one cop to Geri while the other, a larger man, stood by.

To the best of her ability, Geri recapped the details of what had transpired.

Rather than convey hostility, the cop showed a semblance of sympathy. Unlike his hulking, russet-haired partner, who seemed to have the map of Ireland drawn on his generously freckled face, this nice cop was his physical opposite: slighter in frame and weight, older, and with a mop of salt-and-pepper hair. Even if he was faking it, the officer's warm brown eyes communicated a kindness that was a welcome reprieve from the two jerk hotel employees who had started this mess.

"Why don't you come with us and we'll straighten this out?" said the cop.

"Umm," she hesitated. "I don't know…"

"Are you hungry?"

She nodded. It might be a trap, but it had been so long since an adult had been kind to her, it was a reflexive action.

"Come with us. It'll be okay," he said while leading Geri to the squad car parked outside.

Then, whether it was a stroke of serendipity or rotten luck—depending on one's point of view—Dez waltzed through the revolving door into the hotel, his arm draped around some woman who didn't look like Lily as Geri, flanked by the two cops, was about to exit.

In a manner that was pure Dez, he elevated his hand, as if he were a king commanding his subjects, to stop the police officers. "Wait a minute. What's going on?"

"Excuse us, sir. This doesn't concern you," said the quiet officer to Dez. "Please step aside."

"You don't know who I am?" asked Dez, aghast. The woman, who seemed only a few years older than Geri, had one hand on Dez's shoulder and the other planted on his butt.

"Officers, this is Dez Deacon," Geri interjected. "He's my legal guardian." Her voice lowered an octave, as if mortified by this fact.

"Is this true?" the nice cop asked Dez pointedly. "Can you vouch for this?"

"You really don't know who I am?" Dez repeated, nearly gasping from apoplectic shock at not being recognized.

"Yes, I've heard of you, Mr. Deacon, and I must say," added the nice cop, "you might be a talented musician and impressive performer. However, your skills as a legal guardian of a minor female leave a lot to be desired."

Mocking the cop, Dez made a face to the young woman alongside him who kept pawing and groping him, even after she had found out that the girl in front of him was his legal charge.

"We're going to let this go," said the nice cop. He raised his voice so Nancy at the front desk, who had been watching the entire scene unfold, would notice they weren't going to take Geri in.

The larger cop, the quiet one, whirled around to Dez. Geri could see just how imposing he was in comparison. It was a small wonder Dez didn't resort to his usual bluster when dealing with the man. The officer would have pulverized him easily and without an ounce of hesitation.

"Sir, I don't care who you are or how much money you make, but you're a disgrace. This young lady needs guidance, which clearly you don't provide. I'm going to give you a break today, not because I'm in awe of who you are—because you mean nothing to me—but because I don't want to make things worse for Miss Randall, who deserves better than your lack of supervision. You're no role model for anyone. I will give you fair warning: this happens again in our city and I'm taking you in."

Beads of sweat forming on his forehead, Dez bit his upper lip as the cop brushed past him and marched to the squad car.

"How long are you going to be in Chicago?" the nice cop asked Geri.

"Tomorrow is our last night here, then we're off to Detroit," Dez chimed in.

The kind cop gritted his teeth. "I didn't ask you. I asked the young lady." He pulled a card from the upper pocket of his uniform and handed it to Geri. "If you run into problems again and need someone to call, wherever you are, just give me a ring."

Geri nodded bashfully as the cop followed his partner to the cruiser, but not before frowning at Dez.

"I think I need to get some rest," Dez told his hookup, who was still groping him.

"No!" she moaned, crestfallen.

"Yeah, baby. Let's reconvene tomorrow night." He laughed. "What am I saying? Let's reconvene later tonight. Okay?"

They kissed and she vanished into oblivion with all of Dez's other hookups.

Geri glared at Dez, who was rubbing his eyes.

"Let's go up to the room," he muttered.

She trailed after him but not before catching Nancy at the front desk turning her eyes back to her computer after eyeballing them both.

"I'm sorry," he mumbled, as they stepped into the elevator.

"What?"

"I said I'm sorry," he repeated, lightly jacking up the volume of his voice.

"Why didn't you pick me up from the green room?"

"Huh?"

"The green room? Remember? You told me to wait there for you."

"Lily—"

"I don't give a shit about Lily."

"Don't talk to me like that, Geri," he hissed. "*I'm* still the adult here, and I'm still responsible for you."

What she wanted to say to him was that her sister must have been zonked out of her mind when she'd made that stipulation in her will, but she refrained from doing so.

The elevator door opened.

"I didn't fetch you from the green room because Lily had an upset stomach," he said as he strutted toward the suite, Geri in tow. "I told her I had Tums back in my room and brought her there instead. I thought you were going to text me, asking me where I was."

Indigestion? *What a load of crap,* she thought. They probably wanted to snort some coke and then get it on. Geri knew Dez had his stash in his suitcase.

"So you're making this my fault, not yours? Shouldn't you have texted me to tell me where you were?" Before he could answer, she threw her hands up in the air in disgust. "It doesn't matter. My phone died and I fell asleep. But when I woke up and made it to the room, the red bandana was tied around the doorknob with the 'Do Not Disturb' sign."

"Oh that... I'm sorry about that. I guess I forgot to take them both off when Lily left. She didn't stay long."

"Not if you had time to hook up with whoever that was."

"Heather," he corrected.

"I'm surprised you know her name."

"Stop." He yawned. "We'll talk more about this later. Go to sleep. It's been a long night."

Geri did, and woke up six hours later to the epic sound of Dez's guttural snoring in the adjoining room reverberating in her ears. She pulled the thin hotel blanket over her head, hoping to drown out the ruckus. Unfortunately, it didn't do the trick.

Minutes later, she found herself barfing into the toilet. She wasn't sure what had caused this cataclysm of nausea. Was it fatigue, coupled with the nocturnal schedule wreaking havoc on her insides? The diet of fast food and candies? Or the cumulative stress that ripped through her intestines, making her wish she had insisted to Dez that she wanted—or rather, needed—to stay in school just to have a modicum of normalcy injected into her life? She yearned for some peace and calm like what she found in Aruba when Michelle took her there. That was awesome.

Instead, she went along with Dez, doing anything he wanted, when he wanted. It was easy for her to feel defiant when she was by herself, but the moment she was around him, she'd dissolve like a slab of spineless jelly, ready to be at his beck and call. It sickened her, and yet there was nothing she could do. Not yet.

Chapter Ten

Michelle

July 2018

"You see them? It's cool, isn't it?"

"Yeah." Geri stirred closer to observe the swarm of tiny fish swimming in the water. "They don't bite, do they?"

Michelle giggled. "No! Don't be silly."

"What are they called?"

"What?"

"The fish?"

"I don't know. Little Aruban fish."

"They look kind of like eels, don't you think?"

It was the third day of a two-week vacation in Aruba. Geri was off from school for the summer and Michelle had finally been able to squeeze a break in between the constant rounds of photo shoots and fashion shows her agency had booked for her. The frenetic pace and grind were wearing her down. She needed a rest, and what better place to do that than in this Caribbean island paradise?

Michelle had discovered it during one of her photo shoots and loved it so much, she'd vowed that the next time she had some time off, she would go on vacation here and bring her little sister with her. What especially appealed to her was the luminous white sand and the lack of humidity—although it could get very windy. The temperature held steady every day at eighty-five degrees and the light blue ocean waters were so transparent that you could spot the tiny fish, which looked more like elongated tadpoles, coasting underneath.

It was a tourist haven, but she didn't care. Lanie always gave her a lot of flak about that whenever Michelle extolled the virtues of Aruba.

"Why don't you go to St. Barts? It's much more luxurious and exclusive there."

"You mean, it's not full of the riffraff you see in Aruba? The common people? Decent, salt-of-the-earth people who raised you and me and gave us a decent life?"

"That's not what I meant, Michelle, and you know it," Lanie retorted, testy. "Besides, let's face it, Michelle, you are not 'of the people' anymore. You're not. You're a successful model, you travel the world, you're engaged to a rock star, you live in a three-million-dollar penthouse in Manhattan. You might think you're one of the masses, but you're not. That ended a long time ago. You're a member of the elite, and so am I."

"You're a snob," Michelle snapped back, disgusted.

"I may be, but I don't pretend I'm not."

Michelle was fond of Lanie, but sometimes it really bothered her that her friend could be such a pretentious, status-obsessed social climber, considering she came from a background similar to Dez's. Except rather than Philadelphia, Lanie had grown up in a rundown area of Clifton, New Jersey, a product of a single hairdresser mother and absentee father. The only other difference between her and Dez's upbringing was that Lanie's mom, Sandy, was a good woman who loved her daughter and had tried desperately to pay the bills and raise both Lanie and her younger brother. Sandy had taught Lanie all about makeup, and even sent her to one of those rip-off modeling schools, whose fees she ended up paying off for a few years, long after Lanie finished one of their programs.

The classes were good for one thing though: they had helped Lanie get started as a makeup artist at a mall in New Jersey. There, a photographer spotted her applying makeup on a customer and asked her if she had ever thought of modeling. After shooting a few test photos of Lanie in his Lower Manhattan studio, the photographer sent the pics to an old friend of his who was working as a booker at Magnificent Models. Lanie got signed, and began doing the usual rounds of go-sees.

Lanie aced a few of her early go-sees, booking catalogs and a string of fashion shoots. On one of the latter, she met Michelle. But unlike Michelle, Lanie got caught up in the extracurricular activities—the partying and drugs. Soon, she began either showing up late for jobs or missing them altogether due to hangovers.

Eventually, the agency dropped her and she quickly became persona non grata in the industry.

After entering rehab and cleaning up her act, Lanie landed a gig as a makeup artist at a fashion shoot in which the star model was her old friend and former colleague, Michelle. Originally, the client had been very reluctant to hire the former wayward model-turned-makeup artist based on her checkered reputation, but Michelle persuaded them, saying Lanie needed a second chance, which was granted.

Soon, Lanie became far more successful and in demand as a makeup artist than she ever had been as a model. Even though she steered clear of the temptations that had waylaid her previously, she did fraternize with a crowd of superficial posers that Michelle found insufferable.

"You're not being fair," Lanie said to her one time, after Michelle told her point-blank that she considered her new friends to be a bunch of phonies. "My friends are so much fun. I don't know why you won't give them a chance."

After that, Michelle learned the best way to discuss Lanie's new social set was not to bring them up in conversation. They were never going to agree on the topic, so a tenable solution was to leave it alone. Still, Lanie's one-percenter wannabe proclivities bothered Michelle so much that the two friends, who had once been very close, began to drift apart from one another. Then when Dez entered the picture, that space widened into a chasm. They still spoke on the phone and texted each other, yet it wasn't with the same feverish regularity of their early association.

Michelle watched Geri swim, her head bobbing in and out of the no-wave waters. At one point, after doing the butterfly stroke, Geri stood up in the shallow part, her body glistening as if she were a sea nymph. Seeing her sister, Geri broke into a wide smile.

It had been eons since she had seen her sister so ecstatic! The beach was agreeing with her. Well, it agreed with Michelle too. That's why she was seriously toying with the idea of speaking to a broker about buying a place here and being a snowbird in Oranjestad.

Of course, Michelle would time their annual escape from New York City's frigid, blistering winters when Geri was on winter recess from school. But there was a hypothetical scenario to consider: suppose a client booked her for a commercial or a shoot or a fashion show during Geri's break. What then?

That did it. A steely resolve developed within her. When they returned to Manhattan, Michelle was going to devote more time to having a life, even if it came at the expense of her career. She was twenty-six years old and had been working nonstop as a model for over ten years. It was her time now. Dez was pressuring her to join him on tour, to take their relationship to a new level, and she was chomping at the bit to do that.

Yeah, her agency was going to throw a fit, no doubt. But that was their problem. Besides, they already had enough models in their roster that they could work to death and jettison like human debris when they were of no further use. As a model, she was well aware she had an expiration date, and even though to the outside world she appeared to be in the full flush of youth, in her profession she was fast on her way to becoming a relic.

Apprehension seized her when she thought about Geri. Her overprotectiveness, coupled with her promise to her dying mom to always take care of her little sister, had robbed Geri of a life herself. The kid barely had any friends. She couldn't remember the last time the girl had been invited to a classmate's birthday party or anywhere else. And it was all because of this pledge to her mom, a pledge that had ended up being counterproductive to Geri.

Look at her. She was almost sixteen. She should be doing teen stuff, like going to proms, or the mall with friends, hanging out. Michelle hadn't done these things either, because she was already modeling by that age. But Geri should have had that option, and Michelle had taken it away from her by smothering her. Regret flooded her in a flurry.

It was ridiculous. Geri had a learning disability. That was different than being stupid, which she wasn't. And yeah, she was a bit awkward socially, but she wasn't autistic or on the spectrum, as her family had once feared.

Stephanie Fenster had spoken to her at length about Geri's strengths and weaknesses at a parent/teacher conference a year before.

"'Geri is very visual, asks a lot of questions, and has a pronounced curiosity about the world and things around her,'" the teacher told Michelle, reading aloud her evaluation of the girl. "'I am concerned about her isolation from the others, and wonder if her sister's efforts to have her constantly at her side in order to shield her from harm have done her more harm than good.'"

A light bulb had gone off in Michelle's head. In the future, when she trekked out of town or the country on shoots, she would stop taking Geri along as she had done for a slew of them. Securing a tutor and working remotely were more trouble than what they were worth. She would dispense with both. But there was no way she would leave Geri alone in New York City those days she was away.

She arranged for Stephanie to take Geri in during those times when she had to travel for work. Fortunately, that worked out. But she had another concern: what provision should she make for Geri in case something unexpected happen to her? What then?

These thoughts invading her mind, Michelle stepped out of the water and turned back to find Geri still swimming happily. Stephanie is right, Michelle reflected. *I need to stop suffocating my sister and let her start exercising some independence. In just over two years, she'll be a legal adult, and what then?*

The wind gusted hard. Donning her Betsey Johnson straw hat and shades, Michelle slid languidly into her chair. Wrapping a towel around herself, she craned her neck to watch Geri from afar. To suspend her worrying, she reached over to the beach bag on the sand to grab a paperback that had been touted as a top-ten summer read by a number of sites and news outlets. Five pages in, her eyes grew heavy. Michelle tossed the book back into the bag.

Geri was still swimming. Maybe she should try and retrieve her from the water. Even with the wind, the sun was especially unrelenting today. She might get scorched and her skin was even fairer than Michelle's. No, she had to stop. Let the kid enjoy herself.

Her thoughts reverted to Dez. They were getting far more serious now, with Dez talking to her about their future. It was madness. They hadn't known each other that long, but when you met your soul mate, didn't you just know?

She had spoken to him about Geri and their bond. Surprisingly, Dez was very amenable to it, considering he was estranged from his mother and brother.

"Maybe I should have tried to form some relationship with Kevin," he lamented to Michelle after learning about her relationship with her sister. "But if I had done that, I would have still had Gloria in my life, leeching off me for everything, and I couldn't do that. She was a viper I had to get rid of. Kevin was collateral damage, I guess."

They were in bed together in a deluxe honeymoon suite at the Four Seasons hotel in Paris. After repeated tries, Michelle had finally gotten Dez to open up about his past.

"You can still try to reach out to him," Michelle reasoned.

"Nah. It's over. That's one part of my life I never want to revisit. You see, any opening I give Gloria will entice her to try and worm herself back into my life and I can't do that. Kevin comes with the package. I hate to say that, but it's true. So I appealed to her with the only thing she cares about—money. As long as she stays away and never talks about me to the press—and that includes any idiot blogger—the money will keep coming her way. That was the compromise I had to make."

"Sounds so cold and ruthless," Michelle said, massaging his arm.

Though this conversation had happened only a month earlier, it felt like an eternity. Maybe because her lifestyle could be so nomadic, very often the passage of time was suffused with a dream-like quality, making it seem that things that had taken place only a short while ago were locked in a calendar from twenty years past. It was eerie.

Dez needed an infusion of sanity and order in his life, she ruminated. Maybe she could fill that void in his life and hers. They could have a kid—that was one option, and, judging by how reckless she had been with birth control lately, a potential reality that might come true a lot sooner than she'd envisioned.

Having a kid around could certainly be a stabilizing force to Dez, considering how out of control and untethered his life was at times. She cited the craziness of the music business as the main factor that contributed to Dez acting out toward others. Even though it was a side of himself which she hadn't witnessed, she had heard about it from people like Lanie, who'd had a brief fling with Larry, Dez's manager, a few years back. It concerned her.

If she hadn't become a model, Michelle probably would have become a social worker or a therapist or maybe a healthcare worker. The inordinate need to heal broken and damaged people seemed to be embedded deep within her psyche. That informed how she treated Geri, Dez, Lanie, and literally everyone she came into contact with, be it on a job, the agency, or in her everyday life. She could neither explain nor dissect the reasons other than they were catalysts driving her, and it was useless for her to deny or intellectualize them.

"What are you thinking about?"

That simple question shook Michelle back to reality.

"Oh, it's nothing," she said.

She watched Geri wipe herself with a towel and plop onto a beach chair.

"You need to get the sunblock," Michelle told her.

Geri rolled her eyes, fishing through the bag for it. "I know, I know. It didn't look like it was nothing," her sister said, referring to Michelle's reverie.

Geri dabbed the ointment on her face, arms, and any available swath of flesh not covered by her purple two-piece bathing suit. "You looked like you were thinking seriously about something."

Michelle broke into a half grin. The kid was clever. "You like it here, right?"

Geri nodded enthusiastically.

"Yeah, so do I. When we get back to New York, I'm going to contact Marianne and see how she can help us get a permanent place here."

Marianne was her Manhattan realtor who had facilitated the sale of the Village penthouse to Michelle. Marianne worked at a brokerage that had offices all over the world. If there was anyone who could spearhead and close a transaction anywhere, it was real estate supernova Marianne.

"That would be awesome," gushed an exuberant Geri.

"Well, let's see what Marianne can do first," Michelle chuckled, responding to her sister's infectious gaiety. "Let's not jump the gun. I'm just thinking here."

In the end, that plan was put on hold when Michelle and Dez got engaged.

Chapter Eleven

Geri

June 2019

"There's too much echo in this mic," he shouted. "I need a different one."

They had only arrived in St. Louis a few hours earlier when faulty equipment stopped the sound check cold. Dez was slated to perform in a few hours.

The technical director, Kerry, had been corralled by Larry to work this tour. A lanky, curly-haired redhead, Kerry had worked with Dez on previous Prophets tours, and, fortunately for the army of roadies, stagehands, backup band, and even Geri, Kerry had loads of patience. You needed that when dealing with one of Dez's tantrums.

"Okay, I'll swap this out with another mic," Kerry calmly uttered to Dez. "Any brand you have in mind?"

"I don't give a fuck," snapped Dez, standing sullenly, his arms crossed. "As long as the mic works, has clarity, and no goddamn echo. I don't want to be in the middle of a song and sound like I'm in the Grand Canyon!"

"Got it," responded the unflappable Kerry. "No problem. Let's take a break and resume in about an hour, okay?"

"Not like I have any choice."

As soon as they broke, Dez called out for Geri. She rushed to Dez like a thunderbolt of lightning. She always did every time he called out for her. It was a preemptive move lest she be subjected to another tirade.

Poised at the center of the stage, Dez greeted her with a Cheshire cat grin. Flinging his sinewy right arm around her petite shoulders, Dez strolled with Geri to a backstage area where they would be out of earshot from the crew.

When he touched her like this, Geri felt both a twinge of fear and quiver of excitement. The fear she understood, since she'd had a ringside seat to Dez's volatile behavior ever since Michelle had named him her guardian. And her way of managing it was to placate Dez. *Just do what he says. Let him think he has the upper hand.* Early on, she'd felt like his approval was all that mattered, but lately, ever since that whole mess in Chicago, she had started caring less about triggering Dez and more about what she was going to do once she was of age and no longer under his thumb. Still, that tremor of fear and excitement continued to gnaw at her whenever Dez touched her, even if it seemed innocent on the surface. She tried dispelling this notion from her brain, yet there were times when she swore he was straight out ogling her and not looking at her the way he should toward his underaged ward, the sister of his dead fiancée. It was creepy. Sometimes she would chalk that up to his being high or drunk, but what about when she knew he was sober? What then?

Maybe it was her imagination running away from her or her loneliness, combined with a dearth of experience dealing with guys. Maybe she was projecting. She'd heard that term from Michelle, who had told her it was psychological. It was like when you had feelings about someone, and because your subconscious couldn't process those feelings because they weren't cool to have, you accused those same people of having those feelings—and yet you were the one who had them to begin with!

Michelle had talked to her about it one time when she'd been trying to explain why some fellow models weren't friends with her. They considered her a snob, she said, even though she had always been friendly toward them. "They're the real snobs, not me," Michelle said to her, taking a stab at analysis. "They're projecting their feelings about me onto me, Geri. But they're the ones who have the real problem with me."

That was probably the same thing with her and Dez. She couldn't deny that for a long while, she had thought Dez was sort of hot. It was just his personality that was the problem. But after being saddled with him for a few months and seeing the true Dez, whatever attraction she had toward him had abated.

Or at least that's what she tried to convince herself. Her feelings about Dez were a puzzle she couldn't figure out. Did she love him? Did she hate him? Or was it a mixture of both? She was never sure.

That vague, nagging sense of unease she had around Dez was becoming ever more pervasive and pronounced in their private encounters, making her grateful that, apart from that reservation fiasco in Chicago, they had separate rooms on the tour.

His light blue eyes scoured the surroundings, and when he was sure no one could hear, he whispered to Geri in a sultry baritone, "I want some candy." He punctuated his request with a sly wink. Geri knew he wasn't referring to Mentos.

"I'll check the bag. See what's left from your stash."

"Not so loud." He gestured with his hands to reduce her volume in case anyone knew what he might be up to. "Also, I don't want coke." Closing space around Geri, his arm clasped around her shoulder and his eyes narrowed into a lascivious leer. Geri was astute enough to know that the ogle wasn't directed at her, but at the drug he wanted to procure and ingest. But damn, she wished she wouldn't have these jitters every time Dez put his hands on her.

"What do you want then?"

He leaned in and whispered, "Smack."

"No." She shook her head emphatically. "I don't feel comfortable. This isn't right. You should ask someone else."

His eyes flickered with recognition at the monumental recklessness of involving her, a minor, who could also be charged as an accessory. For someone who fancied himself so street savvy, he could really be dense, Geri thought.

He pursed his lips and nodded. "I'm sorry. You're right. That was shitty of me. Really stupid. Forget about it. Just find me that shampoo, 'kay?" He gripped her shoulder again before absconding.

The shampoo was some arcane vegan brand that was sold in select stores. Dez had been introduced to it while he was doing a gig in Paris. One of the local for-hire musicians had told Dez that the shampoo made hair shinier and healthier with repeated usage. Dez tried it and was so pleased with its effects—or rather, what he perceived its effects to be—he constantly sent Geri out on a crazy quest to find and buy that shampoo when he was in short supply. Unfortunately, it was tricky finding it. Whole Foods didn't sell it at every location, and not all health food stores stocked it.

"Why don't you buy it online?" Geri had said in response the first time he'd made that request.

"Because I never know where I'm going to be, Geri! If I was a normie, that wouldn't be a problem. But I'm not."

"I think it's stupid. A rip-off," snarked Geri. "I bet there's no real difference between using vegan shampoo and real shampoo."

"Not true. My hair feels thicker, more hydrated, and lustrous every time I use this shampoo."

She stared at him, skeptical and dubious. Was he a spokesperson for this brand? He certainly acted like it. "I don't get how you can be vegan and still take drugs. It doesn't make sense."

"I guess I'm a paradox," he joked. "Look it up," he added, seeing the girl's blank expression.

"I know what it means," she snapped, rolling her eyes.

"Just do it, okay?" he snarled, before storming out.

Thus began an on-again-off-again expedition for this elusive product. *What a pain in the ass.* Geri wondered if this was some lame-brained scheme on Dez's part to get her out of his hair literally while he tried to score heroin. Besides, it made no sense that he was running out of the shampoo already, since the last time he'd asked her to buy it, they'd been in Milwaukee, which was a month ago. She had spotted eight bottles on the shelf at a local health food store and scooped all of them up, charging it to Dez's black American Express card. No way in hell had he used up half of those bottles, let alone one or two, since then. She knew he didn't wash his hair every day. *This is bullshit, pure and simple,* she grumbled to herself.

Off she went anyway, in search of this dumb vegan shampoo brand. Courtesy of Google, she found that three of them were available in some mystical shop located forty-five minutes away from the hotel. She groaned.

After ordering an Uber to drive her from their hotel to the store and then back, Geri hoped and prayed the three items were still there and not snatched away by another weirdo like Dez.

Fortunately, they were still there. Thank God.

After she got back to the hotel room carrying the plastic shopping bag with the three vegan shampoo bottles in them, Geri barged accidentally into Dez, who wasn't looking where he was going. For some inexplicable reason, the door to his room was ajar, otherwise she would have knocked.

He smiled wildly, his faculties oblivious to the collision. Geri noticed his eyes were glazing over.

"You're stoned," she said, more as a matter-of-fact rhetorical statement rather than an inquiry.

He grabbed Geri for a quick waltz.

"Let me go!" Geri barked.

He cooed, "Oh ye of little faith."

"You're fucked up. How are you going to go out on stage in two hours?"

"The way I go out on stage every night." He stuck his tongue out. "Geri, you really need to expand your consciousness and not be so provincial and boring. I know you're a kid, and that Michelle, my beautiful, sweet Michelle—" his voice choked saying her name "— my Michelle protected you for your own good, but she was wrong to do that. You've been too sheltered. It's time to jump into the maelstrom and experience life in all its glorious, wondrous possibilities. It's time—" Dez stopped, his face suddenly losing all color. He staggered, clutching a table as he tried to regain his balance.

"What's wrong?" Geri froze. "What's happening?"

"I'll be okay," he said, each word slogging out of his mouth as if it were a Herculean labor. "I just have to…uh, lie down, then I'll be okay. Where's the bed? Oh, there it is." He buckled and dropped to the floor.

The gig that night was canceled.

Chapter Twelve

Dez

Thank God for Narcan, because otherwise he'd be in a freezer in the St. Louis morgue right now.

Groggy, he searched for his cell, then remembered: oh yeah. He'd left his Android back in the room with Geri. *Jeez. That poor kid. Damn, she really is getting a serious education in sex, drugs, and rock and roll, isn't she? Michelle, my love, why did you do this to me? What were you thinking, making me her guardian?*

She had only been able to see the best in people. She'd probably thought it was a good contingency plan, not expecting to die when she did. *Christ.*

He lifted his head and saw a tube connected to a vein in his left arm. *What the...?*

He sighed, laid his head back on his pillow, and rubbed his forehead. His head was throbbing. *Good lord.* He needed an Advil. His back ached as well. *Ouch. Unfortunate side effects of an OD*, he guessed.

It was 6:30 in the morning, according to the clock on the wall. *That meant there had been no show last night. Well, of course not—he'd passed out. Like, duh.*

He tried to imagine the scenario that had unfolded after he'd lost consciousness. Desperate, Geri had probably flagged down Larry and he'd called the ambulance.

That scenario sounded a bit sexist to him. He wasn't giving Geri enough credit. Maybe she'd called the hotel reception desk, told them what happened, and they'd gotten an ambulance. Nah, she probably called 911, then contacted Larry, and everything else fell into place. Well, however you wanted to define being "in place," considering he'd screwed up big time by taking too much smack.

This wasn't his first time taking heroin. He'd taken it six years ago when he was with the Prophets. Will, his old childhood buddy, the prodigy who'd played piano, organ, and anything with keys since he was seven—and who'd later betrayed him by siding with the other guys and that record company dipshit, Danny Prescott, by throwing him out of the band he'd started— had told him about an acquaintance at the Chelsea Hotel who was dealing smack. It had been the end of a successful six-month tour culminating in three sold-out nights at Madison Square Garden in New York City.

The gig at the Garden had put them on a whole other plane. He hadn't wanted to mess it up by getting fucked up beforehand. "Let's do it after the final show," he'd told Will.

After the final gig—which everybody who was anybody in show business had attended, clamoring to meet him and the other guys backstage—Dez and Will had met up with the dealer at the Chelsea.

What a glorified fleabag! Talk about overrated. Friggin' dump. He guessed its rich literary history and cheapness were the lures for folks like Dylan Thomas, who'd drunk himself to death at the White Horse Tavern while living there. Edie Sedgwick had nearly burned the place down, hadn't she? Too bad she hadn't succeeded, he thought as the dealer shared some of his junk with him and Will.

They snorted it. Will threw up and his nose bled. To stem the bleeding, he'd grabbed some toilet paper in the bathroom, rolled it up into a tiny wad, and stuffed it into the affected nostril.

Dez was luckier. Outside of feeling nothing but an overweening sense of euphoria, he had been unscathed by the nastier side effects. Like a frolicsome boy, he rolled around on the bed with the dealer, giggling while Will sat in a chair, his finger shoved up his nostril.

It was a fun experience, one he wanted to replicate. But after Michelle entered his life, he put that desire in storage, thinking Michelle would break up with him if he dabbled in smack. Exuding angelic purity, she was like a maiden in a castle in an Arthurian legend. That was how he viewed her the moment their eyes met in that London club. From then on, he wanted to be her knight, her Sir Galahad.

Dez had hooked up with so many models before Michelle. If he had to guess how many, he couldn't. There wasn't a number that high. Hey, he'd been on the road a lot. Superstar athletes got to bang a lot of chicks, too, on the road. What was the problem?

Models were the best. They were all super fine and their bodies were banging. But Michelle had been so different because she had depth and class—real class, which you never saw in the sleazebags that infested the music business, and that went for a lot of those models, too, who would sell themselves to the highest bidder if it meant nabbing the cover of *Vogue* and unending lines of coke.

Guilt tugged at him when he considered how he'd failed Michelle and now Geri, miserably. What a gigantic moron he was. There should be a special place for him in the *Guinness Book of World Records*. Of course, he would never admit that to anyone.

He'd thought scoring some smack would be a nice way to take the edge off. Since Michelle died, he had been under so much pressure, not only with fulfilling her legacy and taking care of her sister, but also from his new record company, Larry, the band—hell, everyone on the tour. A regular militia of flunkies and dependents.

Kids were fickle nowadays, even more so than when he was a kid. In those days, it had taken a while for rock stars to crash and burn and become has-beens. Now, all you needed was one album to flop and that was it. You were done. *Finis.*

There was a lot riding on this tour, and if anything went awry, like last night, he would bear the lion's share of the blame.

Adding to the headache were all those nasty articles in the press about how Dez was a shell of his former self, an example of a once-great talent who'd sacrificed art for commerce and ended up botching that as well.

Then there were the crude blind items that were clearly about him and Geri that proliferated like fungi on all those gossip sites, sites that generated a lot of traffic, sites his publicist tried to pretend didn't exist but he knew about them. They speculated about the true nature of his relationship with his dead fiancée's sister. One bottom-feeder drew parallels between their relationship with the film director Peter Bogdanovich seducing, then marrying, the younger sister of his dead lover, the playmate-turned-actress Dorothy Stratten, after she was murdered by her estranged husband. Those bastards were scum. All of them.

He had spoken to Lloyd repeatedly about suing those lowlifes. His lawyer would tell him the same thing: "As long as it's a blind item and they're not directly naming you and Geri, there's nothing you can do." *Great.*

He'd thought the heroin would be a nice respite from the monsoon of cold reality buffeting him on a regular basis. He should have never involved Geri in this by initially asking her to score for him. *Come on, Deacon, what the hell is wrong with you?*

In the end, he had asked one of the local roadies if he knew of anyone who was holding. An hour later, the smack was dispatched to his room by a courier sporting a gray designer track suit and a blue Cardinals baseball cap.

The dealer had offered to shoot him up. "It'll give you a stronger high than if you smoke or snort it," he advised.

Probably because he always associated syringes with junkies—which Dez was quick to remind himself he wasn't—he was leery about mainlining the smack.

The dealer continued his advocacy of injecting. "If you want a quicker, easier high, it's the way to go."

Well, why not? He prided himself on trying to live his life as an adventure, and that entailed taking risks.

"Give me your arm," said the dealer, who then tied Dez's arm with a violet scarf right above the elbow. "Now squeeze your hand."

A wave of anticipation flowed over Dez as the dealer jabbed the needle into his vein. The dealer pulled out the back of the syringe to draw in some blood, then pushed the smack back into the vein and flipped off the tubing.

Rapture swept through Dez, and off to the heavens he flew.

Thanks to Feral Records's spin doctor, Claudia, the hospital agreed to go along with the narrative that Dez had been admitted to the hospital for "exhaustion," issued in the form of a carefully vetted news release.

At eight in the morning, Larry came to fetch Dez from the hospital. Because he wasn't in the throes of an ongoing addiction and did not require rehab, Dez was discharged.

As he was being wheeled out to the limo parked outside the entrance, Dez ignored the volley of questions fired at him by the horde of bloodthirsty media jackals waiting in ambush to feed on his flesh and throw the carcass to their readership.

"Don't say anything," Larry beseeched him. "Silence is golden here, Dez. Don't take the bait. If you do, they win. You know that."

"Dez, was it really exhaustion?" asked one hack, while another chimed in, "Do you think it was too soon for you to go out on the road, considering your fiancée died not too long ago?"

Then the coup de grâce: "What about the stories that your behavior is out of control and your band is ready to quit?"

Dez gnashed his teeth as Larry and the driver helped him into the vehicle.

"Those bastards are such parasites," he whined to Larry after they were inside the limo. "They just can't wait to pounce when things go wrong."

"Wrong? The gig got canceled because you decided it was a good idea to shoot up smack into your veins."

"I didn't expect the shit to be so potent. I made a mistake, okay?"

"Yeah, well, that move resulted in the loss of thousands of dollars in ticket sales."

"They'll get their refunds."

"That's not the point, Dez. You fucked up, and if this happens again, the whole tour is canceled, not just one gig."

"I'm sorry," said Dez after a lengthy pause. "I have a lot on my mind. Last time I did smack, it wasn't like this."

Another lull ensued.

"Was it too soon, you think?"

"What?"

"Was it what that reporter asked? Do you think it was too soon for you to go back on the road...after Michelle...?"

"I don't know. I thought it would be good grief therapy. Lose myself in work and forget." A beat followed. "Also, I don't know what to do with that kid. I'm at a loss. All that added responsibility, which I never asked for. Man. I don't know what to do about it, Larry. I wasn't prepared to be..."

"Daddy?"

"No, I'm definitely not that. Geri always looks at me like I'm Satan, and not the good kind."

Larry laughed. Dez joined in.

When their mirth subsided, Dez grew pensive. "I guess I'm no role model. That's what this kid needs. I shouldn't have pulled her from school and paid off that teacher. That wasn't one of my better moves."

"That teacher was a phony," responded Larry. "Greedy, too. You showed her true colors."

"Yeah, I know everyone has a price," he said, mocking one of his favorite pet phrases. "I know, but...so what? I didn't think about the repercussions." Another pregnant pause. The silence was deafening while Dez was engrossed in contemplation. "I think we should contact her again," said Dez, breaking the stillness. "This time, we pay her to take in Geri and the teach can help her catch up with school. Or maybe Geri can get a GED. I don't know. I'm just tossing out ideas."

"Oh, shit!" shrieked Larry. He was reading a text.

Instinctively, Dez craned his neck to snag a closer look at the cause of his manager's conniptions. "What's wrong?"

"We're so screwed," said Larry, still eyeballing the text.

Concern lined Dez's face. "What happened?"

"Mike quit. He said he's sorry to give us short notice, but Machine Gun Kelly's manager called. He's on tour in Europe and apparently Machine's drummer quit to go to culinary school. And whatever we're paying him, Machine is going to pay him triple. He's packing his bags and going. Like today!"

"What the hell? He can't do that. What about his contract?"

"He can do that, Dez. He signed a contract that allows him to exit, and without cause."

Dez did a double take, stunned. This was the first time he had heard about this clause. "What?" he bellowed in the car. He was so enraged the blood vessels were popping out of his face.

"Dez, your lawyer was the one who put it together. He was the architect. We had our backs to the wall. It was either this, or risk not getting anyone to back you up. Your reputation, my friend, precedes you. Sorry to say."

"You're an asshole."

"I'm an asshole who protects you, and you should be a little more grateful."

"Yeah, you protect me," scoffed Dez. "You're a traitor."

Good God. Maybe he should have OD'ed.

Chapter Thirteen
Geri

Late July 2019

From the moment she saw him sitting behind the drum kit, Geri was transfixed.

Everything about Val fascinated her. If she had to pinpoint exactly what she found most alluring, she would be stumped. Was it his youth, being that he was in his early twenties, the only other person in the tour even close to Geri's own age—if you didn't count the groupies or hangers-on? How about his tall, sexy bod and super hot blond good looks? Or the way he resembled a panther in the way he moved? So slithery and cool. Combine all that with the manic controlled energy he'd unleash on the drums and hi-hat, and Geri slipped deeper under his spell.

Ever since Val arrived two weeks earlier to take over Mike's spot as drummer in Dez's band, Geri couldn't help but notice her new crush's every movement, gesture, and facial nuance. She was so smitten Dez often had to repeat several times his usual round of requests for her to pick up his dry cleaning, vegan salads, or whatever errands he chose to send her on that day.

Without knowing the source of Geri's distraction—that would come later—Dez tried to stem his fury at his ward's obliviousness. Geri could see this, but she didn't care all that much. She suspected Dez was still feeling guilty about her being inadvertently involved in that heroin bullshit. A total cluster fuck that ended up in the loss of a key musician in his band. It was all Dez's fault, for sure. Until a proper replacement for Mike was found, the tour had to go on hiatus for two weeks. At Larry's suggestion, Val was hired to fill the vacancy.

Meanwhile, the record company kept grumbling about how the tour was bleeding money. Not all the venues had been selling out, so they weren't making back their money. Not good. Plus, the whole process of finding and hiring a replacement for the drummer they lost and then training that person to learn all the songs on the playlist, would cause a minimum two-week delay. That was a serious hassle. Truly.

Fortunately, Val caught on early. He had been the drummer for an alternative rock band that had been signed with Demon Records for a hot minute before the lead singer decided to quit music to enter a New Age seminary while the bassist absconded to Vermont to open a food co-op with his girlfriend. They had recorded and released one album by then, and the only thing notable about it was how quickly it sank to the bottom of the charts. Geri read up all about him courtesy of her friend, Mr. Google.

"Geri!" Dez yelled.

The sound of his scream jolted her out of her daze, a preoccupation induced by the newest addition to the band.

"What the hell is going on with you?" he asked her, in a pique of frustration.

They were backstage at a 3,000-seat theater in Detroit. Dez and the band were on a half-hour rehearsal break, getting ready for a gig scheduled that night. It had been a week since the tour was back up and running.

She apologized and did a double take. "What do you want me to do?"

His knitted his forehead and screwed up the corners of his eyes. "First, I want you to be awake. And second, I want you to go and get me some polish for my boots. They're starting to look scuffed up."

She sulked. "What happened to the polish I bought you when we were in St. Louis?"

"Geri, that was a month ago," he reminded her. "I'm nearly out of it. People are spending their hard-earned money and I have to look good. And that includes my boots."

She nodded her head listlessly and took out the phone tucked into her back pocket. "I'll Google and see what's around."

"Good."

But Dez wasn't thoroughly satisfied. He motioned her to follow him to his dressing room. As she trailed after Dez into the room, Geri let out a groan.

"I can hear you," he responded, his back to her as he opened the door and she shuffled in. "What is up with you? Seriously? It's like you're not here, but off orbiting another planet."

"I don't know what you're talking about," she countered. She knew the reason for her lack of focus lately, and was certainly not going to reveal it to Dez anytime soon.

"Are you still pissed at me because of the smack?" he asked.

Ignoring him, Geri pulled out her phone again. "I'll get your boot polish," she monotoned as she padded out of the dressing room. "Oops," she blurted out loudly after bumping into someone in the hallway. Slowly, her eyes moved up the long, slim torso, the well-built shoulders. and dark blond hair. *Oh no! Shoot me now.*

"I am so sorry." She blushed. "I should have looked where I was going."

"It's okay." Val laughed. "I should have seen you coming."

Still embarrassed, Geri continued to implore Val to forgive her clumsiness.

"Geri, stop apologizing! I'm fine," he replied, his good-hearted chuckling dissolving into a cheerful smile. His cool jade eyes laced deep into hers, sending a tickling sensation throughout her. This run-in marked not only her first encounter with Val, but the first time he'd said her name.

"Well," she faltered, a nervous smile fanning over her face. "I gotta go. Have to do a few errands for Dez."

"Oh yes," he said facetiously. "Have to run around in circles for our fearless leader. Must keep him happy."

"What?"

"I was just kidding, Geri. Really."

She nodded timidly, her tense half-smile fading, before speeding off to find the boot polish. She cursed herself for her awkwardness around Val. *Nice going, Geri. That was really slick.*

Chapter Fourteen
Val

He watched her jittery figure recede into the distance. What an odd kid. Kind of cute, but strange.

He probably had no room to talk when it came to strangeness considering he'd grown up living off the grid with Luddite parents who believed all technology was evil. Rather than be sucked into the vortex of modernity, Eli and Terri had shuttled their family throughout Oregon in an old, rickety SUV while living off the land. And because traditional school learning was nothing more than propaganda designed to lull young minds into mindless conformity—at least according to the gospel set forth by Eli and Terri—they made it their priority to homeschool their children in literature, philosophy, mathematics, and basic survival skills.

It was only when his maternal grandparents had intervened that Val learned how to use a shower and eat with a fork and knife.

"What are you doing?"

Larry's question jarred Val out of his nostalgic stupor. The manager had emerged from one of the backstage rooms where he was doing god knows what. Then Val remembered why he was outside Dez's dressing room, why he'd made a detour for it after rehearsal before that waif barged into him.

"I wanted to ask 'the great one,'" he enunciated the phrase with sardonic disdain while making air quotes with his lissome fingers, "about the encore number 'Slash and Burn.' I'll ask him now."

He was about to knock on the dressing room door when Larry stopped him. "Don't bother him. He needs to rest and gather his thoughts. Meditate."

Larry's recipe for Dez's wellbeing elicited a guffaw so loud from Val, the older man promptly shushed him before leading him away from the door.

"Are you kidding me? He's Mr. Zen?" Val scrutinized Larry's face for a trace of irony. There was none. He was in dead earnest. "Oh my god. Like you all drank the Kool-Aid," said Val. "Starting with that chick Geri, who seems glued to his belly button. What's the deal with her?"

"That, you don't want to know."

Larry's cryptic response only ginned up Val's curiosity. "Why?" Val smirked. "Who is she? Some groupie he picked up in the middle of Kansas? He can't shake her off, so now she's his personal slave?"

"Not quite. She... Geri..." Larry paused as he labored with diplomatic finesse to select the right words to describe the exact nature of the relationship between the teen and Dez. "He inherited her."

"Which band handed her off?"

"No, not like that." Larry scowled, pulling a cigarette from the pocket of his navy blazer. "Let's go outside." He motioned for Val to follow him.

They stopped right outside the stage door. A light summer breeze was blowing, making the humidity less oppressive. The day was turning to dusk.

Larry lit the cigarette and took a puff before gathering his thoughts. Val was intrigued, but also worried. He hoped Geri wasn't caught up in some underage sex trafficking ring. If so, he was going to report that asshole. The hell with the tour. She couldn't be that much younger than his baby sister Sunny, who was a nineteen-year-old sophomore at Boston University.

"Geri is Michelle's sister," said Larry as he carefully deliberated each word.

"What? Who the hell is Michelle?"

"Michelle Randall." Larry could tell from Val's confused expression that the name meant nothing to him. "She was a top model. She was engaged to Dez."

Val shrugged. "Never heard of her but, then I don't read *People* or *Page Six*."

Larry resumed the explanation. "Michelle died in a car accident in Milan a few weeks before the wedding."

"Wow. That's terrible. I mean, I think Dez is a tool, but that really sucks."

Ignoring the dig at Dez, Larry continued. "Michelle and Geri lost their dad many years ago. And when their mom died, Michelle became Geri's parent and guardian. They don't have any other family. All they had were each other." Larry took a long drag on the cigarette, flicked the ash on the ground, and forged on. "Michelle was overprotective of Geri. From what Dez told me, her family thought for a long time that Geri was on the spectrum. Some quack therapist in Colorado told the parents that when Geri was young. Because of that and the dyslexia, she was sent to a special school. And they sheltered her." Taking a final puff from the cigarette, Larry tossed it onto the ground before stubbing it out. "They figured out later on when Geri was older that she wasn't autistic. But the kid was used to the school, and she liked it and they liked her. Then Michelle died." Larry clued Val in about the stipulation in Michelle's will.

Val was aghast. "Are you kidding me? Poor kid."

"What do you mean, poor kid? A lot of kids would kill to be in her position."

Val shot a disbelieving look at Larry. "Was that nicotine you smoked or crack?"

"Yeah, okay. Dez can be a handful at times. I admit that. He can fly off the handle."

"Fly off the handle? Remember the first day I rehearsed with the king?"

How could either of them forget? Still weak and on edge following the heroin overdose, which Val had found out about from one of the tour's techies as a warning should Dez act up, the star had been in rare form, venting his frustration out on the new drummer.

"You're going too fast! Slow down!"

"I set the time, not you!"

"What do you think this is? Jazz? You're doing a solo? Knock it off!"

The litany of complaints was incessant. Grateful to have a gig, as he was running out of money, Val had bit his lip rather than sass back at his new boss.

Oh, how he'd wanted to shout back at him, "Listen, fuckhead. I drive the song. I own the tempo. No one in the band can ever stop the song except the drummer. It ends when *I* stop drumming."

Instead, Val swallowed the bile congealing in his throat and took the verbal hits because he needed the job and didn't want to get sacked. But damn, did he work hard not to lash back at that idiot.

"Don't tell him I said anything about this," Larry cautioned, a shadow of fear crossing his face.

"You're afraid of him."

"No, not at all."

"Yes, you are. That arrogant, overhyped mediocrity has you running in circles—"

"That's not true," Larry retorted, shaking his head furiously. "And shut the hell up with your nasty, elitist assessments of Dez's talents. If it weren't for him, you'd be dealing drugs in Washington Square Park right now to pay your rent."

"Bullshit. You brought me on."

"But he signed off on it. Believe me, you wouldn't be sitting behind him on stage unless he wanted you there."

Val scrunched up his face and said nothing.

"Not everyone is a prodigy like you," quipped a sardonic Larry. "Just because he didn't go to that fancy music school—what was it again?"

Val glared at Larry. "Manhattan School of Music."

"Yeah, that one, and just because he wasn't raised in the wilderness doesn't make him a no-talent. The Beatles couldn't read or write music, and look at what they created. Look at their legacy, and there are more people in our business drawn from the same background than," he pointed at Val, "Mr. Boy Genius, right here."

Val howled with derision. "You're comparing that derivative, fourth-rate Morrison knockoff—"

"Fuck you!"

"—to the Beatles! You've lost it, Larry. He can't even sing on key, and that strutting act he does before each song where he tosses and twirls the mic, thinking he's Plant or Daltrey? Ha! In his dreams."

"I'm not going to listen to this anymore. As long as we sign your paycheck and keep you off the street, you'll do as he says or as we say."

Val crossed his arms in defiance, averting his eyes.

"You might want to get ready," said Larry, glancing at his Apple watch. "The show is in two hours."

Not responding, Val watched Larry reenter the theater through the stage door and then lifted the hood of his jacket over his head as a buffer against the breeze. He needed to get something to eat. Conveniently, there was a deli across the street.

Traffic was at a snarl on Woodward Avenue in downtown Detroit. Honking motorists, mile-long trucks, and jaywalking pedestrians were creating a raucous congestion that Val found perversely comforting as a longtime resident of New York City. While waiting for the green light to signal for him to cross, he was about to scurry toward the deli when he spied a familiar figure of a young woman looming in the distance—Geri.

She was toting several bags full of purchases and heading toward the stage door. Her concentration was so intense, she didn't notice Val flagging her down, nor hear him calling her name above the din of the traffic.

He raced back to the stage door. "Here, let me help you with that," he said.

One of the bags fell out of Geri's hand and all six cartons of boot polish spilled onto the ground.

"Oh shit! I'm so sorry," she said, her face stricken with horror as if she had committed some unpardonable offense. "How can I be so stupid?"

"It's nothing. Don't worry about it," he said as he helped her pick up the boot polish and toss them back into the shopping bag.

She thanked him profusely.

"No problem." He grinned. "Here, let me grab one of those bags for you."

Flustered, she drew a long sigh. "You don't have to do this. I mean, that's not your job."

"Geri, it's fine. It's called having manners. Does he have you go out on these shopping sprees every day?"

"Well, not every day," she said, her eyes darting from him to the ground. Val wasn't sure, but he thought he saw Geri blush, just like she had earlier when they'd collided with each other outside Dez's dressing room.

"I guess we should go in," she said, pointing to the stage door. She reached for the knob and turned it. She tried again to open the door. It was locked.

Geri cursed under her breath.

"Don't worry about it."

With his free hand, Val knocked on the door, and a few seconds later, Jeff, the tour's stage manager, cranked open the door.

"Hey, kids," teased Jeff, a bespectacled twenty-year veteran of the touring circuit. "Time to have some fun."

"Ladies first." Val ceded the right of way to Geri.

Again, Val could have sworn he saw her face redden yet again. Hmm.

"Oh, Geri," Jeff said. "Dez is looking for you. He's frantic."

Val affected a mocking gasp. "Omigod. The boots need to be polished, pronto!"

Her face dropped. "I'm sorry, but can I please have the other bag?"

"I'll carry it. It's no problem."

She stifled a nervous laugh. "Thanks, but he wouldn't like that. I gotta go."

He tilted his head as he watched Geri scamper away like a scared rabbit, her silhouette retreating into the warren of backstage offices.

Chapter Fifteen
Geri

Late August 2019

"Temptation Anthem." It was the only single that The Nameless, Val's now defunct band, had released, and yet, this awesome song kept resounding in her head. The combination of lead singer Jon's raspy vocals, guitarist Marty's crashing riffs and Val's lightning-quick beat, infused her with a thrill that tickled her from her head to toes. It was a sensation to which she was temporarily addicted, and which she kept on replicating by listening to the song on her phone nonstop.

It drove Dez crazy. Of course, she still performed her unending errands for him, but her constant preoccupation with the song, whether humming it when the earbuds weren't stuffed into her ears or listening to it when they were, irked Dez so much that he threatened to demolish her phone. She knew he would never do that because if he did, he'd have to get her another one. How could she answer his texts and calls and everything his heart desired without a cell?

"What the fuck are you listening to?" flared Dez, yanking the earbuds out of Geri's ears.

They were in his suite at the Wyndham Hotel in Hartford, Connecticut, a week before the Boston gig. From there, the tour was going to take a two-week break before reconvening in New York City at the Beacon Theatre. No, it wasn't Madison Square Garden, but it was a respectable venue, and a great way for Dez to further solidify his reputation as a solo artist—or so he kept on telling Geri.

"It's 'Temptation Anthem' from The Nameless," Geri effused.

"What?" Dez scrunched up his nose like he was smelling something rancid.

"It's a song from Val's old band. I'm listening to it on Spotify. It's really great. Want to hear it?"

Horror and disbelief came over him. "Why the hell would I listen to that shit?"

"It's good," insisted Geri. "You should listen to it."

"It bombed. They never even made it to one-hit wonder, and they never even toured because they broke up."

"But it's a good song. Val's drumming is super."

Dez shook his head and rolled his eyes. He stared at Geri long and hard. "Do you have a crush on him?" His lips twisted into a smirk.

"Val?"

"No, the Pope," he sniped. "Who else would I be referring to? Jesus Christ. Grow a goddamn brain." At that last remark, he lightly drummed on her head with his fingers. "Be useful. Pick up my dry cleaning."

She grimaced. "Don't do that!"

"Look at me," he hollered.

Geri's eyes skittered around the room's antiseptic tangerine walls and the dull painting of a sailboat docked at a harbor that hung over the king-sized bed before grudgingly landing back on Dez.

"Ever since that guy joined the band, you have been mooning after him, embarrassing yourself, me, and everyone around you."

She could feel her face reddening. Fighting back the tears, Geri was about to rush out of the room when Dez grabbed her by the shoulders and shook her. She shifted her gaze back to the painting again instead of Dez. *No, you're not going to win, Dez.* Valiantly, she steeled herself as hard as she could not to cry but damn, that bastard made it almost impossible at times.

"If he's nice to you, it's because he feels sorry for you. Nothing more. A guy like that would never be interested in you when he can have his choice of the hottest pussy."

"Fuck you!" she fumed. "You can't stand that someone actually finds me interesting and wants to be my friend. That's what gets you."

Before he could respond, Geri raced out of the room and dashed through the hallway, which reeked of disinfectant. She nearly bumped into a maid's cart. Rather than wait for the elevator, she rushed into the stairway and sprinted down five flights of stairs to the lobby.

She feared Dez would chase her down like a cougar pouncing on its prey, then bodily force her back into the room until securing her unconditional surrender.

But he didn't, and she found that to be both perplexing and a relief. Just when Geri thought she deciphered the conundrum that was Dez Deacon, he threw in yet another twist, completely stumping her.

"Let him go pick up his own dry cleaning," she grumbled to herself. *Or get one of his chippies to do it*, she thought. *God knows they would lick the dirt out of his toenails to please him.*

Dez can go to hell.

She left the hotel, intending to take a walk around the neighborhood. It was a late summer day and the temperature was perfect, late seventies, no humidity. It was ideal for this kind of exercise. Walking always calmed her down and helped her achieve what Michelle called balance.

"It's self-control, composure," Michelle told her one day when she first mentioned that word. They were in Aruba on that vacation in which her sister mentioned the possibility of buying a place there. Michelle was teaching her yoga, explaining its many health benefits, one of which was balance.

Her ringing iPhone jolted her out of the memory. She sighed, then pulled out her iPhone from her pants pocket. She winced. Dez. Who else? She pressed decline on his call and turned the ringer off. Profane texts and lame threats came streaming in, all from Dez. Same old, same old. She tucked the phone back into her pocket. He was going to give her hell later. That was a certainty, but for now, she needed this break, this quiet time. She owed it to herself.

She gazed up at the gorgeous, cloudless sky. A wash of azure blue. Was there anything more stunning than this? She had to take photos of it.

She snapped several shots, adjusting the angle and sizing to get different views and perspectives. Some were wide shots, others were medium. She scrolled through them and posted one of the shots on her Instagram. Dez was going to have a shit fit about this, as he wanted her account to be dedicated exclusively to promoting him and the tour. He can go to hell. She was tired of him monopolizing her Instagram and taking over every facet of her life.

In three weeks, she would be turning seventeen. Then in a year, she'd be eighteen and would legally be on her own. Dez wouldn't be able to do anything. She smiled contentedly to herself as she took in the sights and sounds of Hartford.

Standing in the middle of Main Street, shoulders sinking, she licked her chapped lips as a revelation descended. Initially, when the tour began, she had been excited to get out of Manhattan and see the cities on the itinerary. But that hadn't been the only reason: New York reminded her too much of Michelle. Every block in the Village, every corner and sign, was filled with memories of her sister, bits and pieces of conversation interspersed with some of Michelle's favorite haunts.

The tour had afforded her an escape from grief and an excuse to leave school, an action she now regretted. She never should have listened to Dez. What was wrong with her?

After a month or two on the tour, Geri's excitement had turned to disappointment, then boredom. The details and features were all the same: skyscrapers, hotels, office buildings, crowds of people filing past her when she was on one of her errands. Yeah, some cities were smaller while others were more sprawling. But in the end, you could put a pin on the map and it would be the same. They were interchangeable and oh so predictable.

Once she returned to New York, Geri was going to get in touch with Ms. Fenster. Dez had done something to get rid of her. She knew he did. Blackmailed her or paid her off. There was no doubt.

I'll take the train and stop by her house, she mused, *and park my ass there on her front stoop until she opens the door. I'll make myself such a nuisance she won't have any choice but to listen to me.*

Thoughts of her teacher soon screeched to a halt. She stopped and observed a man, who appeared to be homeless, sleeping on a bench. Ordinarily, she would never gawk at someone in such a dire state, as it went against the tenets of good manners that her mother and Michelle had instilled in her, but she couldn't ignore these wretched souls, either. Those people must have had dreams at one point, families, lives. *Are we supposed to forget them because now they're on skid row?*

What especially drew her to the homeless gentleman on the bench was his style. A black velvet fedora covered his head and a purple silk scarf was slung around his neck. Even under the most abject circumstances, the man hadn't lost his fashion sense. It impressed her. To capture the image, she snapped several photos.

"Now that's not very benevolent of you, photographing people who are in a bad way," tsk-tsked a deep male voice behind her. "You should be ashamed of yourself."

She flinched and jerked her head around, prepared to issue copious apologies when she saw the one reproving her was a familiar person—Val.

Taking two steps back, Geri tucked her phone back into her pants pocket. "Sorry about that." She fidgeted. "I didn't mean to be callous to this man's, um…predicament. It's just, even in his…" she ransacked her brain for the right politically correct word, "condition, he still has flair and style."

"You should be ashamed of yourself. What would Dez think?"

Her mouth ajar, she examined Val's poker face, which was starting to crumble under the weight of playacting.

She nudged his arm. "You faker!" Her eyes danced with glee.

Val burst into fits of laughter. "I got you though," he teased.

"You did not!" Geri protested, giggling.

"So what are you doing out here?"

"I dunno. It's kind of a habit of mine. When we go to a new city, I like to walk around and see what's up."

"See anything special?"

"No. After a while, it starts to get old," she said, a note of dejection entering her voice. Then she brightened. "That's why it's so cool when I see things, people so different for a change, like that man on the bench."

They strolled slowly away from the homeless man toward the next block.

"I'm surprised Dez doesn't have you handcuffed and chained right now, heeding his every demand. 'Yes, Dez,'" he said, affecting terror at being tortured. "I'll do anything you say. Anything. Please, not the bamboo under my fingers! Arrgh! No!"

Offended, Geri turned on her heels and flounced away from him.

He caught up with her. "I'm kidding, Geri."

She scowled, still stomping off, but he kept up with her.

"It was a joke. Remember jokes?" He sighed. "I'm sorry. I guess my jokes are an acquired taste."

Suddenly, she came to a standstill. "Why are you so nasty about Dez? You know, you're on this tour because of him. He signs your paycheck."

Val let out a derisive howl. "Who told you that? Dez? Or was it our second lord and savior, Larry?"

She glared at him and said nothing.

"For the record, I actually respect Dez."

Geri harrumphed as they resumed their stroll.

"I do."

"Yeah, riiiiight," she shot back, disbelieving.

"I do respect him. I think he got a raw deal. The Prophets did their best work with him as their front man." He paused. "Here's a secret. I have most of their albums. With Dez."

Raising her eyebrows, Geri halted in her tracks again. "You do not," she retorted, suspicion clouding her expression.

"I do. Seriously." He put his right palm over his heart. "I swear." He laughed. "Okay, maybe not."

She shook her head. "I knew it."

A moment passed before Val spoke up again, this time in a more somber manner. "I know I never mentioned this to you before, probably because it never came up, but I'm very sorry about your sister."

Geri's lips began to quiver until she tightened them. "Thank you," she uttered softly. "Who told you?"

"It's a tour. People talk." He continued. "I'm sorry for Dez too. I am. Really. That's a very rough break for you and for him."

"So you know the situation and why I'm here?" Geri responded, her voice slightly wobbly.

Without even being aware of it, they had proceeded toward the hotel.

"Oh no, look who's waiting for his favorite slave," said Val below his breath.

Underneath the awning stood Dez, all in black, shades on, arms crossed, head swinging back and forth like a metronome.

Geri groaned.

"We can always make a getaway," Val joked. "Steal away to Maine and hide there."

"We'll need money and food and a place to live," she answered, half serious.

"Ah. You're with someone who was taught survivalist skills at a very young age, Geri," he piped back, injecting a flirtatious tone to their banter. "Remind me to tell you about my family and how we lived until I was ten."

Intrigued, she looked at him sideways.

"Yes, it's quite a story." He grinned at Geri. The smile faded. "Oh, here he comes."

The shades now perched on his head, Dez made a beeline for Geri. Judging by the way he was clomping toward the girl, he was not exactly in a cheery mood. "Where the hell did you go?" he raged at Geri. The muscles in his face constricted with fury. "Rehearsal is in two hours and you run off. I need my dry cleaning and my lunch."

Geri was about to speak when Val cut her off. "How are you doing today?" he said, taunting Dez. "Lovely, bright day, isn't it? Geri and I were enjoying the sunshine, having a very pleasant conversation. It's a shame you couldn't join us."

Instead of a reply, Dez delivered a right hook to Val's chin, sending the drummer reeling to the ground.

Geri screamed and was about to tend to Val when he pushed her away, sprang up, and punched Dez in the nose. Blood spattered as Dez yelped in pain, cupping his hands over his nose.

"You bastard!" he thundered. "I'm going to fucking kill you."

"Stop it!" Geri screamed. "Stop it! Both of you!"

Her pleas fell on deaf ears. Dez and Val tore at each other as if they were street fighters. Her jaw dropped. This was beyond insane.

What especially revolted Geri was seeing a throng of spectators begin to form around the two men.

Omigod. They're acting like this is fun.

"Say, isn't that that guy?" she heard one man say to a woman wedged next to him. "He was in that band. They were on *Jimmy Fallon*. I think his name is Dieter."

Geri ignored the stranger and once again yelled as loud as she could at Dez and Val to stop. Failing in her quest to run interference, she stepped over the fragments of Dez's shades and ran into the lobby to flag down a concierge, a manager, a porter, anyone who could stop the lame, dumb-ass fight between her dead sister's fiancée and the only man to ever show any interest in her.

"Please help!" she implored the desk clerk, a young, geeky-looking redheaded man. "My, uh, guardian and my friend are fighting in front of the hotel. Please help!"

Wearing a nametag that read Miles, the desk clerk was about to speed-dial the police when he stopped. "Are they guests?" He widened his eyes.

Frantic and impatient, Geri responded, "Yes, they're guests."

"Okay, okay. Calm down," he answered before dialing. His voice was measured in a way Geri found unnerving. Why wasn't he upset like she was? Scanning the lobby, she saw a smattering of hotel guests chatting about whatever tourists like to chat about or poring over maps.

Why aren't they trying to stop the fight?

Flustered, she yelled at Miles. "You have to stop them before it gets any worse. Now!"

Geri's emotional breakdown did little to ruffle the mellow desk clerk.

"Don't worry, miss," he assured her. "The police are coming soon. Wait here." He signaled her to stay at the desk as he withdrew into an office. He emerged a minute later with a man so massive, Geri feared for both Dez and Val's wellbeing. This guy was so enormous, muscles bulged from every limb and extremity. He looked like a sumo wrestler, minus the fat.

"This is Tony, he works as our security guard," Miles told her as Tony marched urgently beside him and Geri to the scuffle outside. Miles whispered to Geri, "He's a really nice guy."

"That's wonderful," Geri said, barely listening. Her face was frozen in the same stricken expression as it had been since the fight between Dez and Val broke out.

The crowd of onlookers was swelling into a multitude. Geri thought it was her imagination but she could have sworn she saw some people taking bets on who would win the fight. *Sick. What is wrong with these people?*

Their bloodthirsty glee horrified Geri, but her reaction was nothing compared to the distress that racked her when she saw Dez attempting to put Val in a headlock.

Although Val had a noticeable open gash above his left eye and a welt on his chin, probably caused by Dez's initial right hook, he seemed to have no problem, thank god, warding off Dez's blows.

The whole thing was such a mindfuck for her. Why were they fighting? What was the purpose of this? She couldn't understand it. It would be so stupid if it weren't so pathetic.

It was Dez's fault, yet again, and he wouldn't stop. Even with blood gushing from his smashed nose, spattering all over his black T-shirt and Val's white top, Dez kept going on and on, like the Energizer Bunny.

Gross.

She turned her face away for a second before curiosity got the better of her and then peeked back at Dez and Val.

She wished she hadn't. Dez's face was coated in blood. He tightened his fist, preparing to thump Val once and for all, when Tony intercepted the battling duo.

The mob belted out a chorus of disapproval.

Really? So twisted.

"Aww, no fair. It was just getting good!" squealed one spectator while another hissed, "Go away, you beast! I want to see who wins."

"Enough, guys," Tony warned both Dez and Val as they continued to circle around each other like animals stalking prey. "Unless you really want me to put you both out of circulation, and I will."

When they advanced toward one another yet again, the security guard, who had seemed like such a sweet, gentle soul in the hotel, morphed into a diabolical avenger.

A shiver of fear rattled up Geri's spine as she watched Tony seize Dez by the scruff of his neck as if he were a ragdoll. The moron was stupid enough to sock him in the jaw after Tony tried to stop the brawl. The remaining onlookers gasped.

"I can't watch this," Geri muttered aloud, covering her face with her hands but not before noticing that rather than deal with Tony, Val stopped sparring.

Thank god, he has a brain. Too bad Dez doesn't.

She looked up again to see if her idiot guardian was still in Tony's stranglehold. He was and to make it even worse, Dez was starting to turn blue.

Geri screeched at the top of her lungs, "Stop! You're going to kill him! He's not breathing! Stop it!!"

Racked by terror, she turned to Miles, the desk clerk, who was standing beside her and cried out, "Make him stop, please!"

Miles didn't answer. Geri noticed his complexion turned all pale, the color drained from him as if he had been sucked dry by a vampire.

Finally, a police car pulled up behind Tony. Geri breathed a sigh of relief. She had actually begun hyperventilating, she was so nervous. Unfortunately, that ginormous security guard was still squeezing the life force out of Dez and he wasn't stopping.

"Whoa!" yelled one cop. "Remove your hands from that man, right now," he ordered, cocking his gun at Tony.

The only sound Geri could hear next were the rapid palpitations of her heart. The demon force that had overtaken Tony was ebbing, but his colossal avenger hands were still clamped like a vise on Dez's neck.

"Nice and easy," the cop continued, advancing toward Tony, gun still pointed at him. "I'm going to give you five seconds to remove your hands from this man. One. Two. Three. Four—"

Tony let go. The officer with the gun cued the other cop to handcuff Tony.

His catatonic stupor subsiding, Miles protested, "Officer! Tony is our security guard." "He was trying to break up a fight between these two men."

If she wasn't a girl, she would have bopped this twerp.

Putting the gun back into his belt, the cop emitted a wry laugh. "If my partner and I hadn't gotten here in time, this man would have been dead."

Gasping for breath, Dez grabbed his neck where Tony had nearly strangled him. His face was caked in crusty as well as fresh blood and one eye was nearly shut. To Geri, he looked like a monster from those sci-fi films she and Michelle used to binge-watch on Netflix.

Her eyes then darted to Val. She wondered if he was in shock as he was eerily quiet, standing off on the sidelines. He was stroking his arms and flexing both of his hands repeatedly, a grimace fixed on his face.

She shifted her gaze back to Dez who was jerking his head and craning his neck around as if he were searching for someone, which she assumed was probably her. Maybe. You never knew with Dez.

Geri stiffened in fear as their eyes froze in a lingering stare. Because his face was so beaten up, she couldn't tell what Dez was feeling, either about the fight or her. She expected him to call out to her, raise his voice and start ordering her around like he always did. Instead, Dez's Adam's apple bobbed up and down for a split second, then stopped when he gulped. In a raspy whisper, he let out a hoarse, "Geri."

As if on autopilot, she raced to him like Pavlov's dog, and then cursed herself for doing so.

Standing up, Val mumbled something incoherent as she whizzed by him to get to Dez.

"Be careful. I'm a mess. I don't want to get my blood on you," Dez said to Geri.

"Aww. Isn't that touching?" mocked Val. "He doesn't want to get any blood on his slave."

Geri threw a dirty look at Val, who mumbled an apology. She pulled out a few tissues that had been wadded up in her jeans pocket. Because she was susceptible to seasonal allergies and fall was coming, she always kept a bunch of them on her. She rolled up the tissues like it was a bandage and handed them to Dez, who applied it to his nostrils. Blood was no longer gushing from his nostrils as it had been earlier, but there were still spurts.

Then something unbelievable happened, a miracle. Dez smiled tenderly at her and thanked her. She couldn't believe it. In the time she had known him, he rarely expressed anything resembling gratitude or tenderness toward her. She was so stunned she nearly forgot to say "You're welcome" back to him.

She saw Val was still clenching and unclenching his fist.

"Want some tissues?" she asked, holding up the remainder in her hand.

He shook his head and was on the verge of strutting back into the hotel when the cop, the one with the gun—the other was in the process of shoving Tony into the back of the squad car—thwarted him from making a getaway. "Where do you think you're going?"

"Back to the hotel," answered Val, nonchalant.

"I don't think so. I'm taking you and this other gentleman to the ER for your injuries. But before my partner and I do that, we need to know what happened. Who started this fight?"

Val shot a conspiratorial glance at Dez. Both stayed mum.

The cop sighed. "Okay, we're going to play that game. Fine, we're taking you both to the ER right now." Noting Geri hovering around Dez, he asked him, "Who is this young lady?"

"He's my guardian. My legal guardian," Geri chimed in.

In a wary manner, the cop narrowed his eyes, glancing at the girl and then Dez. "Is this true?" he quizzed Dez, who nodded. "You want to tell me what happened?" the man in blue pressed Geri. "It seems these two have a sudden affliction of amnesia."

"Um. I'm not sure. I was taking a walk and when I came back to the hotel, Dez and Val were at it. I don't know what happened." She shrugged her shoulders in a way that would make Oscar voters proud.

A hint of a smile crept onto Val's lips as he eyeballed Geri. It wasn't lost on him or Dez that she had conveniently omitted certain details of who had joined her on her late-morning walk and what had triggered the fist fight. It still made no sense to her. Maybe it was excess buildup of testosterone needing a release. She remembered her biology teacher once talking about that in class.

"Great!" the cop exclaimed with a world-weariness that made it very clear to Geri that he had witnessed this "see nothing, hear nothing, speak nothing" scenario among perps so many times, he'd literally lost count. "I'm taking you all down to the ER. Maybe your memory," he said sarcastically, his gaze ping-ponging between Dez and Val, "will come back when you're being stitched up." He then turned to Geri. "As for you, young lady, you can stay here. Unless you want to accompany your guardian to the hospital. It's up to you."

"Stay here, Geri," urged Dez. "I'll be okay."

At this, Val sneered.

"What the fuck happened?"

Geri twirled around and saw a horrified Larry, his gray eyes bulging out of their sockets. Next to him was a drop-dead gorgeous brunette.

It never ceased to amaze her how Larry always banged the hottest babes. Forget that he was married and had kids. His hookups were always a hundred times more bodacious than Dez's and he was a damned rock star!

Yeah, she supposed he wasn't ugly and had his charm, whatever, but ugh, he was old. And so pale. One time, she asked Dez what the deal was with Larry and these women.

"What do you think?" he snickered. "They want to get close to, well, you know," he pointed to himself. "So they go through Larry. Besides, you're not giving ole Lar enough credit. He can be very appealing and debonair. And generous. Really. Don't look at me like that, Geri. I swear to god. Ladies love that."

Geri studied Larry's hookup. She was probably a model, just like Michelle, and not a groupie or overzealous fan—or if she was one of the latter, she certainly was better looking than the lot.

With a blank expression, the stunner, whom Larry addressed as Rita, told him, "I'm outta here."

"Good idea," he told her, as they shared a kiss. "We'll speak later."

"Yeah, whatever," said a jaded Rita as she sashayed away, indifferent to the presence of the cops, as well as Dez and Val's beaten-up mugs.

After she left, Larry turned to the lead police officer and Dez. "Will someone please explain to me what happened?"

"I'd like to know that as well," said the cop.

"It was just a disagreement that got out of control," said Dez. When the cop wasn't watching, the rock star winked at Larry, causing the latter to shake his head at the realization that there was more to the story.

"Who are you?" asked the cop emphatically.

"Oh, pardon me. I'm Larry Shaffer. I'm Mr. Deacon's manager."

"Okay, well, we're taking these two to the ER."

"Officer, I'd like to go with them," interjected Larry.

"Fine. Suit yourself," answered the cop.

"Geri," was all Dez mouthed before the cop led him, Val, and Larry into an additional squad car that had been called for reinforcement; an already manacled Tony was in the back seat of the first cruiser that arrived on the scene.

Six months earlier, Geri had watched Dez being whisked away by a squad car after starting a fight with a reporter at Michelle's memorial in New York City. Now she was seeing a similar scene yet again. It was a cycle that seemed to have no hope of cessation when it came to Dez. Was this a side he hadn't shown to Michelle, or had she thought love would conquer all and squelch Dez's self-destructive streak?

She pulled her iPhone out of her pocket and saw it was only one o'clock in the afternoon. That was it? She felt such bone-crushing fatigue that if she could go to sleep and never wake up, she would.

Geri walked back into the hotel and pressed the button for the elevator. Miles was back behind the front desk. Neither of them acknowledged each other, as if they both pretended the events of the last half hour had never occurred.

When the elevator door opened, she padded in. Seeing that no one else was there, she fell to her knees, bursting into tears. She hated breaking down like this, feeling so weak, but enough was enough. *I can't take this shit.*

Chapter Sixteen

Val

Plopping onto a chaise near the front entrance, Val watched as a porter placed his suitcase onto the trolley and parked it by the door. In ten minutes, the Uber he'd ordered a half hour ago would be picking him up to drive him to the train station where he would escape this shitshow.

Because of the notoriously nocturnal schedules maintained by touring musicians and the crew, Val intuited no one in the company would be up at eight a.m. to see him off, so it was safe to make a getaway now and not answer any questions. Peace was all he wanted, even if it came at a price.

Still, he couldn't help but feel depressed.

"So much for nothing," he mumbled as he read a flurry of texts sent to him by Larry in the wee hours of morning. Judging by the time Larry had sent them—two a.m.—they had probably been sent before the manager crashed.

I hope you're not considering quitting because of what happened. Dez said he's cool with everything. He recognizes it was his fault. No bullshit. He doesn't want you to go, in case that's on your mind. No one does.

He scrolled down to another text.

We'll give you a raise. An extra $1K a week?

He pulled up the next one.

How about $5K? Seriously, Val, don't go. I'll connect you with this one band I know in New Orleans that's about to break out in a big way. They lost their drummer a few months ago to cancer and have been using session drummers since then. Atlantic is circling around them. They're putting out feelers for a new drummer. I think you would vibe really well with them. This could be a real coup for you. I know their manager. Really good guy. I can easily connect you with him. But I need you to do a favor for me. Please stay on the tour. It's just one more month and that's it. Anything you want, I'll get for you.

Val drew a long sigh, then read on.

I know Dez can be a real bastard and I have no doubt you were likely provoked into that tiff with him—

"Tiff?" an incredulous Val said aloud, not caring who heard him. "He called that a tiff?"

Suppose one of them had succeeded in beating the other to death—what would he have called it? A spirited battle of wills?

He resumed reading.

I'll get you $10K a week, forget $5K. Dez will agree to a bump. He considers it hazard pay and the rest will come out of my pocket. (But don't tell Dez about the $10K). Seriously, Val, I think the world of you and I know you were put in a shitty situation. What with Geri and all. I want to make it up to you. Don't go. Just steer clear of the girl, that's my advice to you. Think about your career and what's good for you, pal. What do you think?

Luckily, Val had signed an at-will pay for play contract, the same one like his predecessor Mike had signed. This agreement meant he could leave anytime he wanted without penalties being levied against him. Basically, he couldn't be sued. They would have to pay him all the monies owed to him, whether or not he completed the entirety of the tour.

Because Dez's reputation was so tarnished by his backstage antics and that legendary temper—and the music industry could be very tightly knit and ruled by word of mouth like other industries—Larry had found it initially very difficult to snag a replacement for Mike after he dropped out. He had told Val as such when he'd first spoken to him about bringing him onto the tour. So without Dez knowing, Larry and Dez's lawyer, Lloyd, had gone behind their client's back to compose this document, which put Val in the clear if he quit the tour at any time and for any reason.

Why then do the tour? Money—what else? Money made on tours was far more lucrative than what you could make as a session musician on an album. Tours were what made iconic bands like the Beatles, the Stones, and others wealthy, not record sales. Val knew that, and had eagerly signed up.

He hadn't expected to end up living in a mansion and driving a Rolls after doing the Deacon tour, but he knew he'd make enough to pay off some of his mounting bills and perhaps move into a better apartment than the hole in the wall he was currently living in.

After he was released from Hartford Hospital's emergency room unit where he'd been treated for lacerations and contusions, Val had retreated to his room, opened his laptop, and booked himself a seat on the next morning's Amtrak to Grand Central Station. He then pulled a nice fat blunt from his stash and smoked.

The room was probably going to smell like a dispensary after he left, Val thought.

"Who gives a shit?" he muttered as he toked on the blunt, the plumes of smoke swirling around the room. "Fucking nightmare will be over soon," he said to himself, taking one languid drag after another until nothing was left but the roach, which he deposited back in his stash for future use.

The gig that night was canceled. He had smashed up Dez's nose really bad, and there was no way the great front man would be strutting his puny ass out on stage, in front of his adoring fans, looking like he should be in a hospital. Maybe he was still there this morning.

The last thing he remembered at the ER before getting the greenlight to go was hearing a cop trying to get Dez to press charges against Val. First degree aggravated assault and battery. Hilarious when you considered it was Dez who'd thrown the first punch.

"It was just a misunderstanding that got out of control, officer," Dez said. "I'm as much to blame as him."

Val was in the next room, and because the walls weren't exactly soundproof, he could hear everything. What a load of bullshit it all was. It was then Val made his decision to bounce. Larry must have sensed which way was up with him, hence the texts. Too late. His mind was already made up.

His phone pinged. Groan. *Tell me it's not friggin' Larry again, groveling.* Val's strategy of not being responsive was testing his patience.

"What the fuck is it now?" he said in a shrill voice, not caring if the front desk clerk, the porter, or any guests loitering in the lobby or coming from breakfast heard him.

It was a photo of him in profile taken yesterday. Before the fight with Dez. It was from Geri. He wasn't aware she'd snapped any shots of him when they were walking together.

Sneaky little devil.

That pic was followed by two more pics: the homeless man with the fedora and scarf sleeping on the bench, the one whose style she'd admired. There was also a photo of high-rise buildings set against a luminous blue sky. She had an eye, but her potential would have to be honed and developed. She certainly wouldn't get there trailing behind Dez.

She followed up the pics with a text: *What do you think?*

If he responded, he would have to tell her he was quitting the tour, that he was in the lobby right now, waiting for an Uber to take him to the train station. He thought about being cagy and answering her without mentioning he was leaving. He wasn't in the mood for confrontation, so instead, he sent her a thumbs-up emoji. That was the best solution, and a good way to circumvent any unnecessary aggravation.

His phone pinged again.

Maybe she'd sent him a thanks or a like emoji. He pulled himself to the edge of the chair in the lobby, stealing a quick glance outside the hotel entrance before averting his eyes back to his phone.

Nervousness gripped him when he read her message. This wasn't going to be easy to squirrel himself out of.

Thanks. What are you doing up at this time?

Three dots indicated that Geri was in the process of writing and sending another text.

How are you feeling? unfurled her latest text.

Shit. No hope for an easy escape, was there?

HA. I could ask you the same as to why you're up.

Couldn't sleep, she texted back.

I'm okay, he replied. *Sorry about what went down with me and Dez. I'm sorry you witnessed that and were pulled into the middle of it. I really should have kept my big mouth shut and ignored him.*

No response. Maybe he should leave it at that. No, that wouldn't be cool, he thought. Stop being a coward and tell her.

Listen, Geri, I enjoyed meeting you and getting to know you, but I'm quitting the tour. No joke. Right now, I'm in the lobby waiting for a car to pick me up and take me to the train station. Then it's back to NYC. The driver should be here in five minutes. I'm sorry.

A deluge of texts flooded his phone, prefaced by a string of exclamation marks.

WTF? was followed soon by *Larry told me yesterday you were probably going to do this.*

Val frowned at the mention of Larry. He resumed reading the text.

Did you tell Larry that you're leaving?

He typed, *No, but I don't think he'll be surprised.*

You were going to leave and not tell anyone? Geri texted back. *I don't blame you after what happened yesterday. You hate Dez. I get it. But how can you leave and not tell anyone? What about the other guys?*

A moment passed before she sent another text, the one he was dreading.

Or me? You weren't going to tell me?

The Uber he'd ordered, a gray sedan, pulled up alongside the curb outside the entrance. Val grabbed his baggage and gear and strode up to the car. The driver opened the trunk. Val tossed his stuff into it except for his phone. Once he was ensconced in the back seat, he saw that Geri had sent several more texts.

Are you still there? Did you leave already? Where are you?

Pity for her situation combined with compassion overcame him. He started typing.

I'm in the car going to the train station. Geri, I'm sorry things worked out the way they did. I like you. Let's stay in touch. I want to hear how you're doing.

She replied, *K* and a few heart emojis.

As silly as it was, seeing those digital icons warmed his heart. She really reminded him of his sister Sunny. It was uncanny.

If you need anything or someone to talk to, pls get in touch with me. He then added his cell phone number. He was sincere about this, but he also knew that it would aggravate Dez, and anything that stuck in the craw of that asshole was perfectly fine with him. He smiled at the delicious possibilities while dialing down the probable scenario.

If Dez discovered Geri was in touch with his nemesis, she would be the recipient of his wrath.

He pressed "send" before he contemplated the negative repercussions that could await Geri. He rubbed his temple and scowled, cursing himself for not even considering the possibility that Dez might get physical with the girl, hurting her or slamming her against the wall, grabbing her by the hair to do his bidding, or commanding her unquestioning obedience or else.

He fumed, thinking about it. His face reddened with anger. No. He couldn't leave Geri with that brute. Look at how he'd behaved yesterday, like a raging troglodyte. His father had been right years ago: he had a savior complex.

It was after his mom had died, and they were still living in the woods. His dad had ordered Sunny to shoot a deer for dinner. His sister, who had just turned six, refused to do it.

"Then we're not going to eat," Eli announced in an imperious manner, designed to guilt-trip a child. "We'll starve because Sunny is a scaredy cat and would rather see her family waste away and die. What did I tell you about fear? It's a useless emotion designed to control and manipulate people."

Sunny's lips quivered, her tiny hands barely holding onto the rifle her father had shoved into them. "I can't do it," she cried, shaking her head. "I can't kill the deer."

"I'll do it," his older brother Derek cut in. "Give me the rifle, Sunny." Derek motioned for his sister to hand the weapon to him.

"No!" his father insisted. "She has to learn."

The silence that ensued was shattering.

"If you don't shoot that animal in five seconds, it's going to run away. It already senses the presence of humans. See how it's tilting its ears. You have to shoot the deer now or else!"

Tears streamed down Sunny's diminutive face, a cameo of angelic innocence, as her dainty fingers tried grasping onto the trigger. Her eyes boring into the scope, she zeroed in on her target. Nothing. She couldn't fire at the deer.

Val couldn't take watching his sister being tortured like this by their father.

"Give me the gun, Sun," he said to her gently.

Eli was obstinate. "She doesn't need her brothers to step in and save her. Sunny is going to have to learn how to do this on her own, how to survive. That's what I'm teaching you three."

Ignoring him, Val persisted. "Don't pull the trigger, Sun. Let go. Give me the rifle."

"No! She's going to do what I say," yelled Eli.

The deer fled.

"Great!" his father ranted. "Look at what you made me do. All because Val has a savior complex."

Val winced at the memory. Other than a few Kit Kat bars, which he and Derek had shoplifted from a convenience store while Eli got gas for their old, rickety SUV, they had had nothing for dinner. The next day, while Dad was sound asleep in the tent, Derek had woken him and his sister up.

"Let's get out of here," he whispered.

Quietly, they'd gathered their belongings, stuffed them into a bag, and slunk furtively out of the tent like cat burglars after finishing a heist.

Using their father's compass, which Derek had filched after Eli fell asleep, the boy led his brother and sister out of the woods and into civilization. In this instance, it was represented by a small strip mall and the same gas station where Derek and Val had pickpocketed the Kit Kat bars and various candy.

Across the street, Derek eyed the twenty-four-hour sign posted on the front of the convenience store. "Let's go in there," he said, pointing to it, "and ask them if we can use their phone to call Gramps and Grandma. We'll say we got lost."

Fearful their past thievery would come to light, Val resisted. "Suppose they already know we took the candy. We're going to get into trouble," Val protested, his right hand holding Sunny's left.

"They would have stopped us before we left the store," Derek countered. "Don't be a chicken. Let's go in."

"Don't call me a chicken!"

"Okay, don't be a rooster." Derek imitated a rooster crowing in the morning.

Val broke into a grin while Sunny giggled.

"Come on, you two," Derek urged his younger siblings as they crossed the street. A half hour later, Gramps and Grandma picked them up and a new chapter in their lives began.

"We're here," announced the Uber driver as he put the sedan into park outside the train station. He opened the trunk and then the back door. Val was deep in contemplation.

"Sir," said the driver. He cleared his throat. "We're here. Sir?"

His voice jarred Val from his excursion into the past. "I'm sorry," Val responded, still stationary in the back seat. "I changed my mind. Um. How about if you drive me back to the hotel and I'll pay you double? I apologize for the trouble. I...uh..." he stammered a bit as he struggled to get the words out. "I-I-I'm going to stay in Hartford."

The driver shrugged. "No sweat off my back. That's fine. You're the customer."

With that, Val returned to the Wyndham Hotel. His room was already being cleaned for another guest, but that was fine as the company would be checking out after noon. Toting his luggage, he plopped himself back into the same chaise where he'd been seated before the Uber had picked him up. He sent Geri a text. *I'm back. Tell Larry and Dez I'm here to stay.*

Chapter Seventeen

Dez

He woke up to a throbbing headache and the ringing of his cell. His body convulsed with pains and aches all over. Grasping the bandage swaddling his nose, he picked up the phone.

It was Larry.

"Yeah, what is it?" he groaned.

"It's one o'clock, Dez. We were supposed to leave here at 12:30. We're all here in the lobby waiting for you."

"Shit," he replied, rubbing on the bandage.

"This is the third time I've rung you in an hour. Geri said she tried calling and texting you, too, but you were apparently dead to the world. I thought you OD'ed again." There was a lull. Finally, Larry broke it. "What did you take?"

"Vicodin. And I swallowed some oxy too."

"Wonderful," Larry snarked. "Just wonderful."

"Hey, get off my case, alright? That prick broke my nose and it was hurting like hell last night. I needed something extra to help me sleep. Those bogus painkillers that the doctor gave me didn't do the trick. Where are you?"

Dez was concerned there would be eavesdroppers listening to his conversation with Larry. Guilt seeped into his psyche. He was especially worried about Geri knowing he'd ingested Vicodin and oxy so soon after that whole debacle with the smack.

"I'm outside." Larry took the phone away from his ear and directed it toward the cars and sounds of traffic. He put his cell back to his ear. "You hear that? Everyone's inside. How soon can you get ready? I think this hotel really wants us out. Yesterday was not good."

"No fucking kidding. You're a genius, Larry."

"Hey, you should have ignored Val and gone your merry way, but no, you had to slug him, and for no reason other than you don't like him being around Geri. That was on you, my friend. He gave as good as you got and you know you deserved it."

"Screw you!"

"Really? You should be kissing my ass. Yesterday's stunt cost us thousands and thousands of dollars. That's counting ticket sales, paying the local crew as well as ours, the band, etcetera, etcetera."

Dez let out another groan. "Go on," he said, scratching his chest.

"The insurer thinks you're high-risk because of your behavior. You're no longer A-list, like you were with the Prophets," added Larry, thrusting the dagger deep into Dez. "But thank God I was able to get them to agree to cover the loss and compensate for damages by rescheduling last night's show to the end of September, right after the New York City gig."

Dez shook his head. Was that dig about him no longer being A-list necessary? *Jerk.* He really should look for a new manager once this tour was over and done with. Larry was nothing more than a vulture feeding on the flesh of artists.

But he was in no mood to launch into a diatribe against Larry, which he would normally do, had it not been for his broken nose, contusions, and soreness. "Anything else you need to tell me?"

This time, he heard Larry sigh.

"Lar, just spit it out."

"Your fight with Val and your visit to the ER is on *Page Six*, along with all the major gossip sites, and our fave," he added sarcastically, "*Rolling Stone*'s website. Oh and it's on *People*.com and *TMZ*, too."

Dez grimaced and gritted his teeth. "Fuck!" he screeched. "Fuck, fuck, fuck!"

"I know. It sucks."

Of course this would happen, he thought.

"The squealer is either in the hotel or the hospital. Or maybe one of those turds that were watching me and that jerk go at it."

"It doesn't matter. Claudia is doing damage control," Larry continued. "She's working on drafting an official statement from you. Once she's done, she'll send it to me and I'll forward it to you for your approval."

Dez slumped on the bed. "Anything else?"

"You won't like it."

Larry's hemming and hawing was draining his last reserves of patience. Dez would be the first to admit that he didn't have a lot to begin with, but Larry's roundaboutness was getting on his last nerves.

"What?" Dez yelled so hard, he was surprised he didn't hurt his larynx.

"*Page Six* reported that—promise you won't get mad?"

"Larry, I will kill you if you don't come clean. I mean it. I'm going to rush downstairs right now and strangle you if you don't knock off this bullshit."

Larry sighed again. "They reported that Geri was the cause of the fight between you and Val."

A full minute passed before this sank in.

"You bastard!" he snarled. "You've been feeding someone at *Page Six*, haven't you?"

"Not true!"

"Oh yeah, it's true," Dez affirmed. "Weren't you the one who told me there's no such thing as bad publicity in the music business? All publicity is good because it generates attention and drives up views on social media."

"You're reaching, Dez! It wasn't me."

A tense silence followed.

"I will never believe it wasn't you," said Dez, in a low, threatening pitch.

"Listen, we can argue about this forever. We need to get out of here pronto. Get dressed and get ready."

Before Dez could reply, Larry clicked his cell off.

"Son of a bitch," grumbled Dez.

Curiosity got the better of him. He knew it wasn't a good idea, but he Google searched "Page Six" and "Dez Deacon." The item in question immediately came into view. The headline was, as expected, predictably lurid: "Rock Star Deacon Gets Into Violent Scrape With Drummer Over Dead Fiancee's Sis."

Dez's chin stiffened as he sought to contain the ire welling within him. He read on.

"Sources tell *Page Six* that last night, Dez Deacon, erstwhile lead vocalist for popular alternative rock combo the Prophets, and drummer Val Monroe, came to blows in Hartford over the teenage sister of Deacon's dead supermodel fiancée, Michelle Randall. The violent altercation between Deacon, 34, who's currently on his first solo tour since being booted four years ago from the band he founded, and 23-year-old Monroe, who filled in after Deacon's previous drummer dropped out, resulted in a broken nose and contusions for Deacon and a minor concussion for the younger man."

Taken aback, Dez reread that last line. "Minor concussion? What steaming bullshit."

As much as he was loath to admit, next to him, Val had come out of the fight nearly unscathed. If he'd gotten a minor concussion, he'd still be in the hospital.

He resumed reading.

"According to a tour insider—"

"Fucking Larry," growled Dez.

"—the cause of the dispute revolved around the late model's kid sister 16-year-old Geri Randall, who has been accompanying Deacon throughout this outing. According to our spy, the sexy, brooding front man reportedly became incensed at the growing closeness between the nubile teen and the strapping drummer. After catching the teen in a compromising situation with the percussive hottie, Deacon angrily confronted the latter. Accusations exploded into a bloody donnybrook with both men dispatched afterwards to the emergency room in Hartford, the recent stop in a tour that began nearly five months ago. The Hartford gig at the 4,000-seat Palace Theater, a marked comedown from the days not too long ago when Deacon and the Prophets packed 50,000-seat stadiums in SRO shows, was canceled and has been rescheduled for late September following a four-night gig at Gotham's Beacon Theatre.

"Rumor has it that the girl described by our insider as 'sweet and shy,' and the swaggering Philly native Deacon have become an inseparable duo since the glamorous model's tragic death last December in a car accident in Milan. It is not known whether this bond is of a romantic or filial nature.

"A favorite of designers and fashion mag editors, Randall had just finished gracing the catwalk in Milan for Dior when a car taking her to the airport was sideswiped by a drunken Italian motorist. She was only 26 and left no survivors other than her younger sister."

Dez seethed. What irked him about the *Page Six* item—he didn't even want to think about the other sites that had picked up and embellished on the story with their own insinuating takes—was their mention of Geri. Her description by the mole—Larry or the front desk clerk—relieved him. He was glad that the description was innocuous and closer to reality rather than her being portrayed as some sort of jailbait seductress.

It was the fact she had been broached on that tawdry site to begin with that stuck in his craw, especially because Geri had never asked to be in the limelight. If her name appeared on any of those sleazy blogs, it was because of him and Michelle. Their fame made Geri, by association, a target for these gossipmongers.

Venting the wrath boiling inside him like a cauldron, he tore through the suite, smashing the shabby institutional furniture. First, he started with the ugly lamp on the night table. Snatching the plug from the outlet behind the king-size bed, he flung it onto the floor, cracking the light bulb into smithereens. Then he took the wine and water glasses that were on another table, this one in the center of the room, and shattered each one against the wall, the fragments and shards piling up in a heap onto the putrid green carpet.

He was going to start in on the TV and the mirror in the bathroom and the long vertical one above the bureau opposite the bed, but refrained from doing so.

He felt better, his rage fully exorcised.

He knew it was in poor taste to annihilate the room like this, yet how could he not be sure that one of the *Page Six* tattletales didn't work in this glorified fleabag? Even though he was fairly confident that *Page Six* had contacted Larry to confirm the story about his fight with Val, he had a strong intuitive hunch that someone from the hotel—probably that nerdy dipshit, what was his name? Mike or Milton—was the original source.

Despite being fully cognizant that his entourage was waiting for him downstairs in the lobby, Dez took his time to get ready. First up, he took a hot shower. Adjusting the nozzle so the water wouldn't spray directly into his aching face, Dez felt the jet of H_2O hit his back in a baptismal cascade. After the drama of last night and *Page Six*, the shower felt refreshing and cathartic. If he could stay here for the next hour, washing away the memories of yesterday and this tour on which he, Larry, and his record company had pinned their hopes, he would.

After he was finished, he changed the bandage on his nose that was moist from the shower with a fresh clean one. He had been still wearing the bandage that the nurse, not the regular doctor who'd initially tended to him, stuck on his nose. In exchange for an autograph on a prescription pad the nurse had cribbed off some doc's desk, he had been given a generous supply of bandages and adhesive tape. The nurse had also slipped a few oxy and Vicodin tablets into Dez's hands when the attending physician's back was turned. He'd whispered into Dez's ear, "In case the painkillers aren't enough," then winked at him before checking the vitals of the next patient.

Dez exited the bathroom, tiptoed over the broken glass, and tossed on a gray T-shirt, black jeans, and black-and-white Reeboks. He shoved in any clothes that weren't already packed into his red rolling tote. His stage leather ensemble was hanging in the closet in a garment bag. He pulled that off the rack and carried it under his left arm while his right hand pushed the hotel luggage cart.

As soon as he got off the elevator, he was greeted by his entire entourage. His mild-mannered bassist, Gary, saluted him, "Welcome back, our fearless leader."

A round of clapping from the group ensued, except for Geri and Val, who seemed engrossed in some clandestine chitchat. The moment Geri saw Dez appear, she hushed up and stepped away from Val.

Fury surged within Dez at seeing Geri with Val, who was wearing shades even though they were still inside the hotel. *Yeah, probably to cover the bruises and cuts,* he mused. *You may have broken my nose, dude, but you didn't get off scot-free.*

He quelled the urge to confront his ward and the object of her crush. He wanted to abscond from the hotel as quickly as possible, just in case they discovered the destruction he'd left in the room.

Larry nodded at him. "Glad you finally joined us," he said, sidling up to him. A manufactured grin was planted on the manager's face. "I thought I was going to have to call the National Guard."

Ignoring him, Dez addressed the company: "Hey, everyone. I'm sorry about yesterday. But we're going to come back and knock 'em dead when we return here. Now off to Boston we go. Let's rock!"

Dez's exhortation elicited another chorus of squeals and cheers among the group, except for Val. Even with his eyes obscured by shades, Dez could feel the weight of Val's loathing.

Dez's eyes locked with Geri's. As if on cue, the teen made a straightaway to her bruised benefactor. "How are you feeling? I tried waking you up earlier," she said. Because of Geri's personal and professional status, Dez made it a habit to give her his extra room key. Other than the time in Chicago, when he'd been busy partying with Lily, this arrangement had worked out—for the most part.

"I'm okay, kiddo," he responded in a gentle manner that seemed almost paternalistic. Dez threw his arms around Geri and embraced her. In their clinch, with her back toward Val, Dez and the drummer locked eyes until the latter shifted his gaze to take part in a conversation Louie was having with one of the techies.

Moseying onto the bus, Dez noticed Geri was settled in a seat near the front, conspicuously away from Val, who hid in the back like a ghost. Dez guessed she didn't want to further inflame him. *Smart kid.* He took the seat in front of her and was on the brink of taking a nap when Larry thwarted his attempt at early afternoon slumber.

"You piece of shit," he said under his breath, whispering the epithet into Dez's ears so the others wouldn't be able to hear.

Deadpan, Dez's ears perked up. He guessed what this was about. "Oh yeah," he reacted, playing dumb. "What did I do this time?"

"I just got an angry email from the Wyndham. Not only are they suing us for your destroying one of their suites, but we just got blackballed from using that hotel again when we come back here in a month. Nice going, asshole. Who do you think you are, Keith Moon?"

"Let them," Dez responded, his lips curled in a defiant sneer. "It was a dive anyway. Oh, and by the way," he leaned into Larry's ear, also whispering, "I read the *Page Six* item. I swear to God, if we didn't have that much time left on this tour, I'd pound you into next week and not lose a second sleep over it."

Dez leaned back into his seat and closed his eyes. He knew Larry was glowering at him. *Good. Let the POS know that I know what he did.*

Chapter Eighteen

Geri

Early September 2019

"If we're going to be here for a week, then I need a better view," he told her.

They were in Dez's suite at the Boston Omni Hotel.

"Look at this, Ger," he said, pointing to an unobstructed view of a parking lot and garbage depository. "Shouldn't the main attraction of a rock tour get a better view than this? How am I going to be inspired if I have to wake up to this?"

Geri broke into a faint smile. "You have a point. Hmm."

"I do, don't I?" He forced a laugh, hoping she would join him, but she didn't.

A worry entered her head. "Shouldn't Larry do this?"

The late-morning sunlight pouring inside the room heightened the blueness in Dez's eyes. For a moment, she found herself lost in those shimmering pools, but immediately rallied herself back to her senses.

"Seriously, I can't imagine you not doing a better job." He frowned. "That should tell you what a lousy job he's been doing on this tour. No offense."

She said nothing. It wasn't like she was some touchstone of competence. She did what Dez told her to do and that was that. Yet that zinger still hurt.

Still, there was one thing to be grateful about: Dez was in a better mood than he had been at the previous stops. Maybe it was the fact that they were in Boston, the biggest stop for them on the tour so far, which cheered him up. Also, being in a hotel that was a step up from the others might have factored into the equation. For one, the rooms were equipped with loads of cool amenities, like a microwave, fridge and a better-stocked minibar. The furniture looked upholstered in this century and not the last. Also, there was no mildewed odor that wafted into your nostrils the moment you opened the door.

So far, they had been in Boston for two days, rehearsing for the four-night gig that would begin the following night.

There was one thing though that was top of the agenda, even more important than Dez snagging a room with a better view, and that was finding a makeup artist for him.

The cut above Dez's nose that had gushed blood when Val had nearly pulverized it was healing slowly, while the bruise on his cheek was morphing into a shade of yellowish purple.

For some reason, Dez wanted Geri to get in touch with Lanie to find out if she was around and available to be his makeup artist. To Geri's surprise, Lanie texted her back that she was in New York City, back from a job in Paris, and could easily take the Amtrak from Penn Station to get there. However, there was a catch: Lanie needed a place to stay. Her one friend in Boston had married a Dutch businessman and was now living in Amsterdam.

Can you guys put me up in a room at the hotel? she'd texted Geri.

She relayed Lanie's answer to Dez. Geri still nursed a grudge against Lanie for being so self-absorbed and flighty after Dez had abandoned her and flown back to L.A. without telling her.

"You know she and Larry had a thing?" said Dez, an impish gleam in his eyes.

Geri shrugged. *And I should care because...? Oh yeah, I don't.*

"Let's have Larry handle this," Dez stipulated, an idea gestating in his brain. "He's a master at tour logistics," he added sarcastically. "This should be in his wheelhouse, huh? Hopefully, the only room he'll be able to get for her is next to his." He pressed on like a little bitch. "She actually thought he was going to leave his wife and children for her. That's how dense she is."

"If you don't like her, why do you want to hire her?"

"Because she's a very good makeup artist. Your sister, whose opinion I trusted implicitly, told me this. Also, it's so going to get under Larry's skin," he snickered.

"Okay. Whatever."

There was one other thing, something she had been meaning to bring up to Dez, but every time she tried do so, Dez would always sidetrack her with one of his many bullshit dramas.

She summoned up her nerve. It was now or never. *Come on, Geri, don't be a wuss.*

She could feel the sweat on her forehead.

"Um, Dez, I've been thinking a lot about this. I think when we break after this gig and go back to New York, I want to—"

Dez's phone rang. He raised a "one minute" gesture with his finger to Geri as he answered the call.

She bit her lip.

"Hello? Hey, babe!" His eyes twinkled. "How are you? Been a long time. Yeah, I know. I'm here. Finally."

Fidgeting, Geri went over in her head what she wanted to say.

I want to stay in New York. I don't want to come back for the Hartford gig or any gig. I want to stay in Michelle's apartment. I'm going to be seventeen in a few weeks. I don't need a babysitter. I want a tutor to get me up to speed with what I missed in school. I want a normal life.

Dez continued to talk on the phone.

"I can't wait to see you again, too," he said, showing his game to impending tour hookup 13,424. The leering vanished when the genius remembered Geri was still in the room. "Uh, honey, can you hold on for a sec?" He looked up and cupped his hand over the phone.

"Geri, you can go now," he said. "Thanks, kid."

Standing her ground, Geri opened her mouth but Dez dismissed her with a wink.

"See you tomorrow." He waved to her, before resuming his phone chat.

Resigned, she slunk out of the room, frustrated and foiled.

So much for that. Great.

"Nah, that was nothing," she heard Dez giggle as she shut the door. "So where were we?"

She shook her head as she walked down the hallway. Her thoughts drifted to Michelle. Ever since the memorial in Manhattan, neither she nor Dez had spoken openly and at length to each other about their loss. Sure, references had been made between them here and there, but nothing substantial confirming her sister had existed other than being a phantom memory from the not-too-distant past, a specter whose presence was dispelled by conveniently selective amnesia.

Geri counted how long it had been since Michelle's death—nine months. And eight months since the memorial. Not even a year had elapsed, and sometimes it felt like they'd moved on from their grief. Of course, that was a facade. Everything that didn't fit the plan—which was the tour and salvaging Dez's career—had been put on hold. It all seemed so surreal.

Exiting the elevator, she walked to the front desk. Val stood at the desk, gabbing with a pretty hotel employee. Jealousy nipped at her. From the snippets of conversation Geri was able to cobble together through eavesdropping, Val was asking the woman about the weather. Totally innocent conversation. *Yeah, riiiiight.* It was a come-on. Their none-too-subtle body language confirmed this. The woman was toying with her auburn curls. Geri knew what that meant. She read about it in one of Michelle's old psychology books. She was definitely attracted and interested. Little tease.

And Val was even less subtle, with the way his eyes never moved from that woman's boobs, which to be fair, she clearly emphasized with a low-cut white blouse.

Without even thinking about why she was at reception, Geri tapped Val's shoulder.

"Ah, Geri, good to see you," said Val, a flush creeping up his neck. The pupils in his eyes dilated, as if Geri had caught him in the act with the woman.

"Um, Roxanne, this is Geri. She's, uh, Dez's assistant, and um…" Val was at a loss for words, probably because he was reluctant to describe the true legal nature of Geri's relationship to Dez.

Geri exchanged pleasantries with Roxanne, but didn't care to add any more information than necessary. Let Roxanne Google if she was so curious.

"Well, it was nice speaking to you, Val," said Roxanne, all formal and polite, the coquettish tics fading. She put the phone up to her ear. "Best of luck with the concert. You, too, Geri. It was nice to meet you."

Val nodded back, a slight glumness sinking into his features.

"Sorry I interrupted you," Geri said to him, her eyes glittering with triumph as they ambled away from reception.

Val's searching gaze perused the lobby.

"Dez is upstairs," Geri responded. "He's going to take a nap and then go to rehearsal. You can talk to me. It's safe."

The edges of Val's lips curled upward. His head fell forward. It hadn't been lost on Geri that since the fight and the time they'd briefly spoken in the hotel lobby in Hartford after he came back from the train station, he had been studiously avoiding her.

"Sorry. I didn't want to make it worse for you," he responded as they strolled outside down Boylston Street. Though the temperature was far from cold—seventy-two degrees—it was much windier than it had been in Hartford. Pounded by blasts of late summer/early fall air, Geri's trademark bun was blown out of its clip. She removed it and pinned her flyaway tresses back in a ponytail. When she was done, she hugged her shoulders to stay warm. She was clad in a pink-and-white polka-dotted tank top and white capri pants.

Val observed her. "You want my jacket?" he offered.

She nodded tentatively.

He took his jean jacket off and placed it around Geri's shoulders, as if it were a shawl. Because he was six feet tall—another tallie, like Michelle and Dez—and she was only five six, there was no point in navigating her arms through the sleeves as she would literally be swimming in denim.

Though lankier than Dez, who somehow managed to maintain the tone of his biceps on a diet of vegan cuisine, booze, and oodles of drugs, Val's slim, well-proportioned build was nicely offset by a short-sleeved, gray-and-white striped T-shirt and skin-hugging, sun-washed denim pants.

He pulled his phone out of his pants pocket and eyed it for a second before stuffing it back. "I should probably get back."

"Why?" asked an alarmed Geri. "Rehearsal won't start until another two hours."

He stopped walking and bit his upper lip. Even though some of it was obscured by opaque black shades, the same he always wore, Geri could see that the bruises on Val's face were fading to yellow, healing visibly, like they were for Dez.

He stammered. "I-I-I'm not sure it's a good idea for us to talk and spend time together."

"We're doing it right now."

"Yes, I know." He took a breath, pondering the right words. "I don't want to get you into trouble. I can handle myself. But I don't want to make it worse for you."

"It's okay," she reassured him. "Really."

"Yeah." Val nodded. "You're right. Fuck Dez."

Several benches dotted the entrance to the hotel. Val sat on one while Geri followed suit, sitting next to him.

She noticed him flexing his hand, as he did right after his fight with Dez. He was also grimacing, just like before. "Anything wrong?"

He shook his head. "No. These are exercises I like to do to keep my fingers sharp. They did get a workout from..." He stopped short.

She bit her lower lip, then changed the subject.

"So...when did you learn how to drum?"

A beaming smile overtook his face. "Mr. Carney's class. He was my music teacher when I was in the sixth grade. The first day in class he brought us all into this room. It was filled with all these instruments, flute, oboe, cello. Anything you can think of, it was there. I gravitated toward the drums."

His green eyes sparkled. Geri could feel Val's excitement at reliving the memory.

"They became my obsession. Everywhere I went, I would always beat on things as long as they had a surface. My grandparents always joked about it. Then they bought me my first set and I was off."

"This was after...after you lived off the grid?"

"Yeah. After my grandparents got custody of me and my brother and sister." His tone, previously joyful, was now somber. "They blamed my father for my mother's death. She died of lung cancer. In a tent in the middle of the woods."

Part of her wanted to reach out and touch Val to comfort him, but she held back.

"I'm so sorry."

"Thanks. My mother was no innocent either, Geri. She believed everything Dad preached. Hook, line, and sinker. We all did. We didn't know any better. Even after she was diagnosed with stage-three cancer and the doctor told her she had to start chemotherapy or else she would die, Mom and Dad told us they were going to bypass that and rely on natural medicine to heal her. Chemo was a poison, they told us. What would cure Mom would be a diet of greens and vegetables, and hikes where she could breathe in air not polluted by chemicals."

Val's eyes misted. His cleared his throat, then continued.

"The only thing was at that time Mom wasn't breathing well because of her coughing fits. They would last for hours. She couldn't hike either because of fatigue and she couldn't eat because, we wouldn't know this until later, but the cancer was already spreading to her bones and major organs. When she died she was so skinny she was skeletal."

He glanced down at his hands, flexed them once, then stopped.

Silence ensued for the next minute. Finally, Geri spoke up.

"How old were you and your brother and sister?

"I was ten, Derek was twelve, and Sunny was six."

"What happened to your dad?"

Val let out a sigh and shook his head.

"We saw him a few times and then he moved to Mexico. He sent us a postcard. That was over ten years ago. Haven't heard from him since. I can't say it's left a void in our lives because it hasn't."

A beat followed. To change the mournful tone, Geri deflected again.

"How did you get into The Nameless?"

Val nodded to Geri, thankful for that non-sequitur. A smile fanned over his face.

"When I turned 17, I moved to New York to go to Manhattan School of Music. One of the benefits of my parents' homeschooling is that me, my brother and my sister all skipped a grade when we went to normal school. So I was a bit young."

"Weren't your grandparents worried about you being alone in the city? Michelle was always scared about that with me."

"They had a lot of faith in me that I wasn't going to go off the rails. You have to understand, Geri, growing up the way Derek, Sunny, and I did, we matured really fast. We had no other choice. But getting back to The Nameless, I met someone at school who told me about this band that was looking for a drummer. I auditioned for them, got in, and dropped out after one semester. By then, the band already had record company interest. That's when I met Larry."

"I love the songs," Geri gushed. "I listen to them a lot."

"Thanks. You might be one of the few who do."

She paused before asking softly: "Why did you come back?"

Strands of his thick, dark blond hair blew around wildly. He tucked them behind his ears. "I was worried about you."

She furrowed her eyebrows. "I don't understand."

"Geri, maybe I'm overstepping my bounds asking you this," he said, his eyes straying from hers. "I probably shouldn't, but I can't help it. Has he ever hurt you?"

She gulped. "What do you mean?"

"Geri, come on," he responded, narrowing his green eyes into slits as he looked directly at her.

Visions of Dez strongarming her the night he returned to Michelle's apartment materialized.

"Really?" Even with the dark sunglasses hiding half of his face, Geri could see Val shooting her an incredulous expression.

"Why do you think he has?" She leaned forward to watch her feet kick at the ground.

"Because!" He raised his voice. "Look at who he is."

Glancing around, paranoid that hotel guests and passersby could hear, Geri shushed Val.

"I'm sorry. I shouldn't have taken your head off like that." He took the shades off and pointed to the yellowing contusion under his right eye. "See this?" He pointed to another fading bruise, this one on his left cheek. "And how about this beauty, right here?" He put the shades back on. "I'm not going to lie. I've been in fights before. My father taught my brother and me how to defend ourselves. It was part of his," he lifted his callused, nail-bitten fingers in air quotes, "survivalist training."

Expressionless, Geri stared downcast while Val pressed on.

"I've been exposed to all sorts of people in my life, Geri. But I have never encountered a hothead like Dez. One time he yelled at Louie for breathing too hard during a rehearsal. The man has asthma."

"I know Dez can be a jerk," she answered quietly.

"A jerk? He's unhinged. I was joking when he smacked me. What did he expect? That I wasn't going to defend myself? I was going to allow him to beat me to a pulp? For what? Because you and I are becoming friends?"

Geri kept mum as her eyes circled the ground. His eyes were still fixed to hers.

"I shouldn't have asked you if he's hurt you." He glanced away, shifting in his seat.

"He hasn't," she murmured, her voice devoid of any inflection.

"Are you sure?" He turned his gaze back at her.

She was still staring at the ground. Her pillowy lips, which were trembling slightly, compressed into a thin line. A fraught moment passed before she spoke, her voice barely above a whisper. "He did shove me around one time." In a flat intonation, she described the blow-up in Michelle's apartment, recounting the details with a few editing liberties here and there.

Val listened with rapt attention. "Just that one time?"

"Yes." She paused, then stood upright, straightening her posture as if falling into a military formation. "Anyway, it was nice chatting with you. I have to run. Dez wants me to do a ton of things for him and I need to—"

Val cut her off. "It's okay. It's not like I'm going to run back and tell him."

The irises in her hazel eyes darkened to a dull glint. She pursed her lips, nodded faintly, then sat back down on the bench, pitching her gaze straight ahead. She opened her mouth, but no words came out. Finally, she spoke. "Sometimes he threatens me," she said, her voice a soft, whispery cadence. "Like when I don't get him the right lunch or I'm late picking up his dry cleaning. Or I don't do something the way he wants."

"How does he threaten you?"

"What do you mean?"

"What exactly does he say? It's okay. You don't have to be afraid."

"Why are you asking me this?"

"Because...I care about you."

"You do?" The dull flicker in her eyes evaporated. Now they were glimmering. "You're not going to say anything to anybody, right?"

"Absolutely not."

"Not to Larry?"

"He's the last person I would say anything to."

"Sometimes..." She labored long and hard to speak. Then she swallowed a breath, exhaled, and everything spilled out of her. "Sometimes he says that if I don't shape up or listen to him or do what he wants me to do, he's going slam my head against a wall, put me into a coma, or beat the living shit out of me and leave me for dead." The lower ridge of Geri's mouth began to quiver. "He also likes to call me retard. He says I'm a moron who can barely read."

"You're not a moron. You have dyslexia. A lot of very smart people have it. He should speak for himself."

"I've always had problems reading. The words and letters shift. They reverse themselves so what I see is not what everybody sees."

Wrapping a consoling arm around Geri, Val huddled close to the girl and uttered, "You are far from being a moron. You're a sweet, smart, sensitive person."

Geri brightened at the compliment as breakers of warmth swelled and undulated throughout her body at Val's touch. He removed his shades. She looked at him, her face contracting into a giddy smile.

"I think you do a good job as Dez's assistant, putting up with all his crap," Val added. "I like the photos you send me."

Her smile broadened.

"I think you have potential. If that's the area you want to go into, or even if it's just a hobby. But, Geri, you need to go back to school. A tour is not for a kid."

"I'm not a kid." Her smile disappeared, yielding to a frown. "I'm going to be seventeen in two weeks. How old are you? Twenty-three? That's not much older than me."

"Maybe not chronologically, but psychologically, it sure is. There's a big gap between someone your age and someone my age. I'm an adult. You're not."

"I'm almost an adult," she said with a defiant pout. "You're not that much of an adult."

"I think you might have a point." He smirked. She burst into a fit of laughter so contagious, he joined her.

When the cackling subsided, Geri assumed a serious tone. "You're wrong about Dez. I know he can be a jerk, but you don't understand. There's a lot of pressure on him with this tour. It's the first one he's been on since he went solo. Without the Prophets. And it's the first one he's been on since..." Her voice dropped an octave. "Since my sister died."

"I'm sorry. I keep forgetting that. I'm sure that's hard for both of you."

"Yeah, he can be a real tool. But there are times he can also be really nice and funny. And super cool. My sister wouldn't have been engaged to..."

She stopped before another word issued from her lips. Another tense moment arose, then Geri deflected. "I've been Googling about how to get a GED."

"That's great," Val enthused. "When the tour ends and we get back to New York, I'd like to connect you with my older brother Derek. He's an English teacher at a private school in Westchester. I know he does a lot of tutoring on the side. I'm pretty sure he's helped people get their GEDs. He can help you."

Geri's ears perked up. A teacher who was not Ms. Fenster? And the fact that this teacher was related to Val made it even better.

Before Geri could answer, Val's phone pinged. He glanced at it and groaned. "It's from Larry. He wants to know if I can make rehearsal in fifteen minutes. Dez wants to start rehearsal early because he wants to meet up with his yoga coach later. Yoga coach?" Skeptical, Val lifted his eyebrows. "Do you know anything about that?"

"Uh, no," Geri lied. In Dez speak, "yoga coach" was a euphemism for either drug dealer or hookup or both. "I have no idea."

They strolled back to the hotel lobby. Inside, the corners of Val's mouth contorted into a shy, boyish half-smile as he pointed toward his jean jacket presently acting like a shawl over Geri's shoulders.

"Oops." Geri had forgotten. "Here you go."

"It was good chatting with you, Geri." He gripped her left shoulder. "I mean, really chatting." He leaned closer and gave her a hug so hard, Geri was surprised it didn't crush her ribs. His scent of lavender lingered with her after he left.

She was about to approach a hotel employee about Dez wanting a room with a better view but halted in her tracks. She sat down on a gray, velvet-padded lounge chair in the lobby.

A legion of thoughts overtook her.

I shouldn't have said anything to Val. Suppose he gets into another argument with Dez. And then he throws what I told him back in Dez's face. What then? Shit. I should have shut up…But what about the other stuff Val told me? He wouldn't tell anyone that unless, well, unless he…" Her face broke into a big smile. *It has to be that. It's gotta be.*

Chapter Nineteen

Larry

"Guess what? I have a surprise! I'm flying in to see you. I should be landing at Logan at 5:30 tonight."

Oh no! Fuck me!

Rabid fear shot through his veins as he felt his heartbeat racing uncontrollably. He hadn't expected this message from his wife. Certainly not when Tandy was busy launching her own business, a CBD startup she'd co-founded with another ex-model—not to mention their ten-year-old twin sons, Timmy and Tyler, who were starting a new school year.

He groaned. This sucked a steaming pile of shit. Good God. As if this tour wasn't already a nightmare. Now this? He loved his wife but man, oh man, he did not need this. Every day something happened that was more horrible than the day before. It was madness and he did not want to subject Tandy to any of it. It was safe for her to be in California, away from this crap. And also away from his, um, extracurricular activities.

Larry reached for the bottle of Xanax on the night table. He was sucking down so many tablets, he wondered if he would have to go into rehab once his tour-sanctioned servitude to the biggest asshole on the planet was over.

He remembered the first time he saw Dez, in all his anarchic wildman glory, at that dive bar in Philly. Clad in a black leather jock strap, black leather straps across his chest and black leather boots, his long black hair cascading past his shoulders, Dez had been a cross between a rock-and-roll Nosferatu and Iggy Pop.

Sure, that kind of get-up was nothing new. Larry had seen umpteen versions of it so many times from so many wannabe rock stars, seeking to set themselves apart with outrageous gimmickry, designed to grab attention while scoring the ultimate brass ring—a recording contract. But without talent as the foundation of a career, and charisma as the magnet, those over-the-top tactics fell drastically short.

Luckily, in Dez's case, he'd had it all—soulful pipes that actually had range, solid guitar playing, and smoky good looks. And judging by the orgiastic reaction the audience displayed toward Dez in that backwater bar, he exuded a dangerous sexuality that seemed to captivate both the girls and guys.

"I'm telling you, this dude is the next Jim Morrison," he raved to Demon Records's head Danny Prescott while also talking up the other Prophets.

After Prescott checked them out himself at another gig and listened carefully to a demo that Larry had produced, the record company honcho agreed, and the band was signed. When their first album rocketed to the top of the charts weeks after its release, they became the hottest sensation in the biz, and Dez, an international sex symbol. Whether appearing on late night TV or playing sold-out concerts in large arenas, Dez became the undisputed face of the band and linchpin of the promotional advertising. The fact that Dez wrote most of the songs, with keyboard player, Will, and bassist, Craig, making occasional contributions, only solidified Dez's standing as the de facto leader of the band.

At first, the other guys were okay with their front man usurping the lion's share of attention, but when every single frigging reporter in the universe wanted to interview Dez and all the fans would scream for Dez and only Dez, it became tiresome.

They understood the business and that Dez was a big reason they were all millionaires after living on food stamps only a few years ago. Yes, he was always a volatile, impetuous person, even back in Philly, but now, with everyone kissing his skinny butt, telling him how he was the greatest thing that had ever lived, he was unbearable. He even threatened to punch out Prescott after he had the temerity to tell Dez he should learn how to treat people better. At that point, the band's momentum cooled down considerably.

Was it a coincidence or the fickleness of the public? Larry reflected it was both, as well as part of the cycle of an artist's shelf life, in which one minute you were up, the next you could be down.

They were no longer selling out stadiums or charting as high as they had with their first album, Lucifer Laughs. Their third album, Pandemonium in the Graveyard, failed to make the top fifty. In the rock-and-roll firmament, Dez's star had been dimming.

Prescott gave Larry an ultimatum: either replace Dez or he would drop the Prophets from his label. "That bastard is out," he told Larry.

Out of loyalty and friendship, Larry had stayed on as Dez's manager while the Prophets hired another manager at Prescott's suggestion. Larry worked on overseeing Dez's transition to solo performer, advising his pal/client that rehab and anger management classes would suffice if he wanted to redeem a public image badly tarnished by stories—that were mostly true—of his hellraising, out-of-control behavior.

Then, by some stroke of serendipity, an angel named Michelle had appeared on the scene. Like Dez, she shared similar black Irish coloring—the dark hair and crystal blue eyes. Sometimes when they were together, they resembled siblings, prompting a few music journalists to crack that Dez's romance with a female doppelgänger was the ultimate in narcissism, the modern-day version of Mick and Bianca.

She had been good for him, giving him a purpose that fortified his sobriety and kept his tantrums at bay. And now she was gone. Fucking hell.

His throat was brimming with acid reflux. *Ugh. What did I eat last night? I'll have to get an endoscopy after I'm done here. Terrific. If I don't die when this is over, it'll be a miracle.*

He rubbed his temple. God, his head was killing him. Groggy, Larry put on his cheap Walmart reading glasses, which he kept next to the vial of Xanax, and reread Tandy's text, just to make sure he wasn't hallucinating.

Based on the time stamp, Tandy had sent the digital missive at 6:30 in the morning L.A. time. That had been 9:30 here in Boston. He checked the time and saw it was 11:30 in the morning. Shit! He had to get moving now.

He looked over in the bed and saw Lanie snoring. *Good fucking God. Why, Larry, why?*

He stared at Lanie's recumbent sleeping form and the drool on the pillow. Gross. In addition to indigestion, nausea lurched in his stomach.

How did this happen? Five years ago, he'd vowed he would cut this skank out of his life forever after she threatened to tell Tandy about their stupid little affair. He must have been super blitzed last night. That was the only explanation.

He racked his memory as bits and pieces of yesterday started to coalesce. He remembered arguing with Dez about hiring Lanie to do his makeup.

"Are you kidding me? You want to hire her after what she tried to do to me?"

"That has nothing to do with me, Larry. This is business."

Larry gaped at him in disbelief. "Is she the only makeup artist in the country? She's not even in Boston. It would be prudent and within our budget to hire someone local. I have contacts in Boston. I can put feelers out and get you a good makeup artist. I'm sure if I post a notice on Craigslist, I could get someone better than Lanie. What? Are we going to cover her roundtrip airfare and also put her up for four nights?"

"She said she could take the Amtrak from Penn Station. She only needs a hotel room, that's all. Geri's already been in touch with her."

"You can't be serious," Larry snapped, flailing his arms. "Of course you are! Yeah, why not? Sure."

Arms crossed, Dez's silence was as immutable as his arrogance.

Larry shook his head and groaned. "This tour is costing a fortune, and your little stunt in that room in Hartford only made it worse. Oh, and let's not forget the brawl with Val. That was priceless. And now this?"

"Whatever you think about Lanie as a person, she's a solid *pro*, Larry," argued Dez. "She's a great makeup artist, and I need to look good for this gig. You know, a lot is riding on it and New York too. We'll need her for that as well. The good news is we don't have to put her up in New York 'cause she already has a place there. Face it, Larry. Lanie is the best. Patch it up with her and we'll be set. Do it."

Gritting his teeth, Larry had stormed off in a huff.

Though it went against every fiber of his being, he had done as he'd been duly told and texted Lanie. Honestly, he should have called her—that would have been far more professional than texting, which he considered a kid's platform—yet the mere thought of speaking to this woman, who could have tossed a sledgehammer to his marriage, made his flesh crawl. Even the simple act of composing a text and sending it to her required intestinal fortitude on an epic scale.

Hi, Larry, she texted back instantly. *Good to hear from you. It's been a long while.*

Her little miss innocent act chafed at him. *Yeah, that bitch was waiting with bated breath for me to get in contact with her, wasn't she? Damn that Dez. The bastard is forcing me to hire her out of spite. He holds me responsible for that* Page Six *mess.*

In reality, Dez wasn't that far from the truth. No, Larry didn't plant that item. Most likely, the original source was someone from the hotel—probably that squirrely front desk clerk who'd brought out that gargantuan security thug to stop the fight. But the reporter, whom Larry had dealt with numerous times before, did have him on speed-dial. And he had called Larry to confirm the story and ask for more details to spice it up.

Whatever. All publicity was good publicity in the music industry. Everyone knew that. Well, maybe not all the time, but most of the time.

Hi, Lanie, he'd answered. *Dez needs a makeup artist for the Boston gig. His face is still banged up from this scuffle he had the other day.*

Yes. I read all about it in People. *With that hot drummer who used to be in that band that came and went. Very dishy.*

Ignoring her penchant for gossip, Larry continued his Dez-mandated mission and told her they would need her in Boston by Wednesday, the night of the dress rehearsal for the gig that would begin the next night and run until Sunday.

Sounds cool, Larry. Do you have a room for me?

I'm working on that now.

I'm going to be reimbursed for Amtrak, right? Also, I know you guys are heading back to New York for the next leg. Can I hop on the bus with you guys rather than go home on the train all by my lonesome? It'll be fun seeing Geri again. How is she doing? Dez treating her any better?

Larry scowled. What a royal pain in the ass. Steeling himself from going off on her, he texted back. *Yes, we will reimburse you for the train fare and I'll see what I can do about having you join us on the bus. I'll ask Dez. The decision will ultimately be his. It's his tour.*

I get that. That makes sense, she texted back. Then the coup de grâce: *Are you still pissed at me, Larry? Don't you think it's time for us to bury the hatchet? I know what I did was out of line. I'm sorry. I was coked out of my mind, not eating, not sleeping. I wasn't thinking clearly.*

He glowered and glared at the text, wondering how he was going to respond. Should he berate her for how she'd acted back then?

A groundswell of mea culpa overcame him. He was far from blameless. When he and Lanie had their affair, he'd been in Manhattan for a few months; Tandy and the boys were in L.A. The record company had asked him to help launch a few up-and-coming bands like The Nameless. That's when he'd met Val.

One of his ex-girlfriends, Amber, another ex-model, had referred Lanie's makeup services to him, so he'd hired her to do the makeup for The Nameless' one and only album cover. He was lonely. He missed his family. Messing around with Lanie filled those voids. Yeah, he was an idiot and way too priapic for his own good—that, he could freely admit—but he was a guy, and lonely as hell during that time. Sometimes the company of a woman, especially a beautiful, willing one, could make the time pass by so much sweeter. Okay, maybe he shouldn't sleep with other women when he was happily married and with two kids, but he had never claimed to be a saint. He'd never told any woman he met on the road that it was anything other than casual. Lanie had pitched it to a whole new level with her brand of crazy.

Are you still there?

Finally, after a lengthy pause, he answered. *It's water under the bridge,* he wrote back, his teeth set in a grimace. *I think we should keep this above board and professional.*

Lanie agreed. When she arrived at the Boston Omni Hotel, things were awkward until Larry suggested they get a drink at the bar as an icebreaker. That's when one drink became two drinks, then three drinks and more.

He nudged Lanie. "Honey, you're going to have to get up."
She awoke with a start. "Huh? Where am I?" Then she scanned the room until her eyes fell on Larry. "Oh God." She slumped back against the bed, then pulled the pillow over her heard. "Tell me, we didn't...?"

"I think we did," he piped back. "But I'm not sure. Last night is pretty hazy."

"Oh God." Lanie gripped the top of her bedhead hair with her right hand. She licked her chapped lips. "Can I get some water? My throat is parched."

He shoved his naked self into the pair of gray slacks he'd worn last night, the same pair that he'd found on the carpeted floor this morning. He tottered to the minibar fridge and grabbed a bottle of water, which he handed to Lanie.

"Thanks," she answered. In one swallow, she guzzled the water, emptying it in two seconds. "Can I have another?" She cleared her throat. "I get dehydrated very easily."

He tossed her another. She also drained it completely at record-breaking speed.

"Lanie, whatever happened between us last night, let's make it our secret. Okay?"

She nodded. "Yeah. You're right."

She dismounted from the bed. Stark naked, she covered her breasts with her arms and her vagina with her hands. This was dumb, considering he'd seen her in the buff countless times before. She was acting like a virgin, which she most certainly was not.

Hastily, she collected her clothes, a pair of jeans and a paisley halter top strewn on the floor, and got dressed. She fumbled in her pants pocket for her key, her face expressing profound relief at finding it.

"Time for me to do the walk of shame, I guess." She affected a contrite expression on her face, although to Larry, it looked more like she was constipated. Before vamoosing, she staggered over to Larry and kissed him on the lips. "Later."

He tugged at her arm, stopping her. "Um, Lanie. Tandy is flying in today. I had no idea she was coming in until she sent me a text. Please, please, don't say anything. This never happened."

"My lips are sealed. I will be the soul of discretion. Believe it or not, I can be. See ya."

After watching her disappear, Larry picked up his phone. It had been pinging incessantly since he'd first seen Tandy's text. In a subsequent message, she laid out the details of her flight. *No need for you to pick me up at the airport or get a car for me. I know you're going to be busy with Dez and the others when I land. I'll go straight to the theater with my baggage. Or should I go to the hotel first? What do you think?*

Go to the theater first, he typed back. *What about the boys? Who's looking after them?*

The phone rang as Tandy's name appeared on the screen.

"Barb," Tandy said without missing a beat. Barb was an older woman who, since retiring from the post office, had worked part-time as a nanny/babysitter to supplement her social security checks. Tandy had found out about her through her business partner, Kayleigh. "She's staying at the house. She's going to sleep in the guest room and drive Timmy and Tyler to school. So how is the tour coming along? Is Dez behaving himself?"

Larry snorted.

"I guess not. You'll have to tell me when I get there. Can't wait to hear all about his latest antics. Listen, sweetie, I have to run. Have a plane to catch. See you later. Love you."

"Love you too." He heard her click off. "Wonderful," he said aloud, his hand still clutching the phone.

Larry wobbled into the bathroom and unscrewed the cap to Alka Seltzer chewable tablets. He chucked two of them into his mouth and chomped on them. *Maybe that will dispel the reflux.* He undressed and indulged himself in a brief sacramental shower, washing away both the psychological and physical grime this tour was exacting on his body and mind.

What a shitshow. He really should have gone to law school.

Chapter Twenty

Val

"Can you please lighten up on the cymbals when we go into 'Tear My Soul in Half'? Right now, all I hear are the cymbals. They're drowning out the bass and guitar. I can barely hear my vocals."

They were rehearsing for the all-important gig that would begin the following night. Dez's request to Val was the first thing he'd said to the drummer since their fight.

"What are you talking about?" Val spat back, contorting his face in disgust. "I'm playing all of your songs exactly the way you wanted!"

A strained silence permeated the musty rehearsal space at the 3,500-seat Mercury Spotlight Theater. Neither Larry nor Geri was present. The former had apparently bailed even though he was supposed to be there, while the latter had been sent on a wild goose chase to purchase a specific blue crystal that Dez was convinced would bring him the luck he needed to make the Boston gig a smash success. Geri had texted Val about it when he'd asked her how she was doing.

"I can go in a little earlier," interjected Gary, the bassist, "and that can head off the reverb from the cymbals."

Nodding, Louie leapt in. "I could do the same with the guitar. I don't think the problem is Val's drumming. It's spot on. It's the timing that's out of sync."

The guitarist was a big, gentle bear of a man, who always sported his signature bowler hat and was staunchly averse to confrontation, having been a practicing Buddhist for twenty years. He swallowed a deep breath and said in a barely audible gruff voice, "Dez, I think you need to come in earlier."

Dez's lips creased into a stiff smile. "Excuse me?" He addressed his band with a peremptory air, as if he were a drill instructor addressing a band of lowly recruits. "Whose band is this? Is it yours?" He pointed to Gary, who veered his eyes away from Dez and directed them toward the bass held in his arms. "Or is it yours, Louie?"

"Hey, man," replied Louie, raising his palms upward in an appeasing gesture. "You don't have to get that way. I was trying to be helpful."

Still fuming at Dez's dictatorial ways, Val jumped into the fray. "How about I refrain from the hi-hat and only use the drum? I'll hit it once every thirty seconds, marching band style. Would that work for you…Herr Deacon?"

A hush fell over the room.

Dez's blue eyes were so penetrating, they were like bayonets spearing into Val. "What did you say to me?" With a menacing scowl, Dez slowly inched toward Val, who stayed seated behind his drum set.

A jumble of thoughts filtered into Val's mind. *Yeah, come and get me, asshole. I'm so tired of you and your mediocre ways and your autocratic tactics. It would be one thing if you had real talent – that could compensate for being an asshole – but you're a notch above bubblegum. All flash and absolutely no substance.*

The friction between the two men was so intense, so palpable, Louie and Gary both interceded.

"Whoa, whoa, stay down, Dez," yelled Gary as he blocked his boss from lunging at Val.

"You too," Louie cut in to Val. "Jesus Christ. Do you want to screw this up like you both did with Hartford?"

Both Val and Dez were about to speak up in their defense, but Gary spoke over them. "I don't care who started it. I don't care if you were in the right," he said to Dez, "or if you were," he said, turning to Val. "The point is that it shouldn't have happened. It was unprofessional. Like two little boys in a playground."

"Gary is right," added Louie, as he put a steadying hand on Dez's arm. "That kind of behavior does not belong on a tour. I've worked with many different artists. You know this, Dez. A lot of times, these bands didn't get along. Downright hated each other. But, in the end, all of that bullshit, the feuds, the personality clashes, it all got swept away for the music. That's what matters in the end. Only the music."

Dez took a huge, measured breath. "You're right." He patted Louie on the back.

"I know I am," he replied with a light guffaw.

"I think you should both shake hands and that's it," beseeched Gary. "Don't ruin an important gig because of a petty grievance."

"It wasn't a petty grievance," sniped Val.

"Whatever. In the grand scheme of things, it's inconsequential," said Louie. "Come on, do it now. Shake those hands."

The scowl gone from his face, Dez nodded to Louie. He shuffled over to Val. The younger man was less forgiving, but because of his deep respect for Gary and Louie, he complied with their request when Dez extended his hand.

But he wouldn't forgive, nor would he forget, neither their fight, nor what Geri had told him in private, even if he suspected the girl was only giving him a sanitized, edited version of Dez's abuse toward her.

"We still have the matter of the cymbals to hash out," said Val.

His arms crossed, Dez bit his lower lip. "Yeah. Let me figure this out. How about if we take five?"

"Sounds good," answered Gary and Louie in unison.

Not saying a word, Val pulled his pack of cigarettes out of his jean jacket and rushed outside. The ciggie was poised between his lips when he lit it with a lighter. Snapping the lighter shut, he shoved it back into his side jeans pocket. Smoke billowed from his mouth and nostrils as he inhaled the nicotine.

Weatherwise, it was another mild day in the low seventies. Unlike the previous day, where the sun had been blinding, today the sky was overcast and foreboding with rain.

A tempest of thoughts ran riot in his head: *What's wrong with me? I should have bolted in Hartford when I had the chance.* Then he thought of Geri and shook his head, angry with himself for being softhearted when it came to other people's troubles. He wished he could be a ruthless SOB like Dez and not care and do what he wanted. But he couldn't. That had never been in his nature.

He puffed more on the cigarette as he contemplated the remainder of the tour. Not much was left other than this week, the week in New York, and that rescheduled date in Connecticut. That was just over two weeks. From his solar plexus and through his esophagus, he let out a hollow growl that fully encapsulated the depth and breadth of his frustration.

"Aw, it's not that bad," commiserated Louie, closing the door. He stood alongside Val.

"Want to make a bet?" Finishing the cigarette, Val flung the stub to the ground, then stamped it out with one of his boots.

"Can I bum one of those?"

Val arched his eyebrows. "Are you kidding me? The spiritually evolved, mature Buddhist has vices? Nooo, tell me it's not true."

Louie chuckled. "Sometimes it's good to have a nice smoke."

Val held the pack of cigarettes out to Louie. The hefty rhythm guitarist drew out a cigarette, holding it in his fleshy fingers as Val lit it.

Silence descended until Louie, in between drags, broke the stillness. "Do you know what you need? I think you need to chant."

Val laughed, waving his hand away as if to dismiss the suggestion.

"Seriously. I think you need to meditate, open your mind up a bit, and chant. It'll loosen up your chakras and get you to a plane where temporal concerns won't rile you up."

"You mean, like with Dez?"

"Yes. Listen, I've been in this business for a long time, and I've seen a lot of talented young guys like you get chewed up and left for dead because they allowed themselves to fall prey to a shitload of things that didn't mean squat in the end."

"I don't have the patience to chant. I have the attention span of a three-year-old."

"Stop creating barriers for yourself." Louie took another leisurely drag before finishing the cigarette. "Meditate ten minutes a day," he persisted. "Remove all the filler in your brain, the filler that creates these toxins, and let your subconscious float in peace for ten minutes every day and you'll see a difference in your life in no time."

Val shook his head, skeptical. "I don't know."

"Can't hurt." A pause followed. "I'm glad you came back."

Taken aback, Val's eyes nearly popped out of their sockets. "Who told you I almost left?"

"Does it make a difference?" Louie tapped on Val's shoulder. "I think it's time for us to go back in. Remember what I told you."

Val nodded, and both men re-entered the rehearsal space. Gary was already there, tuning his bass while Dez was engaged in a private tête-à-tête with Larry.

Seeing Val return to his post behind the drum set, Larry moseyed over. "Don't worry about the cymbals," Larry murmured to Val. "It's all cool."

Rubbing his eyes, Val compressed his lips. "The leader couldn't tell me this himself?" he whispered back, his gaze reverting to Dez, who was chatting to Gary about their previous stays in Boston. "He needs his little intermediary to do it for him?"

Larry sighed. "Stop it," he admonished Val, his voice pitched low so Dez and the others couldn't hear. "Call it a temporary truce. If not, think of it this way: next month, this will be in the past and you won't ever have to worry about us again."

After rehearsal, Val rebuffed a dinner invitation from Gary and Louie. Instead of Mexican cuisine, Val opted to put eating on hold in favor of smoking a blunt from his stash in his hotel room. Plucking it from the plastic baggie he'd tucked surreptitiously in between overlapping folds in his luggage, Val lit up and toked. Slumping against the bedpost, he extended his rangy legs against the king-sized mattress and closed his eyes.

He pondered Louie's suggestion about meditation, how it would be a good way for him to decompress and reduce stress. Maybe he should incorporate it into a regular regimen starting that night.

Louie probably didn't mean for the meditation to be accompanied by smoking a blunt, but didn't a majority of Americans support legalization? And wasn't it legal in Massachusetts?

He was a musician on tour, and unlike countless others who had sought to take the edge off with extracurricular pastimes ranging from boozing to screwing groupies, his outlet was pot, and he was unapologetic about it. It helped in so many ways, he thought, as he stared at his fingers holding the blunt.

A knock on the door shook him from his mental meanderings. The blunt still in his hand, Val hoisted himself from the bed and glided over to the door. "Who's there?" he yelled out.

A tinny, unintelligible voice that sounded female responded.

He leaned closer to the door and repeated his question.

"It's me, Geri."

Shit. He yelled out, "One minute, Geri! Hold on."

He quickly extinguished the blunt with his fingers, then flushed it down the toilet. He cursed himself afterwards, as he only had a few others left in his stash. But he couldn't have Geri traipse in and see him toking up, even though she and everyone else knew he was a pothead.

He rotated the crank handle of the casement window overlooking the street, getting it to open. The extraneous noise of traffic and pedestrians might drown out conversation, but maybe the room would smell less like a dispensary if fresh air wafted through.

"I'm coming!" he shouted, wiping the residue of the blunt on his jeans. "Be there in a sec." He opened the door, wearing an embarrassed grin. "Hey." His hands were tucked in his jean pockets. "Hello!" He ushered her in.

A perplexed Geri didn't move. "Did I come at a bad time?"

"No, not at all," Val lied.

Upon entering, she sniffed, the pungent scent invading her nostrils. "Oh." The realization sunk in. "You smoke a lot of weed, don't you?"

He tittered. "I guess the fresh air," he pointed to the open window, "didn't get rid of the smell that much, did it? Sorry about that. It'll probably be federally legal before long."

"I don't mean to say anything bad about it," Geri backtracked. "It was just an observation."

"Okay, cool." Val motioned for her to sit on the one chair in the cramped room while he sat across from her on the slightly mussed bed. Unlike Dez's room, Val's was strictly bargain basement, most likely because everyone other than Dez and Larry were on the lower rungs of the tour's totem pole. "So what's up?"

She coughed and giggled nervously. "Nothing. I wanted to see how you're doing."

"I'm doing okay," he replied, toying with his hands. "I almost got into another blow-up with your guardian."

Alarm spread on Geri's face. "It sucks that you two don't get along."

"Yeah, it was in rehearsal. Fortunately, we didn't get an encore of, you know." He steered the forefinger of his right hand to the nicks on his face, which were healing but still visible. "But it was touch and go there for a few minutes. Surprisingly, we called a truce, and everything is now good. Sort of."

"Oh, that's good."

"I'm surprised you're not busy running around Boston proper trying to find some obscure boot polish for Dez."

A shy smile crept up on her mouth. "No. I got a dozen of them when we were in Hartford."

She began to fidget. Other than the roar of traffic from outside, a cloak of silence fell over the room.

"What's wrong?"

"I wanted to ask you something, from the last time we talked," she replied, jittery.

"Sure. Go ahead."

"You told me you came back because of me."

Val nodded.

"You were worried about me?"

"Uh-huh."

"Because of Dez? Was that the only reason?"

Her large doe eyes glistened with hope and anticipation he found unsettling. He furrowed his eyebrows, scrutinizing Geri's face and body language. Before he could process what his intuition was telling him, Geri leaned as close as she could to Val, her derriere barely on the chair, and quickly kissed him on the lips.

He was stunned.

Seeing his expression, Geri turned ashen pale and frowned. The light in her eyes dimmed. "I'm sorry," she waffled, her face turning a vivid shade of crimson. "I thought maybe you liked me. That was stupid of me to think that. I guess not. I'm so sorry." She stood up and was about to bolt from the room when Val stopped her, reaching out toward her.

"Geri, please come back!" he implored.

Slowly and with great diffidence, Geri skulked back to the chair to hear Val out.

He paused to consider the right words to say. After a moment of deliberation, a stream poured out of him. "I'm flattered, I am," he said, still weighing his words. "I do like you but no, not in that way."

"That's okay." She squirmed. "I shouldn't have done that. That was stupid of me. I'm really sorry." As she fumbled out this last apology, her eyes glistened with tears.

"Stop apologizing, and please don't cry," he responded. "Not on my account. I'm definitely not worth it."

"Yes, you are," she replied, a sob breaking in her throat.

"No, I'm not," he argued. "Geri, you know how I've told you a few times that you remind me of my kid sister Sunny? That's how I see you. As a sister."

She nodded. "I understand," she murmured.

Rather than scrape at the wound, Val tried to alleviate it by admitting culpability. "I apologize if I ever gave you the impression of anything more," he said, kneading his hands nervously. "If I did, that was my fault, not yours."

"I have to go." She leapt up from the chair. "Dez needs me to do a couple of things for him and he's going to wonder where I am." She rushed to the door, mumbling, "See you later."

Still sitting in a cross-legged position on the bed, Val called Geri back into the room, but to no avail. She was already gone. Letting out a tortured sigh, he uncrossed his legs and laid down, plopping his head on the pillow. *Nice going. That was genius, Val. Pure genius.*

His phone pinged. He picked it up and saw a text from Sunny. Talk about irony.

She wanted to know if tomorrow night was still good for her to see the show.

Yes, he texted back. *I don't think it'll be a problem. Just tell whoever is at the door that you're on the VIP guest list. I'll make sure you get a backstage pass as well.*

Cool! Can't wait to see you! I'm stoked you're working with Dez Deacon. I used to have such a crush on him when he was with the Prophets. He is so hot! What's he like???? Tell me, pls!!

He wanted to post a few vomit emojis, but refrained out of not wanting to disillusion Sunny. He typed back, *He's interesting. Can't wait to see you too.*

Interesting, huh? Doesn't sound that good, lol! She followed up with a slew of laughing emojis, then typed, *Hey, that girl you told me about, will she also be there?*

You mean Geri? Yeah. She'll be there. I'll introduce you to her...if she ever talks to me again. Which I doubt.

Oh no! What happened?

Long story.

After they were done, Val fished for his stash in his baggage again. He pulled out another blunt. This time, he wasn't going to be thwarted. No matter who came to the door or what transpired next, he would smoke this one through and through—and then maybe smoke another one until the memory of tonight disintegrated into a blur.

Chapter Twenty-One

Geri

September 2019

She polished his leather ensemble exactly how he liked. A little on the top, some extra friction in the middle, then elbow grease on the pants and crotch area. Fit for a star, his clothes had to shimmer like brilliant shafts of light in the pitch darkness.

The music was the most important, Dez had drilled that into her head, but he was also there to titillate and scintillate so that every Jack and Jill in the audience could get the most bang out of their buck.

"It's show biz, Geri," he repeated to her so often as if it were on a loop. "I'm an entertainer."

Geri moved on to his black and yellow electric guitar. Dez only played it for a few numbers, concentrating mostly on singing and putting on a show. His gear, he demanded, must sparkle and be as resplendent as the rest of him.

Unlike the amateurs, Geri never squirted polish on the guitar. That was a no-no, according to Dez's backstage rules. "That will ruin the guitar," he said. "You're going to basically micro-sand the lacquer and scratch it. Eventually, it'll lose the luster and look dull, even if you're the best polisher in the universe."

Always clean the guitar first, before even attempting to polish the instrument. Remove the guitar strings and grab a large makeup brush, the kind women use to apply blush. Use the bristles to get into the corners and crevices, eliminating all loose particles of dust and dirt.

Second, to get rid of any residual gunk, dampen a washcloth. But don't rub or buff. Rather, use a scooping motion to lift and remove dirt. Once it's spic and span, then it's safe to use a guitar polish.

It was part of a tutorial Dez had inaugurated for Geri's induction to life on the road when the tour began seven months ago. "Forget what you learned in school," he said. "Here's the real deal. More valuable than learning algebra."

He had been frustrated with her those first few weeks; everything he'd had her do, she'd bungled, like bringing him a meat sub for lunch when he specifically wanted a vegan burger, or getting him Metamucil when he wanted melatonin.

Since the incident in Michelle's apartment, she feared being the brunt of Dez's temper yet again, so much so that instinctively, when she was around Dez in those early days, she would cower and flinch when he was near her.

"Geri, are you afraid of me?" he'd blurted out in San Francisco while she was grabbing dinner with him on the third night of the tour.

The sheer audacity of the question shocked Geri. *Is he kidding me?* she thought. To save face, she lied. "No, I'm not."

"Really?" His stare was so penetrating, Geri felt like his sapphire eyes were digging holes into her skull. "I would never hurt Michelle's sister."

Obviously, he must have suffered from amnesia, but she went along with the duplicity and the self-deception because where else could she go? The familiar afforded a perverse comfort over the unfamiliar, even if it was toxic and awful. There were no surprises, no horrific twists.

To preempt further outbursts directed against her and make Dez happy, Geri set out to ace this task of cleaning and polishing the guitar. And he expressed his appreciation by giving her more tasks until he freely named her his assistant, describing her as such to everyone in the company. That conferred on her a status she had been lacking during the early days of the tour when she'd been treated like a ragamuffin abandoned at Dez's doorstep, the sad, pathetic waif everyone felt sorry for, but tsk-tsked behind her back and presented fake smiles and insincere, cloying compliments to her face.

The first night of the Boston gig, she'd arrived at the Mercury Spotlight Theater an hour before the others. Reveling in the solitude, an oasis of calm she would enjoy only briefly until the invasion of the backstage horde, she launched into her regular pre-performance ritual. It began with her bringing in Dez's stage leather outfit in the garment bag from the dry cleaner and then hanging it on a rack. Next, she'd open the bag and decide whether the leather needed some polishing or not. Then she'd polish and clean the guitar. That segued her into getting Dez's dinner ready. She would lay it out on a tray in Dez's dressing room, always with real silverware. Dez hated plastic and would throw a fit if he saw plastic near his food.

Since his OD in Chicago, Dez hadn't mentioned scoring any "candy," at least not to her. It was too much of a headache to involve her because of her age and her status as his legal dependent. It never ceased to bewilder her, though, the contradiction of Dez being both a vegan and an inveterate drug user.

Work gave her an excuse not to think about how she'd humiliated herself in front of Val the night before. When she returned to her room after walking in circles around the hotel's perimeter for nearly an hour, she saw several texts from Val, as well as a voicemail message. She deleted them all and blocked him. Her way of coping with his rejection was not to acknowledge it and move on.

When Dez finally strutted into the dressing room, his arm was wrapped around yet another woman Geri had never seen before. This one had light brown hair and appeared to be in her early twenties.

"It's going to be good tonight. I can feel it!" he exclaimed, fired up with fervor.

Without looking up, Geri could feel Dez's scalding stare. No doubt he was waiting for her to look up from polishing his boots. She didn't.

He cleared his throat. "Oh, um, Geri, this is…" He knitted his forehead in confusion. "I'm sorry. What's your name again, babe? Rachel? Renee? Oh, Rayanne. Sorry. Rayanne, this is my assistant, Geri."

Clearly, this wasn't the person Dez was speaking to on the phone the day before. Because, if it were, Dez would at least know her name. But then who knows. That was probably last night's hookup. And this person was probably today's.

She always found it interesting how Dez would introduce her as his assistant to his tour hookups. Like being her guardian made him less sexy somehow.

Geri mumbled hello, then went back to her task. After Lily in Chicago, she'd stopped trying to remember these women's names.

Why bother, when they were interchangeable and just one in a cast of thousands?

"I've got to get ready," he cooed to Rachel or Renee or whatever.

Geri heard the woman loudly bemoan her disappointment at Dez sending her away.

"I'll see you after the show," he placated her.

Her attention still focused on the boots, Geri heard lip-smacking noises. Finally, Rachel or Renee or whatever slipped out, swept out into a sea of anonymity along with so many others.

Dez coughed.

Geri glanced up from the boots. "Yes?"

"I don't think I've ever seen you so single-mindedly fixated on my boots."

"Well, you want them to gleam and shine, don't you? It *is* show business, isn't that what you always say?" She resumed the boot polishing.

He sidled over and seized her right wrist. "What's going on?"

She shrugged.

He continued. "Yes, you are conscientious, but you've never been obsessive when it comes to these chores. I always get the sense you do them to get me off your back, and once they're done, you're happy because they're finished. Now you seem weird."

"I don't know what you mean."

"You're acting like something out of a sci-fi movie, an efficiency robot. I expect you to be speaking to me like this soon." He cupped his hands around his mouth as he monotoned, "Yes, Mr. Deacon. One minute, Mr. Deacon. Your boots are ready, Mr. Deacon." To complete his imitation of a robot, he moved his arms in an exaggerated rigid motion. He punctuated his gag with a dry chuckle as Geri remained inexpressive. "Oh, come on," he teased her. "It can't be that bad."

She held the boots out for his inspection. "I think they look good, don't you?"

He shook his head and threw the boots to the floor.

"Now you ruined them!" she snapped. "They're going to be scuffed."

He scratched his head, then grabbed her by the shoulders. "Geri, they're boots. They look great. Even if they're ruined, I'll get another pair."

"But tonight's the big show," she protested. "And you're always the one who wants to look perfect for your fans."

"Yeah, and we have three more shows in the pipeline in case tonight sucks. I don't think it will. I think it'll be awesome." He brandished two clenched fists in the air, before sitting down and eating the salad.

Geri sulked as she picked up the boots.

"Geri, they're fucking boots! Snap out of it. You're starting to scare me."

It figures he'd be in a wonderful mood, she thought, while she wanted to hide in a ravine and never come out.

"Seriously, what is up with you? Hmm, let me see. Would a certain drummer have something to do with your strange mood?"

She glared at him.

"Ah, I'm right. So, what happened?"

Pouting, she averted her eyes. "Nothing," she responded, her back turned to Dez, who was in between bites of his salad.

"Good. I'm glad," he said, savoring the lentils and arugula. "I don't like him—"

"*Ha!*" Geri let out a guffaw to that understatement to end all understatements.

He rolled his eyes. "You're too young for him, and what do you see in him? I don't get it. Is it because he's a young guy? Is that it?"

"He talks to me and he listens to me."

"Are you saying I don't?"

She ignored his attempts to discuss Val. Given their recent fight and yesterday's near fisticuffs, there was no way she was going to discuss this polarizing subject, both for him and her. "You don't need anything else from me, right?"

"Are you saying I don't talk to you or listen to you?"

"Do you need anything else? I'm going to get something to eat."

"No, don't go," he replied, wiping his mouth with a napkin. "I want you to answer my question instead of running away. You do that a lot. I'm sick of it."

"No," she answered quietly. The pout vanished, replaced by an expression that could only be described as jaded resignation. "You don't listen to me and you don't talk to me. You bark at me. Was this a side of yourself you never showed my sister? I'm always walking on eggshells with you. I never know when you're going to blow up, when you're going to…"

"When I'm going to what? Finish what you were saying," he ordered, his throaty baritone plunging to a pitch Geri found ominous.

"What are you going to do? Hit me? Pound my face against a wall like you've threatened to do many times?"

"I've never threatened you!"

"Then you must have either amnesia or a split personality. Or you think your threats aren't real threats."

"They're not! Yeah, I do a little tough love sometimes, but I have to do that to get things done the right way."

"Tough love? That's what you call it? Michelle never spoke to me the way you do. My mother never spoke to me the way you do. And even though he died when I was really young, I doubt my father ever spoke to *anyone* like that."

"But Val doesn't? He's perfect!"

"I never said that. Just that he listens to me and he's kind."

"He was never going to be interested in you, Geri. He's gay."

She snorted with disgust. "He's not gay. Just because he doesn't fuck everything in sight, that doesn't—"

He slapped her hard across the face.

Shocked, she put her hand on her right cheek, still smarting from the slap. "I hate you!" she raged, her eyes blazing with fury. "I hate you. I don't know what my sister ever saw in you. You're the worst person in the world."

"I'm sorry," he replied, the color gone from his complexion. "I didn't mean to do that."

"You're sorry a lot, but then you do it anyway. And then the next day, you expect everything to be okay and fine, that we'll forget about it. Well, I haven't. I haven't forgotten anything you've done to me. Not one thing." She recoiled in horror when he reached toward her. "I tried looking for the good in you. I tried doing everything you wanted, the way you wanted, because I wanted you to…" She stopped. She was breathing so hard, she was practically panting.

He stared at her, his face clouded in disbelief as she gathered her energy and equilibrium to continue.

"I tried to convince myself that you cared. I wanted so badly to believe it, because I had no one else. I was alone. But it was an illusion. Just like your whole Dez Deacon act is an illusion. You've never cared about me, or even tried to. Not one minute. The only person you care about is yourself. You probably didn't even care about Michelle, but because she was such a good person, she fooled herself into believing you did."

She was ready to race out of the room, but not before Dez said in a tone half mocking, half conciliatory, "Geri, come on, don't be like that. The show's going to start in a few hours."

"You'll be fine. Like nothing happened, as always," Geri flared, then rushed out.

Disappointment hit her on every level as she paced briskly through the streets of Boston. The scenario she played and replayed in her head hadn't gone as planned. Yeah, she'd thought he might strike her, and he did. And she'd thought he would apologize, and he did. But it wasn't with the depth of emotion she wanted or the nuance. It all seemed canned on his part.

And Michelle, the sister she adored, had been planning to marry him, to seal her fate with him—*that* she couldn't understand. Maybe Michelle had gotten seduced by the glittery packaging, the way his fans did, and everyone who entered Dez's lair.

She heard her phone ringing incessantly, punctuated by shrill pings. She contemplated throwing her cell into the nearest trash can, but desisted when she thought about the photos she had taken throughout the tour, the photos that weren't of Dez or anyone connected to him. Instead, she silenced the call, shut off her phone, and tucked it back into her pants pocket.

It was dusk. Although the weather was still warm, the days were getting noticeably shorter. Fall was in the air.

Stopping at an intersection, she waited for the red light to switch to green. The traffic at Boylston Street was becoming more heavily congested as rush hour peaked. One driver rolled down his window to scream obscenities at another driver he accused of cutting him off.

This would be an interesting photo, she mused, yet she hesitated to take her cell phone out. She wasn't keen on seeing a flood of irate messages, texts, and voicemails from Dez. For this one night, she yearned to live in her own insular bubble, free from distractions and turmoil. Quiet and peaceful. That's all she wanted.

She walked and walked and walked until her soles and toes began to ache. Noticing a bench in front of a restaurant and an adjoining deli, both of which were now closed because they clearly catered to the nine-to-five crowd, she sat down and pulled off the black flat espadrilles from her feet. She rubbed them tenderly, then muttered "shit" to herself after hearing the sky rumble with thunder.

Damn. She had no umbrella to shield her from the rain, nor did she have a sweater or jean jacket to act as a makeshift covering. Unlike the squalling wind of the previous day, today's weather had been idyllic, the temperature hovering in the mid-seventies, no humidity, and no wind. She cursed herself for not checking her weather app and being ill-prepared for this impending downpour, but then again, she'd had other things more pressing on her mind—like dealing with the fallout from that cringe-inducing situation with Val and the ongoing toxic melodrama with Dez.

She felt a few raindrops and moaned. Seeking shelter, she cased the area until her eyes landed on a plain and ascetic looking building located at the end of a block. Bolting from the bench, she advanced toward the structure and saw a steeple topping it, a sure giveaway it was a church. A sign announcing evening services heralded the entrance to the Madison Christian Church.

Though her family had technically identified themselves as Presbyterian, they'd rarely, if ever, attended church. Other than the Cathedral of St. John the Divine for her sister's memorial earlier in the year, Geri couldn't remember the last time she'd stepped foot in a church.

Opening the door, she saw a dozen people seated in pews. She was struck by what a lively cross section of races and ethnicities this small crowd represented. All were listening intently to a youngish man with short, light brown hair and a meticulously trimmed beard at the podium. Geri presumed this was the minister.

He was talking about the power of prayer, asking his congregants if they or anyone they knew who was going through a difficult time, needed it. A few people raised their hands.

One by one, the minister called on each congregant and asked them the name of the person who needed a prayer and the reason for it.

A distraught woman said her father was dying of cancer in hospice and currently slipping in and out of consciousness.

The minister nodded solemnly, rubbing his beard. "Do you know how long he has?"

"The doctors aren't sure. It could be two months or two weeks. I don't want him to linger and suffer," she answered, her voice choking with pain.

"I understand," the minister replied. "Was your father a devout man?"

She sank into her seat and shook her head. "Not really. He didn't go to church that much. Only if someone was getting married. Does this mean you won't offer him a prayer?" she gulped.

"Of course not, my daughter," he responded with a soothing inflection. "I simply wanted to know your father's relationship to God. Everyone's relationship is uniquely different and indigenous to that person's life experience. Your father might not have been devout in the traditional sense, but that does not mean he is not deserving of god's benediction and infinite compassion as he transitions. Every person in the eyes of God is worthy of prayer."

"Thank you, Father." The woman nodded, her face aglow with gratitude.

"What's your father's full name?"

"Timothy Scott Crawford."

Clasping his hands, the minister closed his eyes and intoned. "God, help Timothy Scott Crawford discover your peace. Please bless him with a peaceful, relatively quick death. Let him go quietly and in his sleep as he enters heaven. Amen." He opened his eyes and then glanced at the teary woman. "God bless you."

She wiped her eyes with a tissue, whispered a thank you, and slipped out into the rainy night.

And so it went for the next few minutes, with the minister reciting prayers in someone's name. Usually the prayer centered on a beloved relative's illness; only one person asked for good luck for his daughter who had just started college.

"What school is your daughter attending?" asked the minister, flashing a warm smile.

"University of Pennsylvania. She's going to be pre-med," responded the beaming dad.

Geri felt a pang of jealousy, and not simply because the girl was starting a rite of passage that was normal for someone her age, but because she had a father. A parent. Just like the little girl with the doll. That especially gnawed at her.

After asking the congregants to recite a final hymn, the minister signaled the end of the evening services with a final prayer. Then he announced the schedule of services and activities for the next day before calling it for the night.

As Geri watched each congregant file out, all toting umbrellas they were hastily unfurling, she knew it was her cue to follow. But she couldn't. She didn't want to go back to the theater and face Dez's wrath or Val's discomfiture after she'd made a fool of herself. Or Larry's neuroses or Lanie being a flake and pretending she cared.

Curiosity got the better of her. She pulled out her cell and turned it on.

"No cell phones are allowed."

Sheepish, Geri replied, "Oh, I'm sorry." She powered the phone off.

"I was only kidding."

It was the kindly minister. He was standing in front of her, exuding a benign tenderness she rarely saw in any adult—at least, not in any adult she knew currently.

"I guess I should be going," she said, not budging from her seat.

"What brings you out here on a school night?"

Caught unaware, Geri hesitated, unsure of what excuse to invent.

"Did you get caught in the rain? Or did you have a fight with your parents?"

Chagrined, Geri bit her lips.

Noting her distress, the minister's concern deepened on his unlined, ruddy face. "I'm sure it was a misunderstanding, young lady. Would you feel better if you told me what happened?"

Geri shook her head forcefully. "No, sir. It's not that. I wish it were." She heaved out a sigh, took a pause, and continued. "My parents are dead. So is my sister. I'm an orphan. Literally. And I have no family."

"I am so sorry," the minister replied. "Is there anything I can do? How old are you? Who are you staying with?"

"I'm going to be seventeen in two weeks. No, there's nothing you can do. I do have a guardian." She grimaced. "You can see him for yourself tonight at the Mercury Spotlight Theater. Just shell out seventy-five bucks, or a hundred and fifty if you want one of the better seats."

Confused, the minister narrowed his eyes. "I don't understand," he responded slowly. "Are you saying your guardian is a musician? And he's well-known?"

She scrutinized the minster before answering. There was no trace of condescension in his remarks. He was in earnest. The man was the very incarnation of goodness. Dez and company ought to take a note from this holy man's playbook.

"Yes, sir. That's what I'm saying."

"I'm Bob Farrell, but my congregants call me Minister Bob," he said, a twinkle in his eyes. "Surely your situation would make you the envy of a lot of girls, no?"

The corners of Geri's lips creased into a wisp of a grin that quickly evaporated when she resumed speaking and the reality of her circumstances weighed down on her. "I'm Geraldine Randall, but everyone calls me Geri. Unfortunately, Minister Bob, it's not a fantasy. It's more like a nightmare."

"It can't be that bad."

Geri grunted in revulsion.

"Okay," he replied, his voice calming, "maybe not. But there is one thing I've learned in my life, while counseling people like yourself, who feel lost, or betrayed by life or events beyond their control: everything and everyone has a purpose. That there are no coincidences. For example, why did you come here tonight?"

"Because it was starting to rain and I didn't have an umbrella," Geri answered dully.

"Yes." His mouth extended into a smile. "On the surface, that might have been the reason. But perhaps your subconscious was telling you something else. Maybe it was telling you to come here and seek the comfort and support that's lacking in your present life."

She stared blankly at him. "Minister Bob, I'm not interested in joining this church, or any church."

"I understand that. I'm not looking to proselytize." He fumbled, seeing Geri's puzzled face. "I mean, I'm not looking to convert you.

Why don't you unburden yourself of this turmoil that is causing you so much pain and tell me what's aching you? I might not be able to provide immediate assistance, but I can assure you that you'll feel better once you purge yourself of this suffering."

And so, she did, starting from her childhood in Boulder and dyslexia diagnosis to the loss of her parents and her sister, her isolation from the rest of the world, and subsequent life with Dez.

When she was done, all the torments and travails that besieged her about Dez, Val, and the tour were no longer uppermost in her mind. All she cared about were calmness and normality.

Chapter Twenty-Two

Dez

September 2019

He could feel the pain in his head metastasizing to a pulsing sensation behind his eye. It was that severe. Squinting, he flicked the light blinding his vision off in his hotel room, then dove back into the bed, burying himself under a mantle of darkness.

He had been like this since waking up. Hell, the OD in St. Louis had been kid's play next to how bad he felt now. The irony was it neither involved alcohol nor drugs.

The opening-night show last night in Boston had been terrible. He cringed at the memory: He'd been out of sync with the band, so disoriented and distracted. At one point, the band had stopped playing after he began jabbering about love and loss.

"It's a bitch, isn't it?" he'd rambled, not making a lick of sense. "You love so much and they die. Poof. They're gone. My love was killed in a car going to the airport. A drunken Italian asshole murdered her. He didn't see that the lights had changed, so this piece of shit sideswiped the car my girl was in, killing her."

Ear-shattering silence from the SRO crowd had followed until one audience member yelled out, "Sing 'Mistress of Sorrow'!" That led to a thunderous round of cheers and roars.

Dez sneered. He twirled the mic in a methodical, ceremonial fashion, as if he were a high school majorette, then rotated 180 degrees to glance at Gary, Louie, and Val, all of whom were reactionless as they waited for Dez to end his rant and start the song.

"The people want to hear 'Mistress of Sorrow.' Should we give it to them? What do you say, boys?"

The roar from the fans intensified into a deafening crescendo.

Louie nodded and began playing a few bars of the song on his rhythm guitar, prompting Gary to come in with his jaunty bass. But Val didn't leap into the jamboree. He remained sphinxlike behind the drum set.

Attired head to toe in his prized leather ensemble, Dez swiveled back to the audience. His face was imbued with the makeup Lanie had administered to conceal the still-visible nicks and bruises from his skirmish with Val. Under the glaring lights, globules of sweat began to drip from his artfully constructed countenance, making it appear like he was melting, like the witch from *The Wizard of Oz*.

"I'm glad you like the song!" Dez's mouth stretched into a fake grin. "I like that song too. I wrote it when I was with the Prophets. Do you know that when that song was released as a single, it soared to number two on the Billboard Hot 100?"

Again, the audience squealed with loud, rapturous delight.

Dez's piercing blue eyes darted to the wings where Larry, agog with astonishment at his client's public breakdown, loitered.

"Remember that, Larry? Of course you do. That's why you're here. Hi, Tandy." He waved at Larry's wife, who was standing next to him, her face a clone of her husband's bafflement. "How ya doing?"

Caught unaware and not knowing what to do, she glanced at Larry, then back at Dez before waving him a courteous hello.

"Good to see you. You look great."

She mouthed back thank you. Casually clad in sea-blue slacks and a short-sleeved white and blue blouse, her perfectly blow-dried ash blond hair falling to her shoulders, she looked effortlessly stylish and impeccable.

He remembered Michelle telling him that when she'd started out, she had worked with Tandy on a perfume shoot in the Bahamas. An older, experienced model, Tandy had shown her the ropes on how to comport herself with photographers, creative directors, and other models. At the time, Tandy had just gotten engaged to Larry and was preparing to quit the business in favor of marriage and motherhood. Michelle never forgot how Tandy had taken her under her wing and would frequently praise her to Dez, causing him to wonder how a woman of Tandy's caliber had gotten involved with a creep like Larry.

Dez's eyes homed in on Larry. "Hiya, Larry. What's wrong? Are you squirming?" he asked, dripping with venomous sarcasm. "Why is that? I just complimented your wife. Shouldn't that brighten your mood? Oh, I get it. Could this somehow be related to the lovely lass who did my makeup earlier? You know, the same one you boned last night, and a while back? Sorry, Tandy. This is what happens when class acts like you and my dead fiancée trade down for scumbags like me and Larry. The thing is, Lar, I know I'm a piece of shit, but you don't seem to know that about yourself. Larry, are you getting upset? What are you saying to me? I can't hear you." He cupped his ears melodramatically, like an actor in a silent film, then turned to the audience. "My greedy manager is having a shit fit right now."

He heard the sharp blow of a facial slap coming from the wings. He shifted his gaze back to them. "You go, Tandy!" he yelled as he saw the back of her lissome form fleeing through the hallway, with Larry in hot pursuit. "Make him crawl through mud before you take him back," Dez hissed. He switched back to the audience. "Now, where were we?" He scratched his head. "Oh yes, 'Mistress of Sorrow.' That's a great tune, isn't it?"

The audience clapped, but not as wholeheartedly as before.

"As I was saying, that song topped at number two. Only one artist—Justin Bieber," he opened his mouth, jamming the forefinger of his right hand into it while his left hand clutched the mic, "beat it. Go figure." His eyes glazed over in disdain. "I guess it's a matter of taste, although how much taste does the American public have if bubble gum crap like that shoots to the top? I mean, really? Justin Bieber? Seriously?"

The crowd roared their approval of Dez's appraisal of Bieber's musical prowess.

"Do you know this current faux version of the Prophets?"

Raucous boos emanated from the crowd.

"Yeah, I agree. It's certainly not the band I founded in a basement in Philadelphia, a band I poured my heart and soul into until they kicked me out, the way the Stones kicked Brian Jones out. Oh, you don't know who he was? Google him. You see, Mick and Keith could do that and get away with it because Brian didn't write the songs. But I wrote most of the songs for the Prophets. Most of the hit songs, that is. The thing is I have a smart lawyer. They didn't bank on that. They actually had the gall to try and stop me from performing my own songs. But guess what, folks? I own the rights to those songs; I own the publishing. They are my intellectual property. I can play them any time I wish," he exulted in triumph. "And I'm going to do that now."

He nodded to Gary, Louie, and Val as they launched finally into "Mistress of Sorrow."

The music swelled like the engine of a race car about to break away from the lane. Dez kicked off the vocals as a gut-wrenching fusion of bass, rhythm guitar, and drums grounded the preamble to the song. Dez got as far as the third line before his mind went blank: he forgot the lyrics.

He toyed with the idea of vamping the way jazz singers did, but he dismissed it as super lame. The song was so well-known to his fans, he wouldn't be able to pull that trick on them. Instead, he pointed his mic toward the direction of the crowd, exhorting them to "sing along," which they did. Thankfully, the rest of the lyrics came back to him, but it was a close call.

He had gone too far. Blasting Larry publicly like that, embarrassing Tandy who had never done a thing to him. He didn't regret bashing his former bandmates, though. They had it coming. But everything else that came out of his mouth—that was a mistake. Michelle would have been ashamed.

As for the rest of the concert, he plodded through the motions, choosing to stay emotionally detached lest he forget more lyrics. He just wanted to get the night over with.

They only played one encore number instead of their standard three. Depleted and humiliated because he knew he'd let down the audience—and himself—Dez bowed humbly to the fans that should have booed him off the stage; instead, they were polite, if a tad lukewarm, in their applause. No standing ovations for him and he didn't blame them one iota.

After the curtain fell, Val laced into him. "What the fuck was that? My sister was in the audience tonight. Jesus Christ! You might as well have pulled your dick out and jerked off in front of everybody."

"I know," Dez mumbled, chastened. "You're right."

"Okay, it was a bad night," Gary interjected, trying to defuse another potential blow-up between Val and Dez. "It happens. Tomorrow," the bassist tapped on Dez's shoulder, "it'll be better."

You know what they say? If the first night of a gig is a disaster, then it means the remaining shows will be a big hit."

"What about that bullshit with Larry?" Val flared. "That was out of line. So unprofessional. As if the fans could give a shit. Then you're spouting off that crap about him cheating on his wife with what's her name?"

"Lanie," Dez corrected, his voice a near monotone. He rubbed his forehead in frustration at his actions, then added, his mortification not diminishing, "I shouldn't have done that. I need her to do my makeup for the rest of the tour. I'll pay her more. It'll be hazard pay." Dez glanced around, looking for the lady in question. "Speaking of Lanie, where is she?"

"I saw her leave before the show," answered Louie, with his usual Zen-like calm. "She told me she was going to go back to the hotel and unwind."

Most likely, she hadn't wanted to run into Larry with Tandy, Dez thought, even though he was unsure whether Larry's wife knew about them. Well, she did now.

"The kids want to see a good show," Val seethed. "One they paid their hard-earned money to see. They don't want to see Dez Deacon throw a tantrum."

Dez's pupils darkened. He zeroed in on Val. "What happened with Geri last night? What did you do to her?"

"Nothing," the younger man snapped. "She came by to see me and that was that."

Dez always had very little patience when people were clearly and brazenly lying to him. It made him think they were insulting his intelligence. Gloria might have had many faults as a mother, but raising a mentally deficient, obtuse son was not one of them.

"Wow. You really take me for an imbecile, don't you?" reacted Dez, his anger growing. "She has a crush on you. You know it. I know it. Everyone in this company knows it. You did something to make her run away. Admit it."

Indignant, Val shook his head furiously. "You don't know what you're talking about. Yeah, she might have liked me a little, but that's only because I'm one of the few people who actually pays attention to her, talks to her, and is there for her when she needs someone. I told her nothing can ever happen between us because I don't see her that way. I see her as a little sister. Like my own sister."

Surprisingly, Dez seemed to believe Val and backed off from getting into another heated physical altercation with him. As much as he was inclined to discount anything that came out of Val's mouth, he couldn't dismiss it either; it struck him as the truth.

"She's probably back at the hotel," Louie intervened, putting an arm around Dez. "She probably needed to let off steam. I have a daughter Geri's age. I see her running hot and cold all the time. It's those hormones working overdrive. Nothing to worry about."

He nodded appreciatively at Louie. "I hope you're right."

"Are you going to be cool?" asked the stocky musician.

"Yeah."

At that, Dez decamped for the dressing room while Gary, Val, and Louie dispersed. Dez wanted to check if Geri had returned any of his calls and texts.

Two women, one short brunette and the other tall and fuchsia-haired, were waiting for him. He'd forgotten their names. The only thing he remembered about them was that he'd met them the previous night at the hotel bar. They'd told him they were aspiring models and actresses. *Ha!* They all were.

They were both cute and dressed like hookers, which they probably were. One wore a red bustier and black lace shorts while the other was wearing a see-through yellow dress. Ordinarily, he wouldn't dismiss the company of attractive women, but he was not in a sexy mood.

"Out, ladies," he ordered, pointing to the door. "Sorry, but not tonight."

They both moaned with disappointment. The brunette nuzzled alongside him, trying to stroke his crotch, hoping to change his mind. He stopped her.

"Not tonight, babe."

"How about if we come back tomorrow night?" purred Miss Fuchsia.

"We'll see." He kissed them both and watched them leave.

Spread out over the top of the table was some of Lanie's makeup accoutrements, such as a contouring brush, a concealer, and foundation. He breathed a deep sigh of relief. If her makeup gear was still here, she wasn't gone for good. Thank God.

His phone was tucked in the pocket of his black denim pants that were lying on the chair, along with his black T-shirt.

Grabbing the phone, he grunted when he saw and read a lengthy text from Larry. He was resigning effective immediately and flying back to L.A., but not before calling him every name in the book. And he was going to sue him, too, for defamation of character.

Dez snickered at the threat. "Yeah, you do that, asshole."

Underneath the bravado, he didn't blame Larry. If he was in his shoes, he'd probably do the same. Still, he couldn't apologize to Larry — that would make him weak. And anything that made him look weak he'd rail against.

He deleted the text and was about to block Larry from his contacts and social media platforms when he realized his erstwhile manager had gotten there before him.

"Aw, too bad," he snarked. His sardonic mood degenerated to a more worrisome one when he noticed that all of his calls and texts to Geri had continued to go unanswered.

No, he shouldn't freak out. Not right now. Maybe Louie was right, and she was back at the hotel, nursing her wounds.

Or maybe she was lying in a ditch somewhere in Boston, the victim of a predator.

Fuck. He quickly changed his clothes. He sent another text to Geri. When that went unanswered, he called. Voicemail. Goddamn it!

He heard a knock on his dressing room.

"Yes?" he answered.

"It's Dave, Mr. Deacon. Are you ready?"

Dave was his Boston bodyguard. He had been introduced to him the previous evening. At every stop on the tour, there was security detail to protect Dez from overzealous fans — probably one of the few things Larry had done on the tour that he liked.

He hung up his onstage leather ensemble and placed it in the garment bag, then slung it over his shoulder. This would have to go to the dry cleaners. They always did after a show because of how profusely he sweated under the hot lights. Tonight had been especially messy. Fortunately, he had a fresh duplicate of his onstage costume back at the hotel, ready to go for tomorrow night.

If Geri didn't return, he'd have to enlist one of the roadies with the dry cleaning task. No, he had to put that fear at bay. She was back at the hotel. Louie was right. She wasn't answering him because she'd either powered her phone off or was still pissed at him because he'd slapped her for mouthing off to him like that. But she shouldn't talk that way to him. He was the adult and she was still a kid, whether she liked it or not.

Teenagers were a pain in the ass. He had to remind himself of that.

He opened the door. Like all of his bodyguards, Dave was very tall, about six foot six, hulking and buff. Dez especially liked this one as he bristled with excellent manners and charm.

"Let me take that for you, Mr. Deacon," offered Dave. "A man of your stature shouldn't be seen handling that."

Dez chortled. A man of his stature? He didn't know if Dave was being facetious or not, but he took it in stride and surrendered the garment bag to the Goliath in front of him.

Dave led him through the backstage labyrinth, proceeding past the stage door toward a hidden exit few knew about, but Dez asked him to stop.

"Anything wrong, Mr. Deacon?" Dave was so rigid and upright in his posture and carriage, it was obvious he had been in the service.

"Um. Are there fans at the stage door?"

After tonight's performance, he was surprised if anyone, save one or two stalwarts, would be hanging out there.

"Yes! There's literally a mob outside. Would you like to see and maybe say hello to them?"

Taken aback, Dez hesitated. "I was terrible tonight. Probably one of my worst performances."

"You weren't that bad. I mean, yeah, you had some stage jitters, but overall, I really enjoyed the show."

"Really?" Dez raised his eyebrows at the bodyguard, skepticism shading his features. "What about when I insulted my manager? Oh, excuse me, my ex-manager?"

Dave chuckled. "That was hilarious! My girlfriend and I thought it was a riot. We saw you five years ago when you were with the Prophets. I love all the stories you tell in between the songs. They really add to the show."

A rare moment of vulnerability overcame Dez. His crystal blue eyes shone with gratitude as his mouth curled into a crooked grin. "Thank you," he told his bodyguard, shaking his hand. "I appreciate that."

Pushing open the stage door, Dave ushered Dez outside the building, where he was greeted by a throng of screaming, jubilant fans held back by a police barricade. Maybe the size wasn't the teeming multitude of the past, but given the developments of the last twenty-four hours, he was surprised and elated to see them cheering and clapping at the sight of their idol.

It was the first time on the tour that he'd ventured out to meet and wave to his fans. Since going solo, he was loath to do this, not out of any snobbery or condescension—two charges Larry had been quick to level against him—but because he felt deep in his heart that he needed to foment an air of mystery around himself to sustain that aloof rock star aura. Being standoffish was a more viable image to promote when you didn't have the support of a regular band. Or so he'd thought. As he perused the crowd, Dez revaluated that opinion.

Feelings curdled up inside him. *Even after tonight, they still love me,* Dez thought. *Maybe I'm not that bad if I can inspire this kind of loyalty from the fans. Maybe I have some redeeming qualities, and I'm not such a rotten bastard.*

Accompanied by Dave, Dez did something he rarely did, not since those early days with the Prophets. He acknowledged and shook the hands of nearly every fan clamoring for his attention; he autographed photos and articles, and took so many selfies he lost count.

Geri was still nowhere to be found when he returned to his hotel.

His eyes fell on the two bottles of Dom Pérignon that had been gifted to him by a marketing executive at the record company. He stifled the urge to swig them down. Grimacing, he dialed a member of his security detail.

"I need you to call the police and report a missing person. It's my sixteen-year-old ward, Geri Randall. Please make sure this is on the QT. I don't want the press to get wind of this."

Chapter Twenty-Three

Val

"It's not your fault," said Sunny, comforting her brother.

"Then whose fault is it?"

"Dez's, maybe?"

He and his sister were in his hotel room sharing a blunt. Although Sunny wasn't a regular user like her brother, she did partake in smoking nature once in a while. Val had finished telling her about what had happened in his room the night before with Geri, and how he'd suspected it might have been the final straw—aside from Dez's abuse and neglect, of course—which had led her to run away.

"I was so dumb, the way I handled the whole situation, Sunny. I thought I was going to save her."

"Here we go again. Remember what Dad used to say about you?"

"I have a savior complex." He sighed. "I know. I've heard that my entire life. What is so wrong with that? What is so bad trying to help someone who's in need?"

"Not your call."

He ignored her, pressing on. "I had this idea. She seemed really cool with it. When we got back to New York City after the tour is done and I'm no longer forced to breathe the same air as Dez, I was going to ask Derek if he could tutor Geri so she can get her GED. Did you know that the asshole pulled her out of school so she could be his slave on the tour?"

"Come on, you don't know that." She took a long drag on the blunt before handing it back to her brother. "Maybe that's what she wanted. What about us? We didn't exactly have a picture-perfect childhood either, remember?"

"You have to agree that Gramps and Grandma getting us away from Dad was a good move."

"Yeah," Sunny said tentatively. "But… I don't know. I think a lot of how you feel about Geri has to do with your hating Dez."

"Justifiably. He's a dick."

"You see him as the devil, and you the angel, when it comes to Geri."

"Not true." He puffed on the blunt, handing it back to his sister. "She was so lost. Spinning her wheels. I don't blame her for running off."

"She'll be back," Sunny replied, taking one last drag on the blunt that was nearly at the end. She handed it back to her brother, who eagerly finished it off. "Where else is she going to go? We used to run off on Mom and Dad all the time."

"I sent her a text and left a voicemail right after the guys and I had our meeting before tonight's show. That was when Dez told me Geri was missing and he hadn't seen her in nearly seven hours. He asked me if I'd heard from her. I said no. Then he asked me if I could get in contact with her because maybe she'd respond." He let out a bitter laugh. "Riiight. I'm the last person she wants to hear from."

Sunny fidgeted, scratching her neck. From his sister's body language, he knew it was his cue to drop the subject.

"So, let's talk about tonight's concert. Was that a shitshow or what? Be honest."

"I liked it. You played really well. Dez was..." She giggled. "Really out there. Loved watching him flip out. I know you hate him, but he really is fun to watch, and so hot."

Val groaned. "Here we go."

"He is. He's so cute. I love the way he wiggles his ass in those tight leather pants—"

"Oh, puke!" Val cut in, thrusting his tongue out in repulsion.

His sister persisted in her Dez praise. "Even if he couldn't sing—which he can—he puts on a great show. His voice rocks. You have to admit that, Val."

Val rolled his eyes. "Whatever."

"I liked how he bowed his head to me when you introduced us. He also winked at me when you weren't looking."

"No, he didn't." Val shook his head.

"He did!" she insisted.

"You are fantasizing." He made a crazy gesture pointing to his head.

She tittered, then leaned over to slap her brother on the shoulder. "I'm not. He did."

"When?"

"Backstage," she added, a huge smile engulfing her creamy, oval face. She tossed her shoulder-length dark blond hair, the same shade as Val's. "Before you all went on."

"I don't believe this. Sunny, get it out of your head."

"He also slipped me a piece of paper with his number, saying I should call him."

"*Whaaaaat?*" He jumped off the bed and paced angrily up and down the room. "This is fucked up. This is seriously fucked up."

He stopped when he saw his sister was trying to rein in her amusement.

"You little bitch." A mischievous glint lit up his jade eyes. He leapt back onto the bed where she was reclining and began to tickle her furiously.

"Stop it!" she squealed, her hands trying to thwart her brother from tickling the most sensitive part of her body—her feet.

"That's the punishment you deserve for nearly giving me a coronary," he teased.

"Oh, I forgot. He also asked me if I'm free to elope next Thursday, in between my English lit class and intro to psychology."

"Ah, this is death, Sunny!" Val gibed, a playful grin spreading over his high cheekboned face. He knew he and his sister were behaving like children, they were being silly. But they were having fun and he needed this welcome escape from reality.

Twenty-four hours later, as Val was preparing to leave his hotel room for the theater, he stopped when he heard his phone ping. His heart leapt, hoping Geri had sent him a message.

Instead, it was a text from Feral Records owner Ty Nelson and the record company's legal department. It had been sent to everyone on the tour. His face grew increasingly grim as he read the message. He closed his eyes and gripped his forehead, then foraged through his stash, looking for another blunt. Fortunately, one remained. His fingers were trembling so hard, he couldn't hold the lighter steady.

His face blanched. Saying nothing, he breathed heavily and reread the text, the blunt dangling from his mouth.

Pending the disappearance of Geri Randall, a minor who had been traveling with the Dez Deacon solo tour, we're suspending the remainder of the tour. This was a very difficult and painful decision to reach, but in light of present circumstances, we believe we have no other recourse. We have been in contact with the Boston Police Department and the detectives in charge of the missing persons unit. They have reassured us they will do everything possible to find Geri. We requested they keep this search in the strictest of confidence given Geri's age and her status as a non-public figure.

Unfortunately, they could not guarantee that the press would not avail themselves of this development as a filed missing person's report is within the public domain. Henceforth, until Geri is found, we are putting this tour on hold indefinitely. We apologize for the inconvenience this has wrought. You all have worked incredibly hard on this tour and we commend everyone for their outstanding contributions. You should feel proud of what we were able to accomplish these past months. I know Dez and I feel tremendously indebted to all of you.

Lastly, we intend to honor everyone's contract and will pay you for the remaining engagements. We will also reimburse everyone for the travel arrangements they will need to make to return to their home base. Until then, we extend our most heartfelt and deepest warm wishes to all of you. Fondly, Ty.

Chapter Twenty-Four

Michelle

December 1, 2018

"Please get me on an earlier flight," she told her modeling agent. "I need to be back in New York sooner rather than later. I'm getting married in a few weeks and I have to make last-minute arrangements."

Originally, she was supposed to fly out of Milan and into Kennedy Airport two days later, but with her wedding coming up, Michelle found it very difficult to concentrate. Initially, when the booking came up, Michelle had hesitated about accepting it because so much was going on in her life. Plus, she couldn't believe that the Dior people had the audacity to schedule a job like this during the holidays! What was wrong with them? Did they think no one had the right to a personal life? Well, of course they did.

Truthfully, she had no else to blame but herself. She knew that and had often taken jobs because her agency had manipulated her, or so she liked to tell herself.

The fashion world always operated within their own glass silo, completely impervious to the mundane concerns of everyone else. She remembered how, after her mother died, her agency had had the nerve to book her on a five-day shoot in Morocco for a cologne advertisement!

"But it's for French *Vogue*, Michelle, and Jean specifically asked for you!" her agent countered after Michelle had objected to working so soon after her mother's funeral. Incredible. Also, what was she going to do with Geri, her kid sister, who attended a special school in Boulder and needed extra TLC? She was planning on moving her sister to New York to stay with her, but that was after the school year was over. Right now, she was still in Colorado.

Jean was one of the hottest fashion photographers working in the industry. He could make or break careers, and if she said no to this job, he could have her blackballed. That was how much power he wielded.

"He's a cross between Demarchelier and Testino with a little bit of Avedon tossed in for good measure," her agent said as she tried to coax Michelle into taking the job or else.

Her agency was way too skilled in the art of politesse to ever deign to use ultimatums. No, they were far too subtle to sling pedestrian vulgarities at her in the form of threats, yet they made no pretense of caring that Michelle was a flesh-and-blood human with emotions and values. To them, she was nothing more than a disembodied dollar sign that could easily be replaced.

After arranging for a neighbor to put her sister up in her home temporarily and drive her to school until Michelle returned to Colorado, she went off to Morocco. There, she and another model on the shoot had been subjected to Jean's unending volley of verbal abuse during the actual shoot.

"Stop posing, you pig! What's wrong with you?"

"I want sexuality and sophistication! Not dementia and hardened arteries! Be honest: Who did you fuck to get to where you are? That's the only explanation."

Or this lovely zinger: "I can't believe either of you are models. You both should be bagging groceries at a supermarket. What a disgrace!"

And he'd specifically requested Michelle for the shoot? Either her agency was lying—which wouldn't be the first time—or this star photographer was a sadomasochist. Michelle chose to believe the latter.

As unpleasant as the entire experience was, the shoot did elevate Michelle to a higher plateau in the industry hierarchy. It had given her a cachet that made her more in demand while hiking up her fees.

No, she wasn't world famous like Cara Delevingne, Kendall Jenner, or Bella Hadid. The industry was vastly different now than it was in the 1980s and '90s when icons like Linda Evangelista, Naomi Campbell, and Cindy Crawford had ruled the catwalks and graced the magazine covers. With digital media superseding print as the dominant platform, working models like her had to compete with celebrities and reality TV stars when it came to scoring magazine covers.

Then she'd met Dez and relegated work to the backburner. For once, her personal life had taken precedence over her career. It was only after her agency had read her the riot act that she risked being cut from their roster that she took bookings again, albeit reluctantly.

Considering her success in a cutthroat field—which she had attained due to toil, a dedicated work ethic, luck, and resisting the overtures of certain male power brokers who made preying on underaged models a sport—she knew she had no right to complain about anything. Professionally, she was in an enviable position, but with Dez in her life and her taking care of Geri, she wanted more. That was all. Wasn't she entitled to it after working nearly nonstop for over ten years?

She was thrilled when her agency finally came through for her. They texted her that they had spoken to the Dior people and were able to get another model to cover for her for the last two days. She would be flying back to New York on an earlier flight.

She texted Dez, who was at her place in the Village. The last time she saw him, she had given him a duplicate of the key.

I'm coming home early! Yippee! she texted him, giddy with joy.

She waited in the lobby of her hotel for the car to pick her up and take her to the airport. The weather worried her as the sky was starting to become overcast.

She quickly checked the weather app in between texting. Thunderstorms expected for tonight. Damn. Her flight was in two hours. *Maybe the thunder and lightning will happen later, after I'm already in the air*, she thought.

Yeah! Did it wrap early? he texted her back.

No, I asked my agency if they could arrange for me to come back early. I have a wedding to plan! To a wonderful, super hot guy. She punctuated that line with two rows of heart and kiss emojis. Dez reciprocated with several rows of the same.

She giggled. *Hey handsome, do you miss me?*

I miss you every second.

Good answer. See you soon.

Next, she sent a message to Geri telling her she was coming back early. She gazed at the time on her iPhone: It was 3:30 in the afternoon. She calculated the time difference. This meant it was 9:30 in the morning on the East Coast.

School policy dictated that other than lunch break, all students had to turn their cell phones off. Most likely, Geri wouldn't see her message until she turned her phone back on during lunch. By then, Michelle would probably be in the air unless the rain turned into a monsoon, causing the flight to be delayed. If that happened and she had time to kill, she could always sext Dez. And check in with Geri again.

She wondered how her fiancé and sister would get along after they got married. Except for a dinner at Balthazar, the French eatery in Soho, the three of them hadn't spent a lot of time together, so it was hard to judge. What she saw, she liked.

"Gloria — that's my mother — threw me out," Dez had said over a plate of fettuccini and a mushroom tart. He was recounting to Geri how he ended up in a shelter when he was fourteen.

"She was always getting involved with these losers she'd meet at her job. She was a waitress at a local diner. They'd feed her some sob story, and the next minute, they'd be the man of the house. My little brother didn't mind. He wanted a daddy, even a fake daddy for a night would do. But not me. I'd get in fights with these jerks. I mean, she would spend most of her money on these creeps — money that should have gone for rent, food, clothing. One night, I had enough and confronted her about it. I told her it was either this guy — I don't even remember which one it was, there were so many of them — or me. She chose him and told me to hit the road. I moved into a shelter and it was like being in prison. The first night, I was stabbed in the ear, Geri. I kid you not. This elderly man felt sorry for me. He made a makeshift bandage for my ear with a paper towel! He was very resourceful."

A huge smile took over Dez's face.

"He was also very kind. And a great musician. His name was Harrison, but he told me to call him Harry. He had this old acoustic guitar and he used to play all these classic hits from the sixties and seventies. Told me he was once a session recording artist for PolyGram. Well, I don't know about that, but he played really well and he saw how my eyes lit up when he played. So one day, he asked me if I wanted to learn how to play. I said yes and he showed me, every day for a few months.

"Gloria fetched me from the shelter. She had a black eye. I guess it didn't go well between her and her latest boyfriend. I went to say goodbye to Harry. I tried to persuade Gloria to take him in as well, but she wouldn't hear it. He gave me the guitar as a gift. 'You keep it, son. I know you'll go far.'

"When I got rich and famous—" he scoffed when he enunciated those words "—I went back to that shelter to find out what happened to him. I wanted to pay him back for helping me, for changing my life. They had no clue what happened to him. They had no record of a Harry or Harrison living in the shelter during the time I was there. Nothing. To them, it was like he never existed. But to me, he still does. In my head."

Seeing how raptly Geri listened to Dez's stories of his rough-and-tumble childhood and how easily he was able to open up in her presence—a stranger, despite her relationship to his fiancée—reinforced Michelle's crazy, whimsical decision, as her lawyer had deemed it, to name Dez as Geri's legal guardian in case anything happened to her. But at twenty-six years old, that wasn't a reality she envisioned happening anytime soon.

She saw a black Mercedes loom outside. That must be the car coming to pick her up. The driver emerged and walked into the lobby. He was clad in the usual limo driver apparel—black cap, black suit, and white dress shirt, replete with skinny black tie. She was about to flag him down when she heard a woman speaking French, asking her if she was going to the airport.

Michelle spun around and saw it was Selene, another model from the shoot. She was heading back to Paris and wanted to know if there was room for one more person in the car.

"You don't mind, Michelle, do you?" she asked in French.

"*Non pas de problème*," Michelle answered. "I could use the company," she continued in French.

Feeling fatigue roll over her in waves, most likely caused by residual jet lag and anxiety mixed with excitement over her upcoming nuptials, Michelle shut her eyes, hoping to steal a short cat nap in the car until they reached the airport.

The sky began to rumble. Michelle shook her head, still keeping her eyes closed.

And so they went.

Chapter Twenty-Five

Dez

December 2019

He stared at himself in the mirror. He was a mess.

Eyes bloodshot and bleary. Humongous dark circles under his eyes.

Skin sallow and pasty. Lines, deep and grooved, crenellating his forehead. He was only in his mid-thirties, but looked a good decade older.

Clothes that had fit him perfectly only a few months ago hung loosely off his body like a door barely hanging on its hinges.

Whatever had made him tangibly human was now unrecognizable.

He grabbed another bottle of vodka from the twelve-pack on the floor. No use in stacking them on the shelf since he knew he would be downing them in no time.

He liked this brand. He didn't have to uncork them or resort to elaborate methods to open the bottle. Also, there was no stopper. All he had to do was turn the cap and voilà, the coast was clear.

He guzzled the entirety of the bottle in one long, purgative swig. He sucked the last drop down, licking it from his lips as if he were a parched desert nomad convulsed by severe dehydration. He flung the bottle to the floor amid a mountainous pile of empty bottles.

Shuffling around the apartment, he glanced down at his bare feet. His toenails were coated in dirt and longer than they should be. He couldn't remember the last time he'd taken a shower or left the apartment. Other than drinking booze, the only thing he was diligent about was recharging his Android to see if there were any updates on Geri's disappearance, any texts or calls from Boston police. He even held out the faintest of hope that Geri herself would finally get in touch and let him know her whereabouts.

"We have a development," he was told a day after the tour was suspended. A cop from the local precinct had called him.

At that point, everyone in the company had left except for Dez, who stayed in the hotel for nearly four weeks. Fortunately, management was able to accommodate him—he just had to move out of the suite, which was already booked for a private equity investor who was attending some tech summit, and into a smaller room.

Fine. He was cool with that. Fear rattled him so deeply that the thought of acting like a spoiled diva—an offense he'd been guilty of on more than one occasion—dissipated.

Unfortunately, as expected, news of Geri's disappearance and her connection to Dez filtered out to the media. Less than forty-eight hours after Dez reported her missing, a platoon of reporters, ranging from national outlets to the tabloids, were deployed in a battalion outside the hotel. They were waiting for Dez to emerge.

Rather than take the bait, Dez cloistered himself in his hotel room.

"What is it?" Dez's blue eyes glimmered while his hands clung to the phone as if it were a life preserver.

"We got a tip from someone in the neighborhood that Miss Randall was seen inside the Madison Christian Church the night she was reported missing."

Dez was confused. A church? Geri had never expressed any interest in religion. Neither had Michelle. "Are you sure that was her?"

"A congregant of the church saw a young lady fitting her description in the church the night in question. This person is a member of the church and regularly attends services there. She distinctly remembered someone we believe was Miss Randall sitting in the back pew during the evening service."

"Did this person say anything more?"

"No, other than when she was on her way out, she saw the young lady talking to the minister."

"The minister?"

"Yes, Minister Bob Farrell. He's a very popular and beloved member of the community."

"Oh, I bet he is." Dez fumed, his mind aflutter with dire scenarios revolving around this minister whom he'd never met. He probably sex trafficked underaged women like Geri.

"We did speak to Minister Bob an hour ago," the cop continued. "He told us he spoke to Miss Randall for an hour, called a cab to take her back to the hotel, and gave her some money to pay the fare."

"Why would he do that?" countered Dez, still incensed at how forward this minister had been with Geri.

"Sir, the church is nearly a mile away from the Boston Omni Hotel," the cop answered in a calm voice, not missing a beat. "Plus, it was raining very heavily. We have no cause to doubt the minister. He has a spotless record within our community and has helped many people."

A brief lull transpired before the cop spoke up again. "Does she have any relatives or friends she might have reached out to? Maybe she traveled to see them?"

"No. Nobody. The only next of kin she had was my late fiancée. She was the one who named me Geri's legal guardian in case anything happened to her." Dez paused. "Obviously, that was a big mistake."

"Sir, you're being way too hard on yourself. Miss Randall is a teenager, and we see this happen too often, in which a young person gets into a fight with a parent or guardian like yourself and runs away. Eventually, they turn up. We have no cause to lose hope here or believe there's anything sinister going on. It's still early in our investigation."

Soon after, the police mounted a campaign to mobilize and generate awareness of the latest missing person in their community. On every available surface in the city, they plastered posters with Geri's photo that included a hotline number for anyone with information to call, plus a $250,000 reward. Within days, the police were fielding numerous calls of sightings from people with visions of money dancing in their eyes, but upon further probing, none of these tips were forthcoming.

Frustrated by the department's lack of progress, Dez decided to venture out of his self-imposed isolation at the hotel and confront the police directly about Geri. He phoned the concierge, asking him to order a car to drive him to the precinct. But first, he had to brave the gauntlet of media camped outside the hotel, all of whom seemed ready to pounce on him like the jackals they were.

"Dez, any news on Geri?" one low-life hack yelled at him.

Another screeched, "Do you think this would have happened if Michelle was still alive? Are you concerned about what may have happened to Geri, considering her age?"

Dez stopped and glared at this jerk.

"Of course, I'm concerned," he told the reporter, who was scribbling furiously on his pad while several others thrust their microphones into the rock star's face. "I wouldn't be here if I weren't."

"Was there a misunderstanding between you and Geri that led to her disappearance? An argument, perhaps?" one pesky blonde reporter from a tabloid news show quizzed him. "Sources tell me that Geri became very close to a musician in your band—Val Monroe, I believe is his name. Would he have any information as to Geri's whereabouts?"

What the fuck? Stay cool, Dez. Don't let this slimebag cause you to blow up. Dez was very familiar with this despicable blonde because in a past broadcast story, she had insinuated in no uncertain terms that he played an indirect role in Michelle's death. According to her warped rationale, if Michelle hadn't been as focused on her upcoming wedding, she would have stayed in Milan another day or two and missed the car crash that killed her. If there was a special place in hell for reporters, he wanted this smarmy bitch to roast there in eternity.

"I'm not at liberty to discuss the details of the ongoing police investigation," replied an officious Dez, suppressing his bile. "What I will say is we will find Geri soon. I have full confidence in the Boston Police Department."

With that, he excused himself and made a beeline for the car. Three weeks later, after the police told him they had no more updates to share, but they would let him know once they got them, Dez had left Boston in despair and utter desolation.

Rather than fly back to his home in Laurel Canyon in L.A., he returned to Michelle's home in the Village. It was a calculated move, as it was the home that Geri knew, and he figured it would be the one Geri would return to either of her own volition or once she was found.

"We still don't have any news, other than sightings that haven't panned out," one police officer told him after he called for the latest on the case. "We'll keep you apprised should we get any more information. We're so sorry."

That was at the start of October; two and a half months later, there was still nothing.

He had even texted Val a few times, asking him if he'd heard from Geri.

No, I haven't, but I will let you know, the drummer had responded.

Great. Just great.

Other people, like Lanie, texted him to ask if he'd heard anything.

Shocking him most of all was a text from Larry, of all people. *I know we didn't part on the best of terms, but I really hope you find Geri soon. She's a sweet girl. I always liked her. Dez, I know you won't believe this as you seem intent on only believing the worst when it comes to me, but I'm truly sorry for you and Michelle's memory that you're going through this. If there is anything I can do, please let me know.*

He wrestled with himself on whether he should answer. Maybe if he had been dead sober, he wouldn't have, but the incessant vodka intake emboldened him not to care. He swallowed his pride and sent a reply. *Thanks, Lar. I appreciate it.*

His ex-manager reacted swiftly with prayer and angel emojis.

Dez tried to piece together for himself what may have happened to Geri. Unlike the police, he was still very skeptical that the minister had nothing to do with her mysterious vanishing. He frequently phoned the police department to voice his suspicions, but they would always respond with the same canned dismissal: "We have no reason to think Minister Farrell had anything to do with the circumstances surrounding Miss Randall's disappearance."

"How about he was the last person she was seen with before she went poof?" Dez argued.

"Mr. Deacon, we understand you're frustrated, but we're doing the best we can to find Miss Randall. Unfortunately, the trail has turned cold. That doesn't mean, however, that we won't get a breakthrough at some point that allows us to close this case and return Miss Randall safely to her home."

Fatigue wore at him, as he recalled fragments of conversations with law enforcement, conversations that had gone nowhere, conversations he replayed in his head in a loop. The conclusions he drew were always the same three possibilities: Geri was dead, she was living incognito, or she was trafficked into some underage sex ring. For her sake, he hoped it was the second alternative. But if not, her being dead, as horrendous as it was to him, was far better an outcome than being enmeshed in some Epstein-like pedophile operation.

His phone rang. He bit his lower lip. Probably the police responding to his text and call from yesterday asking about Geri. No updates, he was sure.

He contemplated putting his phone on silent, until he saw that it was his record company's owner, Ty Nelson, calling.

He picked it up, weighing whether he should answer. His hands shook.

Fuck. I'm in no condition to speak to Ty.

He let the call slip to voicemail. After waiting a minute, he listened to the message.

"Dez, how are you? How are you feeling? First off, have you heard anything about Geri? I'm so sorry. Please keep your hopes up. No news is good news. Second, I know this is bad timing, but I have great news for you. *Afterlife* is now back on the *Billboard* charts. It's in the top twenty. It will probably climb much higher. Isn't that great? Yeah, maybe there's morbid curiosity going on here with Geri's disappearance—some of the news coverage is driving the chart action—but I don't think that's the only reason. The tour also helped. It wasn't a failure like you think it was. Momentum was really picking up. Before we put it on hold, the gig in Boston was selling out. New York looked to be the same. We were very excited. I know you don't want to hear this, but we would like to reactivate the tour for 2020. We could do it as a tribute to Geri—"

Dez pounded the phone against the kitchen wall, smashing it into smithereens. He'd heard enough. That greedy bastard. Son of a bitch.

"A tribute to Geri?!" he raged. "She's not dead!" he screamed at the top of his lungs, his voice becoming raspy from the guttural impact on his throat. "Until there's a body, she's not dead!" Tears streamed down his face. "I'm so sorry, Michelle. I failed you. And I failed Geri."

When his crying subsided, Dez tore a paper towel from a perforated roll on the kitchen cabinet and used it to wipe his eyes.

His still-soggy gaze scurried around Michelle's smooth, gray-white stone countertops, sleek oven, and shiny white subway tile backsplash. How cold it all was. It was like a museum. No wonder he was more comfortable drinking in the far-homier living room.

His eyes fell on the art nouveau clock affixed on the wall above the sink. It was almost seven o'clock. Even though intellectually he railed against the idea, his instinct took over and he wobbled into the living room, grabbed the remote, and turned on the TV. *Insider* or *Entertainment Tonight* or one of those interchangeable trashy TV tabloid shows was going to come on soon. He wanted to see if they were running anything on Geri.

About a week ago—or was it a few days ago? he wasn't sure—Lanie had texted him to suggest that he watch an episode of one of those shows. She was being interviewed about Geri's disappearance.

Dez had been planning to text her back and ask her what she had said. Specifically, he wanted to know if she talked shit about any of them—himself, Michelle, or Geri. But he'd passed out on the living room sofa minutes after reading and receiving the text.

CNN came onto the wide plasma screen. Breaking news. Groan. He reached for the remote. It wasn't in his hand or anywhere. Shit. Where was it? Must have fallen on the floor and slipped under the couch. He pushed the couch back to find it, a Herculean feat considering how heavy and unwieldy it was.

The anchor was intoning in an ominous baritone: "A top epidemiologist at the Centers for Disease Control and Prevention in Atlanta has expressed concern about the exceedingly high number of patients coming down with unexplained pneumonia in Wuhan, China. What is especially alarming to the medical expert is how contagious this pneumonia is, despite efforts to isolate these patients. This has led her to conclude that this virus, if not successfully contained, could lead to a worldwide pandemic not seen in our country since 1918..."

Chapter Twenty-Six

Val

Late March 2020

"You're a scaredy cat, a real scaredy cat," his father had taunted him. "How did I raise such a scaredy cat?"

"I can't do it," Val whined.

"Break the goose's neck!" bellowed Eli. "Take your hand and twist his neck, like this." He demonstrated to the boy.

Quivering, Val stared at the goose, then at his father. "I can't do it," he said after a prolonged silence.

Sensing it was in danger, the large bird began honking loudly. At his father's urging, Val threw tiny pieces of bread at the goose to entice it to totter out of the pond to eat from his hand.

"If we starve, it'll be your fault," his father jeered.

Val grabbed the goose and snapped the bird's neck, but not before hearing the worst bloodcurdling scream he'd ever heard spring from an animal. His heart broke as he saw the goose slump onto the ground, dead.

"I hate you!" he screeched at Eli, who snickered as he snatched the carcass and started plucking off the feathers.

"Are you going to help me or blubber?" he asked him point-blank.

His son refused.

"Scaredy cat. Val is a scaredy cat," his father sang while cutting open the bird with a hunting knife.

"I hate you."

"Val is a scaredy cat."

He woke up with a violent start.

"Are you okay? Do you need any more sedatives?"

He looked up and saw a nurse wearing a surgical mask inside a face shield, her hands encased in latex gloves, hovering over him. She was garbed head to toe in a thick garment he'd heard one hospital worker refer to as "PPE." He wasn't sure when exactly he'd heard this weird term first float into his head, other than he was pretty sure it was while he was being wheeled into the intensive care unit.

Val shook his head. He tried opening his mouth, then remembered he couldn't speak due to the tube stuck inside his throat. He gasped, his fingers pointing to the ventilator that, for the past week, had been breathing for him.

"Your oxygen levels were very low," said the nurse, as if she automatically knew what Val was asking. "That's why we need to keep you intubated."

He tried to croak out the words, "How long?" but to no avail. Desperate, he mimicked a writing motion with his thumb and forefinger of his right hand.

"Sir, you need to relax and not place any undue stress on yourself," the nurse responded.

He wanted to know how long he had been there, and if his brother and sister knew where he was.

Insane that this was happening to him. He had first known something was off while he was in the recording studio in Manhattan's Hell's Kitchen neighborhood. He had been asked by a musician pal of his from the pre-Nameless days if he was interested in drumming on his demo, which he planned to shop to various labels. Finding himself bored and idle since the aborted Dez Deacon solo tour, Val agreed. Why not? It would give him something to do.

Both Sunny and Derek had pleaded for him to be careful.

"Val, you need to wear a mask and socially distance," his brother had implored him in a phone call. Derek had begun teaching his students remotely after his school was shut down by order of the governor. "You can't go out galivanting around the city without a care in the world. This virus is serious. And you have an underlying health condition, need I remind you."

Rheumatoid arthritis. He had been diagnosed with it five years ago by a doctor after Val complained about nagging joint pain. At first, he'd thought the doc was humoring him. Wasn't this an old person's disease? How could this happen to someone who was only nineteen years old? It was an autoimmune and inflammatory disease, he was told. His immune system attacked healthy cells in his body by mistake. Treatment could help, but it couldn't be cured.

Val suspected the years of living off the grid with his parents might have caused this condition, which the drumming only exacerbated. He asked the doctor about it.

"No one really knows what causes it," said the stone-faced doctor. "The good news is that you can live a long time with it. It's not uncommon for people who have it to live to their eighties and nineties."

Val's face brightened at the positive outlook, but sank when the doctor gave him the bad news: If he wanted to slow the disease's progression, he'd need to take a regular protocol of meds and undertake physiotherapy.

Maybe his father and mother's survivalist training was still embedded in his psyche, but he resisted the conventional medical approach. Instead, he opted to rely on a regimen of pot, with occasional dabblings in CBD. Other than his siblings and doctor, no one knew of his condition, and no one was ever going to know. He was more comfortable with everyone thinking he was an incorrigible stoner rather than someone, who, at the prime of his life, should be stricken with a potentially debilitating condition.

His disease wasn't exactly conducive to romancing women. Like any hot, red-blooded male, he had a libido and loved to express it with scores of attractive, available young women. Unfortunately, sex was exhausting and left his joints in spasms of excruciating agony. So Val consigned sex to the margins of his life, and as a result, that often made whomever he was dating wonder if he was either asexual or gay. The outcome was always the same: in a preemptive move, he would find something wrong with the woman to give him a pretext to break up with her. Or she would dump him before he had the honors of sabotaging the relationship.

He could have told them all the truth about his condition, but that was his secret and his cross to bear. Nothing would change his mind about that, no matter how insistent Derek and Sunny were when it came to them telling him to be honest to his various girlfriends.

Now it didn't mean anything anymore. It was the end. He knew it in the core of his soul. Twenty-four years old. He never expected to live a long life. Lodged in the stratum of his subconsciousness, he'd always harbored a presentiment that his days were limited. Was it the rheumatoid arthritis or an overwhelming sense of foreboding that contributed to his fatalistic, existential perspective? He wasn't sure, other than he knew that it was best to live in the moment and avoid making long-range plans.

Still, this wasn't the way he wanted to go. Not like this. Not in the hospital on a frigging ventilator, his body ravaged by this evil virus. Dying of exposure while hiking in the middle of nowhere would be a more appealing option. That would be better than simply being another statistic. Soon he would join the death tally he'd seen being regularly calculated on TV before collapsing at the recording studio.

He'd known it was a bad idea to go to that session when the virus was exploding in New York City; just as he'd known it wasn't smart to ride the subway, a likely underground petri dish of infection. But he'd done those things anyway because there was a ticking time bomb already in his body, so why not expedite matters by inviting COVID into his immunocompromised system?

"Are you okay, Val?" the engineer had asked him at the start of his session. "Maybe you need to go home and rest."

He had been coughing so hard he thought he was going to throw up over the drum set. "No, it's cool. Just need some water. That's all."

The coughing subsided slightly when he drank a glass of water, but it didn't alleviate the dull, nagging pain racking his chest or the fog in his brain.

"Are you sure you're feeling okay?" his musician friend asked him from the protective glass partition of the control room. He and the engineer were engaged in a serious conversation while glancing with concern at Val.

His pal spoke into the talkback microphone: "Val, we think you need to go home and take care of yourself. You don't look or sound good. Should we call an ambulance?"

"No, I'm okay, I just need to…" He was fidgeting at his station behind the drum set. The glaring lights in the recording studio bore down on him, making him feel even more light-headed. "Can you guys lower the lights? I can't see. I can't…"

The next thing he remembered was being strapped onto a gurney. He had never been in an ambulance before. As pathetic as it was, if he could teleport from his body, he would find it pretty cool.

When he wasn't drifting in and out of consciousness, a jumble of thoughts roiled in his brain. He thought mostly about Derek and Sunny. *Do they know where I am? What's going to happen to them when I'm gone?* The more he thought about them, the more his eyes brimmed with tears.

With her latex glove, the nurse brushed away the tears with a tissue.

"You'll be okay, Mr. Monroe," the nurse said, a faltering tone in her voice. "You'll be fine."

If the breathing tube hadn't been shoved down his esophagus, he would have howled right there.

His thoughts segued to Geri. That poor girl. He had tried to be her white knight and failed.

He hadn't handled that well, but what else could he have done?

Her sister had been a fucking moron, saddling her with Dez, of all people. She would have been better off falling through the cracks of the foster system. How stupid people could be when they were blinded by celebrity, status, and their own self-importance. Super model? Super moron.

And then isolating Geri because—gasp!—she had a learning disability? *Are you kidding me? Her and nearly everyone else on this planet.* It didn't make her an idiot. The only idiots were the sister and Dez, king idiot himself.

He consoled himself with the knowledge that despite what the public, police, and Dez thought, perhaps Geri was alive. There was no basis for him to think so, no incontrovertible proof of anything, just intuition interwoven with fraying threads of hope.

He closed his eyes and remembered his mother telling him, right before cancer ravaged her, "Karma is all cause and effect. And for karma to work, good things need to happen to good people, otherwise the cosmic order won't work."

He had no faith he was going to undergo a drastic ninth-hour turnaround. His mom hadn't experienced that either. But maybe it could happen to Geri. Just maybe.

He closed his eyes, remembering a daffodil Sunny once picked while they were living in a tent in the woods somewhere outside Portland. She refused to part with that daffodil, her little hands clutching it even after most of the petals fell off. Dad called her a baby for keeping it.

"Leave her alone!" he'd yelled at Eli. "Let her keep it."

In the end, a strong gust of wind had torn that daffodil from Sunny's grip. In the days, weeks, and months afterwards, the plaintive anguish of his sister wailing had echoed in his head. It still haunted him.

Chapter Twenty-Seven

Blu

July 2020

When she got the alert on her phone letting her know the transaction had cleared, she squealed.

She tasted the freedom in her mouth and it was exhilarating. To exult in this moment, she pushed her foot down on the brake and pulled off the road. Euphoria surged within her. She'd won. At last.

She examined her grinning self in the mirror. She was going to keep the hair color and the length. It suited who she was now, who she was always meant to be.

Memories of the odyssey that began in September 2019 reeled in her head like a kaleidoscope. They began when she'd snuck away in the middle of the night on a Greyhound bus heading to Tucson.

"Take this," Minister Bob had told her as he'd stuffed a wad of cash into her trembling hands. He was advising her where to go for her escape. "Fran Meadows is a good friend of mine and a former congregant. I just called her. She'll help you get situated. But you have to go now. The police got a tip that you were in the church last night and they spoke to me this morning. I told them you left after we talked. I know they'll be back. Posters with your face and a hotline number are being put up all over the city. And from what I heard, there's a $250,000 reward being offered to anyone who knows your whereabouts."

Before she left Boston, Bob's wife, Lori, who owned a salon, said she would have to change her look so as not to be spotted.

"Bob and I think you should go dark because it's so different from your normal hair color," she said, holding up a box of blue-black dye. "This might be too dark for you, but you can always lighten it to a more normal-looking shade once you're in Tucson. Right now, this," she pointed to the girl's messy strawberry blond bun clipped onto the top of her head with a silver barrette, "has to go."

At first, she was resistant because black had been her sister's hair color. She didn't want to be judged or characterized in relation to Michelle. Now, with a new identity, the comparison was moot.

"Just go with it," Lori had urged, after she blow-dried Blu's freshly dyed blue-black hair and trimmed a few inches off her thick, wavy mane, which now ended above her shoulders in a bob. "If not, you're going to get picked up and we'll be accessories."

She scrammed at the crack of dawn, arriving in Tucson two and a half days later. On September 17, 2019, on what would have been her seventeenth birthday, Geraldine Maisie Randall died and Lynda Barbara Garretson, born a year earlier but on August eighth, came into existence, courtesy of a packet of fake identification cards fashioned by Minister Bob's underground help-a-minor-out-of-bad-situation network.

Lynda Barbara Garretson? The name made her squirm. It sounded so old-fashioned. Like it wasn't even from this century. But if it was her ticket to a new life, she would have to put up with it.

After she got off the bus in Tucson, before she could even take a breath and explore her surroundings, she was approached by an older woman with greying short brown hair. With a crinkly grin, Fran Meadows introduced herself and led the girl to her car.

Maybe it was the gleam of warmth in Fran's brown eyes or her friendly, gentle manner but instinctively she knew that whatever would happen from then on, she would be safe with the fifty-year-old widow. She was going to be okay. Relief swept over her as it was a feeling she hadn't had in a long while.

Because of that, she didn't ask where Fran was driving her nor did she care. The only thing she yearned for at that moment was a bed or a comfortable surface on which she could plop and sleep for days on end. Wipe her mental slate clean and start over.

Fran kept the chitchat to a minimum. She was grateful for the silence, which was like a balm to her frayed nerves. Peering out from the passenger window, she squinted at the blinding Arizona sun as her sleep-deprived eyes took in the varied landscape that unfolded around her: the flowering desert, rugged canyons and pine-topped peaks, all beneath a clear, blue sky.

She thought about taking a photo of this amazingly picturesque scenery until she remembered she currently had no phone. She'd given her old iPhone, the one she'd had on the tour, to Minister Bob the night she met him. It had pained her to give away that phone because it had contained all the photos she'd snapped that weren't of him, all those photos of... She stopped. No, she couldn't go there.

Bob had said her phone would need to be disconnected and she'd have to get a new phone once she arrived at her destination, replete with her brand-new identity.

Her eyes flew open when Fran pulled the car to a stop and parked. After gazing awestruck at the scenery, she had shut her eyes, hoping to steal a little catnap. They were on a driveway that belonged to a two-story white and brown stucco colonial home outside Tucson. She assumed this was Fran's house. It was pretty cool looking, all that Native American architecture. Really sweet and kind of exotic—well, more exotic than in New York City, that's for sure.

Fran and her twenty-year-old college student son Teddy lived upstairs while the teen formerly known as Geri stayed in the guest room downstairs.

She crashed those first few days. If Fran had not woken her up and insisted she eat breakfast or lunch, she wasn't sure what meal it was, she probably would have crashed some more and then some.

When she finally woke up from her long slumber, just like Sleeping Beauty, she couldn't help but notice the décor in the house. The kitchen had this simple rustic feel: brown cabinets, gold and brown wooden walls, a wooden table in the center and a gold and brown countertop.

The living room had a big black leather couch that was flanked by two black leather chairs. In front was a rectangular glass table topped off by a ceramic bowl of fake fruit and a couple of coffee table books. On the walls were paintings of what she guessed were supposed to be Arizona as well as a few framed shots of Fran and Teddy.

She didn't want to be rude but she couldn't help but check them all out. I mean, she was there. She still had all her senses. *He couldn't rob that from her.*

It was hard, though, for her to ignore this neat black and white print of a desert landscape that hung above the black leather couch. That shot, with its massive sand dunes and canyons, had an otherworldly quality, like it had been taken on Mars.

Teddy caught her staring at the photo.

Flustered, she was about to apologize when he said quietly, "Ansel Adams."

"Huh?"

"He was a great photographer. Specialized in taking photos of nature. Mom has a book of his photos. I should show it to you."

As he spoke, her eyes ping-ponged between Teddy and the photo before finally resting on the photo.

Teddy continued, "That shot was taken at the Canyon de Chelly. It's a national monument here in Arizona. Unfortunately, it takes about ten hours to drive there. Mom and I went there for a visit two years ago. We stayed overnight at a local motel. It's not a day trip but it's amazing to see in person. Maybe one of these days, we can go up there and you can see it in person."

She found herself gravitating toward Teddy, whose lanky frame and brooding, blond good looks reminded her of... No, she couldn't go there. She steeled herself to move on. *The past is dead. Don't look back, look forward.*

Because of the blue sheen in her hair, Teddy had christened her Blu.

"You're not a Lynda," he said one night as they sat together on the porch, gazing up at the constellations in the sky. "That name is too dull and ordinary for you."

"You think so?" She winked coyly at him. Her new identity gave her a boldness that her old one never had.

"Yeah," he said softly as he snuggled next to her, their hands interlocking.

She and Teddy kept their growing romance under wraps, or at least they thought so until one blissfully temperate evening as they all sat outside on the porch, Fran told her son, "It's okay, Teddy. You can hold her hand."

Both she and Teddy cringed.

"*How?*" her son asked nervously.

Shaking her head, Fran's thin lips burst into a huge smile. "Neither of you are exactly discreet. Just be careful. And, for God's sake, please sleep in your own rooms."

Without waiting for Teddy to follow his mom's behest, Blu grabbed her beau's hand. They beamed at one another before their eyes circled back toward the inky sky.

Her old self would have never reveled in being as forward with guys as she was now. But Blu was different. She was fun, sexy, smart, and independent—everything Geri had not been.

In exchange for room and board, Blu had to clean her room several times a week, help out with the cooking and food shopping, and attend services at the local Christian church where Fran was an outreach volunteer, serving as a literacy coach for people of all ages.

Next to what her old self had gone through on a daily basis, life in the Meadows household was a breeze. Yet, even after her culture shock wore off and the exciting newness of her situation began to ebb, she still felt exactly like she had months before—stalled and at an impasse. What was next for her? Could she actually remain here for the rest of her life? Did she want to?

Before Blu could process and answer these questions, Fran did them for her.

"So, kid, what's on the agenda?" she asked her one night over a dinner of spaghetti. It was just her and Fran. Teddy was attending a night class at the university.

Blu's fork fiddled around the spaghetti. There was only one goal in her head, the same goal that had lodged in her head the last six months and refused to budge. As Blu was about to open her mouth, Fran put her hand up.

"We're going to start tomorrow," she said, with a sweet, crinkly smile, the same one she used to greet Blu when she first picked her up at the train station.

Blu's tongue faltered.

Fran let out a dry chuckle. "You want to get your GED?"

Blu's hazel eyes widened.

"How did you know?"

"Hon, I'm an old hand at this. I know the drill. I've helped many others like you in the same situation. It's the next step in your journey."

Blu's eyes watered.

Fran lightly tapped her shoulders.

"It's okay, kid. It's no big deal. We're all in this together."

At night and on the weekends, when Fran was home from school where she taught English and social studies to tweens, she would tutor Blu for the GED. They sat down at the table to do this four to five days a week, in between the driving lessons.

At first, Blu stiffened at such a breakneck pace because of her dyslexia. "I'm a slow learner." She hesitated, not alluding to the special schools she'd always attended that had specifically focused on helping her erstwhile self overcome her disability.

"Is that what they told you?" Fran asked, the only reference she'd ever made to Blu's past life. "Well, they were wrong and if anyone was slow, it was them. You had special reading classes, correct?"

Blu nodded tentatively. For a second, vestiges of that other girl reared its unedifying head.

"You want to go to college, don't you?"

"Yes. But I want to study visual arts…photography."

"You'll still need a GED. I've coached so many kids like you over the years, and no one has ever failed. Neither will you."

Math, social studies, and science didn't terrify Blu; she only balked at the reading and language arts portions of the test.

Fran dismissed her worries with a cavalier wave of her hand. "I bet you're better at it than you think. They gave you a complex, that's all. We just have to build up your confidence in reading and writing."

For six months, Blu, under Fran's guiding hand, boned up on her reading and writing skills. After bungling the first test, a failure Fran attributed more to fear and less to aptitude, Blu excelled at the subsequent practice tests.

"You see, I told you you can do it," Fran gushed. To celebrate, she and Teddy bought Blu an angel food cake topped with icing that read "Congrats! You're Almost There." Blu gorged on a large piece of cake, not remembering the last time she ate this type of confection. She racked her mind. Maybe when she was in Colorado on one of her early birthdays. But the memory was so blurry, she couldn't figure out which birthday it was.

One unseasonably warm mid-March morning, Blu was about to go to the local community college to take the test when her plans were waylaid by the pandemic. Schools, restaurants, movie theaters, gyms, water parks, and stores—all were shut down except for those businesses deemed essential, like pharmacies or supermarkets. Even Fran's church suspended its in-person services.

"It's okay," Fran reassured Blu and Teddy over dinner the day the state commenced the shutdown during the public health crisis; there was no mask wearing mandate though, at least not in Arizona. "We have food, we have shelter, and we have Netflix," she told them. "We're going to hunker down here in our very nice shelter for a while. It'll all be okay."

"Mom, the 1918 pandemic lasted for two years," groaned Teddy, picking at his food.

"It'll be okay," Fran repeated.

A week later, Blu took the test online and aced it. This time, Fran, Teddy, and Blu cooked a three-course meal from food they bought right before the lockdown: pasta, vegetables, fish, and soup. Halfway through the meal, Fran began to cough. Three days later, Blu and Teddy found out they were negative; Fran was not.

After Fran was admitted into the ICU, guilt consumed Blu. She had never gotten to thank this gracious, generous woman for not only taking her in, feeding her, and tolerating her romance with Teddy, but helping her pass the GED. Even more important, Fran had never pressed her about the circumstances that surrounded her departure from Boston.

She found that curious though, like a key piece missing in a puzzle. One day, three months after Fran died, Blu quizzed Teddy about how much he and his mother knew about her past life.

"We thought you were trying to escape an abusive home," said Teddy, his eyes blinking more than usual. They were still in the home that he'd inherited from his mom, the home he planned on selling so he could use the proceeds for graduate school tuition.

Blu was aware that she was one of many who were part of that church's underground railroad when it came to offering safe houses and secret routes to minors and adult women fleeing dangerous home situations.

Beads of sweat began to form on Teddy's forehead as Blu studied his face. She also saw that his breathing was uneven.

It was then the revelation dawned on her. "You know, don't you?"

He bit his nails, saying nothing.

She persisted. "What do you know?"

"Blu... I... Mom thought it was—"

"Do you know my real story? Yes or no?" Her volume rose, as did her anger.

"Um," he averted his eyes.

"Why is this so difficult for you to answer my question?"

"Mom told me you should never know," he blurted out.

"I want to see it!" she shrilled.

He registered confusion. "See what?"

"I want to see your mother's savings account—from September 2019, when I first came here!"

"What are you implying?"

"Teddy, don't insult me. I'm not an idiot, contrary to what he thought of me or my sister or those on the tour—"

"I don't know what you're saying," he replied, wildly gesticulating. "You're speaking in riddles."

"You damn well know what I'm saying. Show me your mother's account."

"Geri." He winced as soon as the name issued out of his larynx. "I mean, Blu."

"You got it right the first time." She stilled the slight quiver in her voice to a near monotone as she crushed the fury that had seethed in her moments ago like a cauldron.

Their eyes locked. Unlike their previous staring contests, there was no tenderness in this optical exchange. Just a cold, ruthless understanding on Blu's part that she had been betrayed yet again.

"Okay, I'll get it for you."

Her eyes followed him as he shambled out of his bedroom, which she had initially shared with him before decamping back to her room downstairs. Blu might have been more outwardly adventurous than Geri, but physical intimacy was a challenge. Maybe they had waited too long to have sex—a few weeks after his mother died. She wasn't sure whether it was her or Teddy that was to blame. Probably both. After the first few times, which felt more like a wrestling match and less like sex, both agreed they were better off as friends and remained as such.

Blu heard his steps move down the hall, in the direction of his late mom's room. Then the sound of a drawer being pulled out, the rifling of papers, and the drawer snapping shut.

Reentering the room, he tossed Fran's bank statements to Blu.

"Here it is. It's right there. But it's not from when you first came here. You're wrong about that. Bob told Mom your real story. I thought you were like the others. It was only when she got sick and she knew what was going to happen to her, with the bills and all, that she begged me to get in touch with…"

"Dez Deacon. You can say his name. Dez fucking Deacon. The rock star. My legal guardian. My late sister Michelle's fiancé."

He compressed his lips. "I called the number on the poster with your picture. It's on his website. Mom told me it would be there. I didn't know anything about your real story or your connection to him until Mom told me."

"But you'd heard of him."

"Well, yeah. I went to his concert when he was still with the Prophets. My friends and I were going to try and see him on his solo tour but…" He hedged.

"That got canceled after I disappeared."

"I didn't know anything about that."

She scowled at him. "So Dez knows I'm here then?"

Eyes downcast, Teddy nodded.

She pored through the statements furiously, zipping through the remainder of 2019 until she got to March 2020, right before Fran checked in to the hospital. There it was. $250,000.

"How good of Dez to give you and your mom the entire reward instead of a fraction of it. What a guy."

"I didn't deal with him. I never spoke to him. I spoke to someone else."

"Larry? No, it wouldn't be Larry. It was Lloyd then. He's Dez's lawyer." She let out a cynical chuckle. "Why should I be surprised? I always suspected he paid off my teacher, Ms. Fenster, to ghost me after my sister died. I don't have any proof but I know, in my gut, that he did that. It's something he would do. Other than my sister, Ms. Fenster was the only person in the world I thought, stupid me, cared about me. I guess not." Thoughts of Val stirred in her head, but she didn't bring him up.

She started packing while Teddy watched helplessly.

"Where are you going?"

"What do you care? You've got your bounty from Dez and your mom's house and all of her money and I have nothing. My sister left me nothing. Not even her place in New York. I don't know where I'm going, but I'm outta here."

"You don't think you're being unreasonable? Why don't you wait a bit and think about it instead of charging off?"

"Because if I do that, then I'll never be in control of my life and I'll always be dependent on someone else. I have to go now. Not like I have any reason to stay."

He shook his head and let out a long sigh. "Why don't you take the car?"

She stuffed her clothes that she had bought with Fran at a local mall, having left her original clothes and suitcase with the tour, into an old suitcase used by the Meadows. Fran gave it to her after she arrived in Arizona, telling her she could use it in the future whenever the time came. The remaining items, which included a laptop and surgical masks, she tossed into a duffle bag. She stopped when Teddy made his offer. Geri may not have had a driver's license but Lynda Garretson did. "Why would you do that? Give away your car?"

"I can always get another one."

She shook her head and resumed packing. "Of course. You're loaded. I forgot."

With the straps of the duffle bag slung across her shoulder, she wheeled her suitcase toward the front door until Teddy blocked her.

"Stop being so stubborn," he reprimanded her. "Take the car." He shoved the electronic key into her hands.

"Thanks," she mumbled.

Their eyes met in a lingering stare. She thought about kissing him goodbye and giving him a hug, but decided against it at the last minute.

"See you," she murmured as she exited the house and rushed toward the car, a gray-blue 2020 Nissan. She was about to put the car into drive when Teddy, waving his hands like an air traffic controller, motioned her to stop and open the window.

"Here." He handed her an envelope. "Even before the pandemic, I've always had this rainy-day fund. Mom used to have one too. I guess old habits are intergenerational."

Blu tried giving him back the envelope, but he wouldn't take it. "I don't want it. Don't be stupid. You'll need it…wherever you go."

Grudgingly, she accepted the envelope and then drove off, not looking back. When she was safe and far away from Teddy, she pulled into the parking lot of a strip mall. Checking out her surroundings on this mid-morning summer day, she saw a handful of cars and a few people walking to and from stores.

She opened the envelope and saw a thick wad of fifties and twenties. Fingering the cash bundle, she counted and then recounted just to make sure: eight hundred dollars. That wasn't going to be enough. She racked her head until an idea crystallized.

Opening the web browser on her phone, she typed in the URL for a website she never thought she'd would ever set eyes on again. A cascade of emotions, ranging from sorrow to heartache, swept over her as she took in the images coalescing on the screen.

Inexplicably, the Geri Randall Disappearance page was still up. "Last seen in Boston on September 13, 2019. All information is welcome and will be kept confidential." There was a blurry photo of Geri that looked like it had been taken backstage at one of the concerts. Dez's publicist or social media manager or whomever was in charge of updating the site had probably scrambled to get a pic of Geri but could only find this crappy pic. The hotline number was still on there, even though he knew she was alive and not rotting in some ditch.

All publicity is good publicity. Wasn't that Larry's motto, and Dez's to a certain extent?

She guessed her disappearance had caused a groundswell of good will and sympathy toward poor Dez, the down-on-his-luck rock star stuck with the stupid, witless teen sister of his stunning but very dead supermodel fiancée. Could this narrative be any more dramatic? Perfect for the press.

She combed through her memory, trying to ferret out from her mental cobwebs Dez's telephone number.

Wait a minute. There was one telephone number she remembered because it contained the birthdates of her and her mother. 917 and 204. It was a mnemonic device that Michelle had drilled into her head.

She sent a text to that telephone number and waited.

An ellipsis of three dots blinked on the screen.

I'm going to report you to the police. This is not funny.

Blu suppressed a laugh. She should have known reaching out to this person would solicit an over-the-top incredulous reaction.

Impulsively, she shot a selfie of herself and sent it. She then typed in, *It's me, Lanie. Forget the black hair dye. Look at my face. See the features. You do makeup. Come on. Unless I have a clone out there, who else can it be? It's fucking me.*

Again, she saw the ellipsis with the three dots.

Geri! OMG! It's you! I can't believe it! OMG!!!!

Blu sighed at the theatrics. *Very good. Very performative.*

What are you talking about? I don't understand.

You understand perfectly.

She called Lanie directly. Apparently, she must have cut too closely to the truth because the cell rang three times and was probably about to kick into voicemail when Lanie finally picked up.

"Geri?" she answered, sounding embarrassed.

"Knock off the bullshit. You know I'm alive. You've known for a long time now."

"No, I didn't!" she insisted. "I swear. This is the first time I've heard from you since Boston."

"Wow. You really think I'm braindead, don't you?"

"What are you talking about? Why are you so hostile?"

"Oh, aren't you the wounded party? Get off it. So were you screwing Dez when he was with my sister? I saw the photos of you two together."

"No! Not at all. I was a good friend to Michelle. I would have never betrayed her by sleeping with her fiancé."

"Aren't you a saint?" Blu snarked. "You're pregnant though? That's what *Page Six* says. And we know *Page Six* is always right."

"No, I'm not pregnant, but Dez and I have been seeing each other since the beginning of the year. He was in a bad way after you, um, disappeared. This was right before COVID. He drank himself nearly to death one night. When he was in New York."

"Yes, the apartment that should have gone to me," Blu threw in, her pent-up rage simmering to a boil.

A long tense pause ensued.

"I had nothing to do with that, Geri," Lanie muttered. "Do you want me to continue or are you going to yell at me?"

"I know about the epic love story, Lanie. I read about it online. I know Dez moved back to L.A., went to rehab, relapsed, caught COVID, recovered, and you became his sober counselor/coach/whatever. Then love bloomed. I can read. Contrary to popular opinion."

Lanie cleared her throat, then answered, "Well, it wasn't quite like that. But the media never gets anything right. You know that."

"Oh yeah, I know. I also know how wonderful it must be for you to no longer be in my sister's shadow and to come into your own, even if it means you have to fuck a miserable piece of shit like Dez, who I have no doubt is cheating on you with a cast of thousands. But that's your problem. Not mine. Listen, I need to speak to Prince Charming. I don't have his telephone number anymore, so he needs to call me."

After Blu gave Lanie her telephone number, she turned the phone off without waiting for her sister's friend to say goodbye.

To kill time, Blu strolled into a clothing store located in the center of the strip mall. The racks were overflowing with winter apparel marked down for the summer.

There was a snazzy yellow mohair sweater that caught her attention. Michelle used to wear one like that all the time when the weather got cold. She checked the price. It was $75, marked down from the original $125. She contemplated buying it, but resisted the impulse. *No. That was Michelle. I'm not her. I will never be her.*

Her phone rang. It was Dez. Actually, it was from a Desmond but Blu knew his real name. Other than being on his driver's license and passport, Dez never used it, preferring his nickname. She remembered one techie who had called Dez his real name to his face and was greeted with a punch in the jaw. The techie went to the hospital and later sued Dez in an out-of-court settlement.

She accepted the call. "Dez," she said, her voice bereft of emotion.

"Geri! I can't believe I'm speaking to you! It's a miracle!"

"Yeah, real miracle," she answered impassively while walking out of the store and back toward her car.

"How are you? I am so sorry for everything—for *anything* I might have done that made you run away like that. Geri, I've missed you so much. We all have. I just can't believe it. Finally, you're back with us!"

Blu was unmoved. She leaned against the back of the Nissan, the warm summer breeze on her face. "Umm, okay. Riiiight. Uh-huh. So you never wired Fran Meadows the $250,000 bounty?"

An ear-deafening silence followed. Finally, Dez spoke. "You were never supposed to know about that." Another pause ensued. "Are you still in Arizona?"

"Listen, Dez, I'm not calling to catch up with you. I'm leaving Arizona and I want to start over. I got my GED thanks to Fran Meadows. I want to go to college and begin a new life. I can't do that with no money."

"What about the quarter million that Fran got? Why didn't she share some of that with you? That was supposed to pay for your expenses."

Blu filled Dez in on Fran, her battle with COVID, and the hospital bills that had accrued following her hospitalization and death. "Her son needs that money to pay her hospital bills, and from what I understand, that still won't be enough. He also needs it for his tuition. He'll probably sell the house. I'm sure he'll end up doing fine—he has some security—but I don't have anything. My sister, the successful model, left me *nothing*. Not even the house in New York. You got everything. And me as your personal slave and doormat."

"Geri, that's not fair. You were a minor when Michelle died. And it's not true that she left you nothing. Michelle stipulated that you'll receive money when you turn twenty-one. She never expected to pass away—"

"And I never expected to be helpless and hopelessly dependent on you, of all people. A man who sees the entire world as his own amusement park, to do whatever he wants."

"Geri, I know you hate me. I was a mess after Michelle died and during the tour. I took it out on you and everyone around me, and for that, I apologize. I know it's just words, but I've done a lot of thinking the last year. You probably know this already, but I'm sober. I'm in AA—"

"You want to help me?"

"Yes! I want to make amends."

"Okay. Good. That's why I'm calling." She waited a moment, then continued. "I want you or Lloyd, if he's still working for you, to wire one million dollars to my account. I'll give you the account number. I want this done in twenty-four hours, otherwise I'm going to contact every single gossip site out there, *Page Six*, *People*, *US Weekly*, *Rolling Stone*, the *National Enquirer*, I don't care. I already have a long and lengthy list. "

She was bluffing about the list, but Dez didn't have to know that.

"I'm going to contact each and every one of these sites and let them know how you tried to rape me when we were in Seattle on the tour. Remember that, Dez? Remember how you called me into your room that night because you wanted me to do something for you and then you lunged at me? Your excuse was you thought I was Michelle! *Ha*! As if we look alike."

"What the hell are you talking about?" he raged. "I never did that. That's total bullshit, Geri and you know it."

Blu was undeterred.

"Oh, yeah? What about your pre-performance rituals in the dressing room? Remember that one time when none of your groupies were around, you forced me to blow you because you said otherwise you wouldn't be able to perform? It gave your voice a husky tone, the way the fans liked it. You told me if I didn't do it, you'd send me to the foster system."

"You're insane!" Dez exploded. "I never did any of that!" His voice was so loud Blu had to hold the phone away from her ear. "And I know I did a lot of shitty things to you, but that is one thing I *didn't* do. And I never tried to rape you, either. No matter how fucked up I got, I know I didn't do any of that."

"It doesn't matter. Who do you think people are going to believe? You, the out-of-control rock star with the bad reputation or, me, the stupid little victim, the idiot orphan who had nobody and is a nobody until she got handed off to you? Who do you think they'll believe?"

"You lost your mind!" he yelled. "Did the Arizona heat get to your head?"

She ignored his protests. "Doesn't matter. You were still a bastard to me. Still treated me like I was less than human. Val knew it. That's why he came back to the tour after that fight, the one you started for no good reason. He wanted to protect me from you."

She broke at the mention of Val's name. Even though she'd swore to herself she would move on, she had reneged on that vow when she'd Googled Val three months ago, right after Fran went into the hospital. Teddy had been in the kitchen cooking pasta for them while she was in the living room. Immediately, Val's obituary on various media outlets popped up.

She froze. He had only been twenty-four. That poor, beautiful, sweet, talented guy. What a crock of shit life was if someone like that could go so early and from the virus, no less.

She hadn't been able to sleep that night. When Teddy was ostensibly deep in sleep, Blu had snuck surreptitiously out of the house and walked and walked and walked, the way she used to do when the tour would hit its various stops. The only difference was the tour had taken them to cities heavily congested with people, buildings, and the burr and rattle of life; here in this small slice of suburbia a half hour outside of Tucson, where the nearest house was a mile away and you had to hop into a car to buy milk, there was none of that.

At that moment, she was grateful for the isolation. It was a tonic, but it didn't stem the tears. Fortunately, by the time she returned to the Meadows' domicile, her eyes were dry and Teddy was still asleep.

"I can't send you a million dollars," Dez snapped. "I don't have that kind of money. Musicians make money from tours, but my last tour was downsized and stopped short because of you."

"Bullshit. That money is chump change to you. I remember you telling me how Lloyd set you up with a really smart broker from Goldman Sachs and that he'd invested wisely for you. Had offshore accounts, too, accounts the government would never know about. But I know about them, Dez."

"I shouldn't have told you that."

She laughed. "You told me a lot. Good thing for me, you were always loaded. Bad thing for you, of course. Oh, there's one other thing…"

He groaned. "What is it?"

"I want you to file papers to declare Geri Randall legally dead."

"What? Why? You're not. Also, don't you have to be missing for like, ten years, to be declared dead? It hasn't been ten years. Not even a year. Besides, you're not dead. A paper trail can prove that."

"That's where you're wrong." She clued him in on her fake ID and new name.

"Lanie told me you dyed your hair black, just like Michelle."

"It's even darker than Michelle's. It has a blue tint to it, and because of that, everyone now calls me Blu."

There was another protracted break in their conversation. Finally, Dez shattered the stillness, his voice full of resignation. "I don't know how long it takes to declare someone legally dead. I'll have to ask Lloyd about that, but I can wire you the money. If this will set things right between us—"

"It will never be right between us, Dez."

"I know, but I need to make amends to you, Geri. I know I wronged you."

"Yes, you did." Blu gritted her teeth.

"I'll make sure you get that money. I don't know when. I'll text you to let you know when it's coming."

"Thank you," she replied in a choked voice. "After you send it to me, I promise you won't ever hear from me again, and hopefully you'll reciprocate."

He was about to say more, but Blu clicked off. There was nothing left to say. She had said her piece and so had he. Closure was now mutual, with the money sealing the deal.

She jumped back into the Nissan and drove for two hours straight, not knowing where she was going other than she was going somewhere. A smile overtook her face, as the weight of the past lifted off her, purging her of those noxious feelings that had corroded and infected her insides.

She turned the windshield wipers on as the sky, streaked with fleecy low-hanging clouds, unleashed a brief downpour of summer rain. When it was over, a blinding rainbow stretched out against the horizon. Blu gaped at the mesmerizing tableau that seemed to be a metaphor for her life. She stepped her foot onto the accelerator, driving into the limitless expanse that was her future, her destiny.